Although the men dragged the half-clad woman along, their grips tight and threatening, she wasn't fighting or resisting them physically or verbally. She looked beaten, not in body but in spirit. And yet, when she stumbled, the toe of her wear-marred but neatly laced-up boot catching in the cloying mud, pitching her forward out of the men's custody, the crowd gasped. Some stepped farther back to avoid physical contact. The carrion seekers in the mob pressed nearer, set to rend her vulnerability.

They hurled insults at her. She suffered the name calling, if it could be called such. The style of her clothing—or lack of it—and the building itself proclaimed the truth of her profession. She was the whore they called her.

Then he heard the new word, the word that was at first only whispered before it gained a more daring voice: *murderess*. One of the men yanked her upright, uncaring whether he hurt her or not. It was only then, when she raised her head, her chin, in a manner any grand dame reared in the top tier of Eastern society would recognize, that he knew her.

It couldn't be. And yet, when she swept the gathered crowd, the gaze she turned on them was the one she had learned at her mother's knee. At her grandmother's table and at enumerable dinners, balls, and afternoon teas in Boston.

Tal watched in stunned amazement as the once Honorable Miss Noletta Kittridge shrugged free of the man's hand and with a back straightened by years of deportment, stepped from the meager shelter of the porch, moved beyond the hungry, insult-hurling crowd, and strode on her own toward the camp jail.

Praise for Beth Henderson

"Beth Henderson creates characters that you might expect to see walking down the streets of the 1800s. They are so real with all the foibles that make us human."

~*~

"…a great job with characterization, pace, and plot. The characters were believable and interesting. The historical aspect of the book was spot on."

~*~

"If you love historical romances, if you are fond of Americana stories [with]...people who get a second chance, *AT TWILIGHT* is that and more."

~*~

"…action-packed yet character driven as the lead couple has demons (real and imaginative) to overcome before they might pursue their inner feelings."

~*~

"I actually like this book so much, I've read it twice!"

~*~

"This engaging mystery, adventure and love story is a quick and easy read…about moving ahead in life despite the cards that are dealt."

~*~

"The author does a wonderful job of keeping the true bad guy's identity a secret until almost the very end, which I admire a lot."

Until…

by

Beth Henderson

This is a work of fiction. Names, characters, places, and incidents are either the product of the author's imagination or are used fictitiously, and any resemblance to actual persons living or dead, business establishments, events, or locales, is entirely coincidental.

Until…

Contact Information: info@thewildrosepress.com

Cover Art by *The Wild Rose Press, Inc.*

The Wild Rose Press, Inc.
PO Box 708
Adams Basin, NY 14410-0708
Visit us at www.thewildrosepress.com

Publishing History
First Edition, 2021
Trade Paperback ISBN 978-1-5092-3554-4
Digital ISBN 978-1-5092-3555-1

Published in the United States of America

Dedication

To Gail Kamer,
Beta Reader Supreme!
You improved Tal and Letty's story immensely!

Acknowledgments

With thanks to Sherri Denora for her friendship and wonderful feedback on Tal and Letty's journey...particularly a love life hampered by a heroine in jail!

Chapter One

Boise Basin, Spring 1863

The ruckus spilled out of the saloon and into the sea of mud the residents called a street. Coming in off the trail, tired and footsore, his worldly possessions long ago reduced to the pack strapped behind the saddle of the sturdy nag trailing him, Tal Hammond stalled his steps to avoid being swept along with the surging tide of locals milling before the door. The mob was primed to unfolding events, but all he wanted was to rest an elbow while savoring a medicinal shot of whiskey. Or, depending on what its burn cost him, perhaps two shots.

A dozen buildings marched down both sides of what passed for a road. Most were long, low, narrow, and no doubt hastily erected before snow buried the place five months back. A couple boasted second stories and spanned what were intended to be double town lots. Many were crude, raw timber that barely served their purpose, built to last no longer than the last gram of gold in the strike. More substantial places were in progress, seeming to have sprung from a late planting of structure seeds that now stretched fresh cut pine sprouts toward the warming sun.

Saloons made up the bulk of the camp, numbering four in all, and every damn one of those farther down the path appeared to be far quieter and better maintained establishments than the one the crowd kept him from passing by. Whatever the ruckus was that held them cocked, he had no interest in it. Was content and then some to let the camp's drama play out as it would. He was just passing through. On his way to an unknown somewhere else but looking for a likely poker table to round up the size of the investment in his pocket, courtesy of a man possessed of a lucky gold pan but an unlucky hand of cards.

Then the crowd wavered as two men pushed through the open doorway and shoved spectators aside. The mob parted like the Red Sea, but Tal didn't blame them. Given that the fellas were armed and as craggy faced as some of the snow-topped mountains surrounding these gold fields, he'd be inclined to take a step or two back himself. Behind them another couple of men angled through, shoving a third person between them.

A woman.

Her head down, her long hair straggling. It could have been a mousey brown or a faded gold, but with it hanging free like a tattered veil covering her face, she looked a harridan, a witch. She wore little other than serviceable drawers, chemise, and a corset stained by something damp and dark.

The crisp air of the day stirred, swirling coldly under the saloon's overhang, bringing the scents of tobacco, sweat, cheap rotgut, and fresh blood to Tal. His usually docile horse spooked at the last, but a soft word and a soothing pat on the beast's neck settled the animal somewhat.

The woman's entrance on the paltry stage ensured a tragedy would play out under the saloon's porch roof.

He'd seen similar circuses before, knew the script by heart. The part he'd played changed the outcome occasionally, but only occasionally. Two years and a lifetime away and reminders of that reality still rested heavy on his mind.

Although the men dragged the half-clad woman along, their grips tight and threatening, she wasn't fighting or resisting them physically or verbally. She looked beaten, not in body but in spirit. And yet, when she stumbled, the toe of her wear-marred but neatly laced-up boot catching in the cloying mud, pitching her forward out of the men's custody, the crowd gasped. Some stepped farther back to avoid physical contact. The carrion seekers in the mob pressed nearer, set to rend her vulnerability.

They hurled insults at her. She suffered the name calling, if it could be called such. The style of her clothing—or lack of it—and the building itself proclaimed the truth of her profession. She was the whore they called her.

Then he heard the new word, the word that was at first only whispered before it gained a more daring voice: *murderess*.

One of the men yanked her upright, uncaring whether he hurt her or not. It was only then, when she raised her head, her chin, in a manner any grand dame reared in the top tier of Eastern society would recognize, that he knew her.

It couldn't be.

And yet, when she swept the gathered crowd, the gaze she turned on them was the one she had learned at her mother's knee. At her grandmother's table and at enumerable dinners, balls, and afternoon teas in Boston.

Tal watched in stunned amazement as the once Honorable Miss Noletta Kittridge shrugged free of the man's hand and, with a back straightened by years of deportment, stepped from the meager shelter of the porch, moved beyond the hungry, insult-hurling crowd, and strode on her own toward the camp jail.

She looked at no one, met no eye, taking comfort in the inborn dignity of the class into which she had been born.

Her class, Tal thought, heart sore. He'd never been a true part of it, merely a hanger-on, a climber. A friend to her brother.

And that friend had called him a traitor to his country.

But Letty… What was she doing in Idaho Territory? She should be enjoying the comforts of Boston, being fêted by the officers who managed to make it home and the wealthy industrialists who paid other men to take their place in the infantry lines.

If she hadn't stridden down the sorry muddy excuse of a street with her blue blood holding her above the rabble, he might have doubted his eyes. Even so, it was difficult to believe Letty Kittridge and the prostitute with blood and mud drying on her scant clothing were one and the same.

The show over, the crowd dispersed around him. Before they could all disappear, Tal tapped a blurry-eyed man in a threadbare suit coat on the shoulder.

"Pardon, friend," he said. "Could you tell me what that was all about?"

"Gal shot her man, from the looks of it," the fellow said. "Not surprised it happened, just that it took Pearl this long to do it."

"Pearl?"

"The dove they arrested."

"You sure she's the one that did it?" Tal pressed.

"Wearing Rosser's blood, isn't she? Why the interest, mister?"

Tal gave the man what he hoped passed for a harmless grin. "Just making sure no other gal or man's like to shoot my fool head off while I'm here."

"Gold brought you, then?"

"Brought everyone else in town, too, I'd say," Tal observed, his smile widening.

"You're right," the man agreed and chuckled. He offered his hand. "Ebner Melton, mayor of this little burg."

"Adam Cain," Tal said easily and pumped the mayor's paw. He'd been using the alias for too long now to ever stumble over offering it. It was more difficult to remember his life as Talmadge Hammond back in Boston.

Did Letty feel the same?

"Where do you hail from, Mr. Cain?" the mayor asked.

"Anymore, the last gold field that called to me," Tal admitted. "'Fore that, Canada and points beyond."

"And might I ask what you did before you came down with gold fever?"

The mayor was treading on dangerous ground now, wanting to know what sort of man he'd been back East. But considering events at this gold strike, Tal decided the truth needed to be let out at least one last time.

"I was a lawyer, Mr. Mayor. One with a knack for defending the innocent."

****

Noletta Kittridge waited until they shut her in the nearly airless room before giving in to despair.

The scent of blood rose from her clothing, fresh, raw, and frightening. It had seeped through her corset to taint her chemise, to cling to her skin. Mud covered some of her clothing now, clung to her straggling hair and added a further layer to the stench enveloping her. All her efforts to keep moderately clean in the impossibly squalid camp had gone for naught. Would they let her change into decent garments before they hanged her, or force her to meet the rope soiled by the stains of her sins?

Her last act would be one of entertainment as she swung from a scaffold for the crowds, the bloodthirsty, sanctimonious louts and the handful of spuriously pious wives.

Though no window graced the narrow room save the observation hatch in the cell door, the town had splurged in furnishing the jail. Used now to the dirt floors at the makeshift saloon, the echo of her footsteps on a wooden planked floor sounded foreign. A ramshackle cot, just rough boards hammered together, with a blanket folded at the end, crowded the space, but in the gold-rich, godforsaken wilderness of Idaho Territory, its mere existence equated to luxury. She'd seen the bed along the wall before they slammed the door behind her and hastily barred it anew, leaving her alone in the dark dank of the cell. Angry men, frightened men, their sense of right and wrong all turned around because a woman had killed a man.

Except *she* hadn't. Her misfortune lay in proximity, appearances, and an all-consuming desire to want Silas Rosser dead.

Letty's shoulders slumped as the first bout of chills shook her slender form. She'd had pride of her family name drummed into her as a girl, but it was insufficient to the task of keeping the current nightmare at bay. And why should it be? Pride was a sin, and she had become monsterishly adept at sinning.

Letty slid down the solid width of the door, crouching against it, unable to take the two steps needed to reach the cot as despair robbed her of the last of her strength. She wrapped her arms around herself, but they could not keep out the cold or warm the hollow spot beneath her heart.

Cursed, that's what she was. That twisted creature Fate had taken her dreams and warped them, crushed them, and landed her here thousands of miles from home, from civilization, from the life she'd known. Stranded her far from the ballrooms she'd taken for granted, from the future she'd expected. And all because of the war. The damned war.

She had no idea how much time passed before a quick rap sounded on the cell door. Light spilled into the room through the tiny observation trap. One of her jailers had either come to leer at her or to make a few coins by putting her on display. Odd that they knocked politely to warn her. Or was there one fool still mindful of the lessons of courtesy learned at his mother's knee?

Letty pushed to her feet, tossing the straggling mud-splattered locks of her hair back as she squared her shoulders.

The face at the gap was young, undernourished, and cured to a shade reminiscent of lightly toasted bread by hours spent out-of-doors. Obadiah Short cleared his throat nervously, his face coloring with embarrassment to be addressing her. "Ah'll give ya a lamp, Miz Pearl, if'n ya promise not ta burn the place down," the fellow said, his voice breaking with adolescent disharmony.

Letty stared at him silently, judging the roughhewn visage so like others it was nearly undistinguishable from the dozen rawboned boys who had haunted the saloon over the winter. The sort who swaggered, tossing back a drink as they ogled her, eager to paw and take a poke to prove their manhood.

Better eager innocence than a rough handling, though. There had been far too many men like Rosser, enjoying her loss of status and her dependency on their favors.

This one at least bore a familiar face and had never had reason to drop coins in Rosser's hand in exchange for her time. "Thank you, Mr. Short," Letty said softly.

He nodded. "Best ya take a seat on that thar bed then, ma'am. Sheriff'd like ta string me up if'n ya made a break fer it."

As much as her feet longed to flee, there was no place she could run, no place to hide. None to take her in, clothe her, feed her, protect her.

"Yes, of course," Letty agreed, took two steps farther into the cell and, careful not to spoil the lone blanket with residue from her soiled clothing, sat on the edge of the rough cot. From habit, her back remained straight, her knees and ankles aligned, her hands rested together in her lap, as if a lady's deportment could offset the tattered, bloodstained rags of a whore. Oh, how deep in Hades' realm she now lived.

The rasp of wood against wood tore at her nerves as the young man removed the primitive barricade that kept her caged.

The sound of men's voices was hushed, muted by the sturdy thickness of the door. Had someone objected to the boy's courteous offer of a lantern? Or were they gaming on the other side to decide who would sample her wares for free? The dark was preferable if such was the case. If the way was barred, she was safe, if only temporarily. Within its false comfort, she had the luxury of counting her sins rather than having more forced upon her.

Solitude was not hers to claim, however. The hinges complained as the door opened, drawn outward to allow the warm glow of an oil lamp to creep within her dim cell. But it was a man who held it before him, not the boy who had promised it.

"Sure you want to do this?" the sheriff's voice demanded from the outer room. "Got her dead to rights. Barrel of the pistol still hot from the shot and resting at her feet where she dropped it."

"I'm sure," the man with the lamp said.

And with those few words, hope stirred anew in Letty's soul.

****

Tal waited until the sheriff rebarred the door before he took more than the single step inside her cell. By the light of the lantern he'd seen the flash of recognition in Letty's face. And the hope. The combination was enough to buckle a man's knees, for how could he tell her everything would be all right when he knew the chance of the local jury bringing in a verdict of not guilty was slim to nonexistent?

"Name's Adam Cain, ma'am," he said, affecting the frontiersman's drawl he'd assumed along with the new name, crushing the telltale sound of Massachusetts from his voice. "Understand you're known as Miss Pearl."

"I am anymore," Letty murmured sadly, but her gaze never left his face. "Are you here to help me or to gloat?"

Unlike himself, she made no effort to obliterate her origins from her voice. The sound alone shouted her class, education, and her New England home. But for him it did more, drawing memories he'd begun to think were merely half-remembered dreams to the forefront of his mind. Letty in his arms as he guided her through a graceful waltz or rambunctious polka; Letty smiling at him mischievously, daring him to steal a kiss, then another; Letty laughing at whatever ridiculously flamboyant compliment he'd given her.

Letty with her golden hair spread out over a pillow as she whispered his name.

Facing her now in the narrow, rustic cell, the dreams seemed to have spun into a nightmare.

"Help you or gloat?" he repeated. "Now that, ma'am, is what you'll have to tell me."

Seeing no table or other furnishing besides the rough cot upon which she sat, Tal lowered the lantern to the floor between them. A damp chill clothed the air, partly the result of the rough construction of the building, partly the despair that radiated from Letty herself. She looked cold as well as desolate in the shabby, bloodstained undergarments in which they had dragged her from the saloon. Tal stripped off his greatcoat, the only remnant from his Boston wardrobe that had come west with him. Mostly because it was sturdy, weather resistant, and warm, all features that recommended themselves time and again.

"You need this more than I do right now, ma'am," he said. "Just on loan 'til your things can be gathered."

She stared at the garment. He wondered whether she recognized it. Remembered that he wore it the last time they managed to steal a few hours together. How she'd lain her cheek against the fabric covering his chest and, though clinging to him, had refrained from asking him not to go.

She reached for the coat. "Thank you, Mr. Cain," Letty murmured, draping the garment around her shoulders, tugging the lapels to cover her half-naked form.

Tal settled on the floor next to the lantern, his back against the wall opposite her. Even by the dim glow of the wick he noted how drawn she looked. The vibrant woman he'd known back in Boston couldn't possibly live within this bedraggled shell.

"The mayor was kind enough to accept my offer to represent you in the coming court of law," he said, drawing one leg up to rest his arm on. The other sprawled toward her, nearly touching the toes of her scuffed and muddy boots.

"Did he? How kind of him." Her gaze dropped to her hands. They lay in her lap, clasped lightly together. Stained with a man's blood.

"You should know that I have no coin with which to pay you," she said. "Nor gold dust. Did someone lead you to believe the camp would pay you? If so, it was a lie."

"The mayor didn't say." Tal shifted uneasily. "But then I volunteered to act on your behalf, which is as good as a bona fide written contract in this country, ma'am. This is *pro bono*."

She tilted her head in a slight nod of acceptance. "Not the first case you've taken with no chance of payment, is it?"

He looked back at the man he'd once been, the man who had fallen in love with her knowing he had aimed too high to ever achieve her hand. Just her notice had had to suffice. He'd been fortunate to earn more than that. Just not enough to satisfy him.

But then, what he wanted had been the impossible.

"Would you have looked at me differently if I'd eschewed charity cases, Letty?" Tal asked quietly.

Her head snapped up. Her eyes sparked with green fire. "Don't be ridiculous. It's who you are. But whoever I was before, that woman is dead," she snarled. "You might as well drag yourself out to the nearest saloon and just mourn her if you expect to find any trace of her, *Mr. Cain*."

"I'll wait," Tal said. "And hope I don't have to mourn two women when I take that drink."

She remained silent, simply staring at him through the shadows. When Letty looked back down at her tightly clasped hands, he knew she was beaten. He had won this round, but only because for her there was no other option.

"Where's Kit?" he asked softly, to ensure his voice wouldn't travel beyond the door.

"He died," she said simply of her brother.

"Your parents?"

"Gone too." Her voice was flat, dull. Resigned. "Influenza last spring."

"I'm sor—"

Her head jerked up, her eyes blazing with anger.

"Don't be," she snapped. "Our dear father's debts left us destitute. Kit thought the gold fields were our only hope."

"The gold fields," Tal mused, bitterness creeping into his voice. "I thought he would have joined up, trotted about town in Union blue for a bit, then headed for the front lines. You have cousins, friends, who would have taken you in while he was gone."

Her lips curved with rue. "I would have thought you understood society better, Mr. Cain. If you come with an empty purse, no one welcomes you. As for Kit, he had no reason to join the Army. Father paid a substitute to march in Kit's place when he was conscripted."

Tal bit back the angry words that rose in his throat, nearly choking him.

She studied his expression. "Kit called you a traitor for disparaging the war, didn't he?"

"As did many others," he admitted. "Did you, Pearl?"

Her chin rose in that familiar stance. "Women have no head for politics, Mr. Cain," she admonished, hurt and sarcasm mixing equally in her voice. "Surely you knew that. But, no, I don't think of you as a traitor. I consider every loudmouthed idiot who promoted the very idea of this war, much less the reality of it, a fool. A *damned* fool. As I am now."

The tenseness in his muscles eased; the wound Boston had given him healed a little, for he agreed with her. And had never thought there was another soul living in the length and breadth of the continent who shared his repugnance for the conflict.

"Tell me what happened," Tal urged quietly.

Letty looked down at her hands again. They were twisted together in her lap, gripping each other so tightly her knuckles looked white. “No,” she whispered. “I can’t.”

Her voice echoed with pain. She had lost so much in such a short time, but she stood to lose more—her life. Before pressing her further, he’d drop a few questions around the camp, spend a few coins in the saloons priming verbal pumps. And if nothing panned out, he’d browbeat her into relating the circumstances that had led her to this profession and the chronology of events that morning. Both had brought her to the foot of the scaffold’s steps.

In the meager light of the lantern, he could see tears glittering on her lashes, in her eyes. She had let hope drown in them already. The courage she had shown in the street had evaporated, leaving her a woman alone, a woman who was frightened.

A woman who needed him. Or at least his talents in the courtroom.

“All right,” Tal said. “We’ll let the story rest for now. There is one detail about events earlier today that you can tell me.”

Letty brushed the bright tears away with the back of one hand, the only area that wasn’t stained with dried blood or mud. “Which is?”

“The most important fact,” he said. “One the sheriff hasn’t thought to ask—Who *did* kill Rosser, Pearl?”

Chapter Two

Letty stared at him. "What?"

Tal grinned. It was the cocky, self-satisfied smirk she'd seen curve his mouth often in the past. The one that had made her breathless just to see.

Otherwise, his appearance had changed drastically from the last time he'd held her in his arms. Instead of his jawline being neatly shaven it bristled from the once modest muttonchop sidewhiskers into a ragged beard that indicated many months of neglect. The beard disguised the roguish dimple she knew creased his cheek just to the left of his mouth as he smiled at her. A mouth that had first taught her the intoxication of shared passion.

His hair waved, long and tumbling to his shoulders, tangled and wild, the once deep brown strands no longer tamed to Boston standards and sporting a touch of gray—evidence of how difficult his life had been since leaving Massachusetts. He'd been on the road for two years already, she less than a year, though the journey made her feel a decade or more than her twenty-three years. Tal would be thirty now, far too young for silver to steal into the glorious locks in which she'd once loved to bury her fingertips.

His clothes showed evidence of rough usage as well, the boots scuffed and gouged by encounters with an unforgiving terrain. Her own lone pair of footwear showed similar abuse. But though showing wear damage, Tal's clothing exhibited only dust from the trail, not the blood of a dead man, as did her scandalously meager apparel.

"I said who really killed Rosser, Pearl? I know for damn sure it wasn't you."

She sighed and shook her head. "No one would believe me. Whoever believes the word of a whore?"

"So little faith in my abilities, sweetheart? It can be done. All it takes is evidence tying the murderer to the crime, and a bit of dash to begin erasing the fallen woman image from their minds."

It was an impossible task, she knew. Far more difficult than clearing her of the charge of murder—and there was little chance he could do that. The camp residents had already condemned her.

"Pearl is all that's left," Letty said. "The woman she was before ceased to exist months ago."

Tal shifted his position against the wall impatiently. "Like hell she did," he scoffed. "I watched her stride down that dusty track they call Main Street, chin held high and a goddamn look in her eyes."

"Pride, that's all it was, Mr. Cain, and I've spent the last ounce of it I possessed."

"Then let's restock the supply," he suggested, and got to his feet. A moment later he banged on the cell door, the very sound seeming arrogant, confident, and forcefully male.

Letty nearly flinched. There had been far too many arrogantly forceful men doing as they wished with her since Kit's death. Perhaps even before. Hadn't she always done as her father wished? Hadn't she foolishly followed Kit on his great adventure to regain their fortune?

Sheriff Linus Strand's aged and weather-lined face appeared in the narrow opening cut in the door. "You finished your business with the lady then, Cain?"

"With my *client*, Sheriff," Tal corrected. "Nearly finished. I'm glad you agree with me that she's a lady, for the fairer sex deserves better accommodations than this hole."

"We ain't letting her free, Counselor," the lawman growled as he swung the door wide open.

"And I didn't ask you to," Tal countered. "What I *want*—"

Letty noticed he put emphasis on the word.

"—is some privacy for her, a meal, a change of clothing, and the means to wash unobserved by townsfolk, any deputy, or yourself."

"Now, hold on, Counselor," Strand insisted, clearly riled by the demands.

"You'd feed a man," Tal said. "You'd see he got his kit, a bar of soap, and a basin of water. I'm only asking for a dressing screen and whatever else another prisoner receives as a matter of course."

Letty was surprised when Tal turned to her. "Miss Pearl? Did you happen to have such a screen at Rosser's place?"

She nodded. "In the bedroom."

"Was it Rosser's property?"

"No," she answered. "My brother made it for me. Silas packed it into camp after Kit died."

Tal turned back to the man in the outer room. "Bet it's a simple thing, Sheriff. Your deputy can tote it back after we visit Rosser's place of business."

"Visit the saloon! Why the devil would…"

Tal stuck his hands in the rear pockets of his trousers and rocked back on his heels. “Just thought you’d prefer to send a fella along with me when I checked out the scene of the crime,” he said. “Of course, if I’m wrong, I can bring it along when I come back with my client’s other possessions.”

Letty heard the sheriff mutter something under his breath. Probably a string of curses that, until a few months ago, she had never heard any man utter in her presence. She knew them all well now.

“You ready to head out then?” Strand demanded.

“Five more minutes,” Tal answered. “Miss Pearl will need to give me a list of her things.”

“I’ll need to check them before we let her have them,” the lawman said.

“Wouldn’t want it any different,” Tal assured him, then turned back to face her. He waited until the clump of the sheriff’s boots reached the front of the building before moving. This time, instead of taking a seat on the floor, he hunkered down at her feet and took her hands in his.

Where his fingers covered hers, warmth coursed through Letty, chasing the cold of fear away, even if but temporarily. She wished they had let her wash her hands, yet Tal appeared not to notice that they retained the stain of Silas Rosser’s blood.

“And now, my dear,” Tal Hammond murmured in a barely audible tone. The endearment and sound of his voice echoed of Boston a lifetime ago when he’d guided her into the sensuous sway of a waltz. As he had when the music ended, Tal raised their joined hands and brushed a light kiss across her knuckles. This time when his eyes met hers, there was no tenderness, though. Despite his actions, he was her lawyer, not a would-be suitor.

"Tell me the one thing I really need to know," he urged. "Who did kill this Rosser?"

"I'm sorry," she whispered, "but I can't."

****

He needed a name. Lacking one complicated the case beyond measure. Considering he'd only walked into town a short time before, he was shy on information, blind to the lay of the land, and most likely damned if he got her off as well as if he didn't.

He'd wintered in Virginia City, exchanging greenbacks with fellow drifters over innumerable games of poker. A careful fellow, he'd accumulated more than enough to cover Adam Cain's living expenses, which were a hell more modest than Talmadge Hammond's had been back in Boston. Now, in pursuit of information, he'd stand enough rounds of whiskey and purposefully lose many hands of cards to seriously deplete those funds. Saving Noletta Kittridge's life was worth every dollar.

Fate had directed him to Idaho because Letty had need of him, of his courtroom skills, rusty as they may be from disuse.

With the boom towns of the western territories preferring a brand of justice that was swift and had barely a nodding acquaintance with actual law, time was at a premium.

"Tell me about the victim," Tal urged the youngster serving as temporary deputy, one Obadiah Short, or as the kid had insisted, "jist plain *'Diah,*" as they headed back down the main mud track to Rosser's saloon.

"Ya mean Miz Pearl?" the boy asked.

Tal nearly smiled when the boy's face lit up when he said her name. Nearly. There was, after all, the chance that, his youth aside, 'Diah Short had been one of the men to patronize her trade.

"I'd certainly like to learn the circumstances that led to my client's confinement," Tal answered, "but I meant Rosser. What sort of man was he? A flash man? A fighter?"

"A fair enough fella," the boy said. "Hear tell he were one o' the first fellas ta start sellin' whiskey und offerin' games o' chance in camp."

"Just when was it that he expanded his business then?"

The lad pushed the wide brim of his weather-worn felt hat back and scratched at the thatch of untidy jet-black hair beneath. "Ya mean when did Miz Pearl join him? Cain't say. Ma brothers und me wintered further south o' here, then headed fer different camps. Ah jest come up 'bout a month ago after the weather broke. The mayor'd know, though. He's been here since the first strike last summer."

Which meant Tal knew what his next step would be: give Letty a sense of herself again. Reminders of who she really was so the spirited young woman he remembered so well could come to the forefront again. When they faced whatever lout served the office of judge in the territory, whether legally or by local vote, he needed Noletta Kittridge on the stand, not the crushed drab she'd become as Pearl. It would also be well worth his time to learn more of the camp's short history and when the Kittridges entered into it.

"Whatcha lookin' fer at Rosser's place?" the kid

asked.

"Just gathering up Miss Pearl's belongings right now. A lady needs certain comforts that a man can do without. Particularly when the lady in question is incarcerated," Tal said, and waited for the lad to tell him a woman who sold her favors no longer qualified for the status of a *lady*.

He was surprised when the youngster nodded solemnly. "Frippery things like…like…"

"Soap," Tal supplied. "Privacy. A pillow and decent bedding, not a ratty old horse blanket even the horse rejected."

'Diah grinned widely, showing a twin row of stained teeth, an oddity considering there was nothing but a fuzz of dark hair straggling across his upper lip. A smear of dirt rather than stubble painted shadows along his hollowed cheeks and lean jaw. No matter how much he swaggered, the boy was still just teetering on the threshold of manhood. Whether it had covered him or not when he left home, the fabric of his shirt and trousers had been outstripped by his arms and legs over the winter, leaving them inches shy at the wrists and ankles. His boots had obviously been passed on to him by an older sibling. They were too well worn for one youngster's ownership, and so filed down by wear at the heels that 'Diah probably listed backwards when standing still.

The kid also smelled strongly of unwashed body and a meal he'd drunk down at one of the many saloons, emulating men there was no good reason for a lad to idolize.

"Soap," 'Diah mused. "Ain't seen much o' that since ma brothers und me headed out from home. But yer right. Womenfolk set a lotta store by the stuff. Ma walloped us a good 'un if'n we come in from the field without a trip 'neath the pump with that nasty lye soap she boiled up." They continued down the packed dirt of the street with the kid looking thoughtful. "Miz Pearl never smelled like Ma's soap, though. Bet she had that fancy store-bought stuff."

The memory of Letty's scent washed over Tal reminding him of better days. Days when he'd dared to dream the impossible. "You're probably right," he said.

"Think ah should get a mule er a wagon ta cart Miz Pearl's things ta the jail?" 'Diah asked as they arrived before the hastily thrown together building that served as Rosser's saloon. Back in Boston, the Kittridges wouldn't have housed their horses in it, and yet Letty had lived there. Had done whatever it took for a woman alone to survive.

"Bet she didn't arrive in town with much more than what three men can carry," Tal said. "Got a friend you can round up? There'd be a dollar in it for him."

The boy nodded but his expression turned thoughtful. "Ah don't think the sheriff wants ya here alone, Mr. Cain."

Tal grinned. "Thinks I'm light-fingered, does he? Don't worry. I'm only making off with Miss Pearl's possessions. Don't fancy a one of Rosser's." Except Letty herself, he added silently. As far as the camp was concerned, she'd definitely been one of Rosser's possessions. "Besides it doesn't look like I would be alone. We've got company waiting for us."

The kid squinted into the shadows beneath the saloon's overhanging porch until he spotted the man who hung back in the open but shadowed doorway. If the man hadn't taken a further step back when he spotted them making a bead on the saloon, Tal wasn't sure he would have noted the fellow himself.

Beside him, the boy relaxed. "Oh, that's Gately. He tends bar fer Rosser."

Now he was a man without a job, something that apparently hadn't registered with the kid yet.

"Hiya, Gate," 'Diah called and jerked a thumb in Tal's direction. "This here's Mr. Cain. He's gonna be Miz Pearl's lawyer at the trial."

"Waste o' time, that," Gately rumbled, stepping back from the door, allowing them to enter the building. "She done him. Town jest needs ta find a handy tree ta string 'er up."

If Letty had given him a name, would Gately have been the one she identified as the shooter? Seen up close, the former bartender was no prize. Although probably no older than himself, the fellow was already grizzled from a life of hard work and harder drinking. The scent of bad whiskey emanated from him, indicating Gately had drunk his midday repast courtesy of his late employer. It would take a good deal of alcohol to dull the former barkeep's reflexes though. He was broad and bulky of build, yet Tal had no doubt every inch of the man was honed muscle. From the inflections in his voice, he was a fellow of many parts, the echo of the south nudging more northern tones, as if the current contest of arms was being refought over every word he spoke. A traveled sort of cuss, then, but one who favored destinations far from the civilized sections of the cities, if he even crept within their confines. Gately definitely had all the markings of a man born for the long drop.

"The law says she's innocent until proven guilty," Tal reminded the barkeep.

Gately stared hard at him. "Sheriff locked her up, didn't he? Heard she was a wearin' Si's blood when they took her away, too. Sounds damn guilty ta me."

"Perhaps merely *suspicious*," Tal countered.

"Ya'd say so, Counselor, no doubt jest ta wring a fee from the gal," Gately growled. "She didn't tell ya she's nary a penny ta her name, did she?"

"Oh, I'm sure Rosser found her a mine of wealth," Tal answered. "We've simply come for her things. For what reason did you return?"

Gately's gaze didn't waver. "Wages," he snapped. "Rosser owed me."

"Then he no doubt owed Miss Pearl her take from clients as well," Tal said. "'Diah here can wrestle up the sheriff or the mayor to go over Rosser's books and oversee distribution of any monies found."

"What if there ain't none?" Gately snarled. "What ya gonna do then?"

Tal let his right hand rest lightly on the handle of the Colt Model 1860 revolver snugged in the holster at his belt. "I might suggest that the sheriff search you. There would only be a contretemps should it be found you were in possession of a fribble of clearly feminine design."

"Sheriff don't take kindly ta thievin', Gate," 'Diah added. "Fact, he's right righteous 'bout it."

The bartender stepped back, gestured with his arm as if welcoming them to strip the place bare themselves. "Help yerselves, gents. Don't know as takin' any of it away counts as thievin' when the man what owned it is deader 'n yesterday's dinner."

****

Tal waited until Gately left the premises before looking the late Silas Rosser's establishment over. The interior was redolent with the scent of "seegar" smoke, liquor, and sweat. There wasn't much to the place, but it was solid enough to keep out the worst of the winds, rain, and snowfall, which was all a man needed when stranded in the mountains at the hump of winter. He'd spent the snowbound months in a similar place his first year of exile, which was why he'd spent the last one in an established place. Even if Virginia City was latched on to the side of a damn mountain, it boasted a theatre, a comfy hotel, churches, residential areas ranging from fine to bearable, and saloons that ran the gamut from luxurious to dangerous. Even the worst of Virginia's bars was several steps up from Rosser's place of business.

A street-facing window would have provided light and circulation in the building, but Rosser had foregone the luxury. To dissipate the cave-like penumbra of the saloon, 'Diah lit the lantern dangling from a rafter support. Illumination showed a bar constructed of a couple of barrels and a stretch of roughly planed wood, with another four barrels behind it. Three of them rested on trestles and were tapped, ready to draw a cup full of whatever poison they harbored. Just the sight made Tal long for the polished and carved glories that graced the Nevada Territory bars he'd left behind.

Rather than gracefully shaped and polished spittoons, there were a couple of battered buckets at each end of the bar surrounded by evidence that the men who spewed tobacco juice toward them had lousy aim. There were no scandalous paintings of buxom nude beauties on reclining couches, on the windowless walls, no mirror behind the bar, and only a handful of tall bottles in sight, the tapped barrels obviously being the preferred method of drawing a drink. Tables were long and rugged, with seats nothing but sturdy stumps of uncleaved trunks serving as stools. They only wanted for an ax to move from the log stage to a repurposed life as fuel for the stove.

Surprisingly, a cast iron stove angled back in a corner with a supply of corded wood nearby. Just to the right of it, a door that probably led to an outhouse out back, and a partially opened door that led to a rear room.

"That there's Miz Pearl's room," 'Diah said. "It ain't real pretty, Mr. Cain. We took Rosser's carcass out o' it, but he done bled like a slaughtered heifer."

And Letty had been in the room when the killing commenced. She'd probably have nightmares for years, reliving the event.

If he managed to keep her from the hangman's hands.

She had to know who the murderer was. Had to be protecting them. The *why* of it nagged at him as much as the *who* did.

Tal made his way across the saloon proper carefully, ensuring that he didn't disturb the still damp splotches of blood on the packed earthen floor. The dryer ones were fainter and seemed configured to the form of a boot heel or toe, but others created a trail of drops, no doubt deposited when the dead man's body had been removed.

"Where was he taken?" Tal asked.

"Over ta Burl Bergen's place 'cross the way. He

und his wife got ’emselves a general store, but he does undertakin’, too. Built a rough shed where those who didn’t make it through the winter were kept so as they’d be safe from the wolves ’til the ground warn’t froze no more und they could bury ’em. Burl’s already slappin’ t’gether a pine box fer Rosser.”

Tal mentally added Bergen to his tally of folks to visit. He needed to see for himself what had happened to the dead man. Needed to also see the weapon that had killed him. Learn who the weapon had belonged to. The Noletta Kittridge he remembered from two years ago had no knowledge of pistols, but could he say the same about the woman she had become in those lost years?

But first there was a crime scene to see.

Letty’s possessions to collect.

Had she come west with trunks filled with gowns created by modistes? Had they slowly been jettisoned until it seemed her life was being left behind? He’d met a few other women in his travels who sighed over the necessity of giving up their treasures along the trail. Had seen the pain in their eyes over the losses.

Tal fought down the sensation that he was trespassing as he pushed the partially closed door open. ’Diah had been right. It wasn’t a pretty sight, and that had little to do with the rough, blood-soaked blankets on the bed.

The room stretched the width of the narrow building, but it did get light as well as air from a trimmed-out section of the eastern-facing wall that posed as a future placement for glass. Twin shutters bracketed the empty opening, swinging in the breeze that wafted in, banging the boards against the inner wall. They were clearly the only barricade between the room's residents and the elements and had probably failed to keep out the rain, much less the snow or the winter winds. Sunlight streamed in after the breeze. Tal glanced beyond the frame to find a small but natural meadow bordered by a tall, ancient growth of coniferous forest, and the expected necessary.

Despite the pine-scented breeze, the taint of freshly spilled blood cloaked the room.

The bed was the sturdiest piece of furniture. No doubt because the use of it had put cash and gold dust in Rosser's pocket. Shaved-down saplings served as posts at each corner, their cousins notched and tied with rope to create the sides and a support for a thin mattress. Small comfort, since even straw was hard to come by in this wilderness of rock, sagebrush, spruce, fir, and bitterroot. There were no traveling trunks in sight, just a rustic shelf nailed to the wall, holding a small ceramic bowl with a few hairpins resting in it, a hand mirror, hairbrush, comb, a sliver of scented soap, a clear unlabeled medicine bottle of noxious-looking liquid, and a small book of Shakespearian sonnets. Another piece of tree trunk served as a table for a wash bowl, the chipped pitcher sitting on the floor beside it.

Behind a primitive three-part screen of calico and scrap wood, a few nails protruded from the wall to hold her clothing. The jacket of the walking suit that he recalled her wearing while strolling through the Common with him dangled from one. The skirt had fallen to the floor. Both were now so faded and worn only his memory supplied the deep emerald it had been. Another nail hosted a once-white blouse, a frayed chemise, and a petticoat in need of darning. A sturdy gray calico dress hung from a third. At the head of the bed, a paisley-patterned wool shawl of now-faded jewel tones was draped around one of the bed posts and had unfortunately received a splattering of Rosser's blood. The blood had already dried on the cloth.

There was no sign of the type of stylish hat that had once perched at a coquettish angle on Letty's upswept blonde hair, but at the foot of another log bedside table lay a discarded man's shirt, a pair of trousers, a broad belt, and a pair of abused large boots—all Rosser's, no doubt.

It was difficult to picture Letty living in such sordid conditions.

Avoiding the bed, Tal gathered up Letty's meager collection of clothing. He found a reticule dangling from its strings beneath the draping folds of the jacket. It held a delicate handkerchief, the decorative lace along the edges in the act of unraveling, but nothing else.

What bedding there was had soaked up too much of the dead man's blood to merit saving, including a blanket that had dropped to the floor. The bed lacked the comfort of a pillow. Tal added a visit to the general store to his tally of chores. Fresh blankets were needed to improve Letty's accommodations at the jail.

"Looks like we won't need your friend to help us after all, 'Diah," Tal said, hunkering down to look beneath the bed. The drape of the bedding toward the dirt floor had cloaked the existence of a crate of corked bottles, but also the carpetbag he'd hoped to find stored there. Fortunately, the satchel had escaped baptism by blood. Pulling it out, he carefully folded Letty's few items of clothing and tucked them neatly inside. Next came the comb, brush, mirror, reticule, and the rest of what he took to be her possessions. The blood-flecked shawl was packed last, arranged so that the stain was neither visible nor against her other clothing. “Think you can carry the screen on your own?”

The boy stared at the satchel, a hint of hunger clear to read in his face. Was it because he was taken with the woman who called herself Pearl, or was it because the items could be turned into ready money, such as they were?

With a subdued sigh, the lad squared his thin shoulders. “That ah can, Mr. Cain. Miz Pearl’s lucky the blood didn’t get on this thing er her clothes,” he said, folding the pieces of the screen into a manageable load.

Tal let the boy maneuver through the door and into the saloon proper before following him out. “You’re fond of her? Were you one of her clients, ’Diah?”

“No, sir, but ah woulda liked ta o’ been. She was nice ta me. Kind. Didn’t heckle me like some o’ the others do. Jest didn’t have the coin Si Rosser wanted fer a poke with her.”

As there hadn’t been either greenbacks or coins among her things, Tal wondered what the going rate had been and whether Letty had ever received a share of what Rosser collected from the men who used her body.

“Know it’s bad ta say, bein’ as ah’m now a deputy und all,” ’Diah added, “but Rosser deserved the lead he caught. Deserved it und a load o’ buckshot more.”

****

’Diah set the dressing screen against the building and returned inside to close and barricade the shutters over the lone window so that the curious couldn't steal into the building without a concerted effort. Tal took the time to survey the camp's business section. There wasn't much to it. A dry goods store, four saloons, if he counted Rosser's, a fenced paddock and a sad excuse for a barn, the jail, three long, low-roofed buildings advertising themselves as boarding houses, and a scattering of other shacks and tents. He could hear the ring of metal being beaten against an anvil, so a blacksmith was tucked away somewhere. Compared to Bannock City, where he'd stopped briefly, this camp was still in its infancy. Tal wondered if there had been much more than a hundred people to winter there, which made it odd that a jail had been built and a sheriff hired to man it. Which led to a longer list of questions he needed answered.

When 'Diah extinguished the lantern and closed the door on Rosser's defunct saloon, Tal casually broached his first query. "This camp have a name?"

The deputy hefted Letty's dressing screen. "It's got lots o' names but none official, fer as ah can tell. Seems discussions on the topic were what occupied most folks ov'r the winter. Like ah said, ah warn't here then, but Bergen had pulled inta camp with wagons o' provisions fer folks a month er so after the first strikes. Foley got here not much after. They both brought their wives with 'em, but we ain't got even a handful o' good women."

Which meant there wasn't a church hidden away farther out of the miniscule settlement either, Tal decided. Churches grew when the soiled doves no longer outnumbered the wives. If the camp was still pulling sufficient gold from the streams in six months, someone would be campaigning to bring the Lord in, the denomination determined by what the first preacher to ride in practiced.

But why was there a jail, a sheriff, and a deputy in an otherwise loosely organized mining camp?

"Pollard, the horse doc und blacksmith, arrived same time ah did, 'bout a month er more back. 'Course the girls at Madam June's were carted in soon as word got out 'bout the gold," 'Diah continued as they headed back to the sheriff's office.

If there had already been prostitutes plying their trade in the camp, why had Rosser pressed Letty into selling herself?

"Which of the saloons is Madam June's place?" he asked.

"Ain't in the town proper," 'Diah said and pointed farther up the path. "It's down the road, just 'round that outcrop o' pine. Nice proper house like back East. Ya might o' passed it on yer way in, Mr. Cain."

"If I had, I wouldn't have made it the rest of the way into the camp yet, bucko." Tal gave the boy a broad wink. "But I arrived from the south, not the north."

'Diah nodded. "Me, too. Come up through Mormon lands, though ah hail from Missoura."

Though the kid was probably expecting a confession of his own antecedents, Tal changed the topic. "Which saloon's got the best whiskey? Having a drink was all that was on my mind when I strolled in and got sidetracked with the excitement. Once we turn Miss Pearl's possessions over to her, are you free to introduce me to this fine camp?"

'Diah's eyes lit at the offer. "If'n the sheriff don't need me," he said. "Most fellas'll be back at their claims, but there's always a few in the saloons. Seein' as how yer plannin' ta save Miz Pearl from the rope, ah'm not sure how friendly their greetin's might be."

Tal doubted cordiality would be high on the list, but opening his wallet to anyone willing to bend his ear as they bent an elbow with several rounds might supply answers to some of his less pressing questions.

The harder ones…well, his experience back in Boston would get an airing. It might well take every trick he knew to save Noletta Kittridge's life. Fortunately, he was a hell of a persistent man.

Particularly when it came to Letty.

Chapter Three

Letty heard the sheriff and the mayor talking in the outer room, discussing who to hire to build a scaffold for the hanging. While the camp was surrounded by forest, it was a coniferous one, pine, spruce, and fir abounding. Trees not configured for use when the required outcome was that the victim dangle a yard or so above the ground.

She should be frightened. Instead she was empty. Cold and empty.

On one hand, Silas Rosser had saved her. He had come to her rescue after her brother's death, albeit too late to stop the three men who had invaded the tiny shack she and Kit had shared outside of the settlement from doing as they wished with her. On the other hand, Rosser had used her, both to increase his income and personally nearly every night after the saloon closed. He'd never said the words to her, but she'd overheard him tell more than one of the men who bought the use of her body that she belonged to him.

There had been no affection. No freedom for her, just a constraint. He would keep her safe, keep the worst men from enjoying her favors, but he had sold her to any other man who met his price. There had been no way out for her. A woman alone couldn't survive in this wilderness. Not a woman like her, who had been cosseted, courted, and constrained to society's rules of behavior. By her parents' expectations.

A life in the strict confines of Boston society had landed her here, in a countryside that was beautiful. Dangerous. Vicious. There was no golden opportunity awaiting her in Idaho Territory or any other territory of the West. All that awaited her was a noose, the final payment for a crime she had not committed but would accept as her due. She had been foolish beyond measure to follow Kit west. Had been damned from the moment her family cut Talmadge Hammond from her life.

Oh, if only she'd been strong enough to follow her heart and not the dictates of those who claimed to love her and yet hadn't loved her enough to allow her happiness.

Letty wasn't sure what happiness was any longer. She only knew what it had been like fleetingly.

Happiness had fled early in the spring of 1861.

It had arrived the previous autumn when her brother had appeared at Hester Moorehouse's ball with a friend at his side. A friend named Tal Hammond.

****

Boston, November 1860

"Your mother will be peeved with me. I told Kit to bring a friend tonight. A man who is new to Boston and most definitely not of our set," Letty warned the plain young woman reflected next to her in the mirror as they did a final primp before joining Boston's most select families.

"Qualities that made him irresistible to you," Hester Moorehouse said. "Is he handsome as well?"

"I've no idea. What makes him of interest is that my parents were quite disparaging over the idea that I wished to meet him. Well, that and the fact that he's a friend of Kit's. You know what they think of my dear brother's taste in companions."

Hester sighed. "Yes, and I also know that if Kit is bringing this paragon of inappropriateness, they will arrive late to my ball. We shall both expire of anticipation before getting satisfaction in shocking our parents. At least, you will, dearest. I'm too timid in company to be more than a wallflower even when Mother and Father wish to push me forward."

Letty linked arms with her friend. "Then I will help you shock them. I shall insist that Kit dance with you. We will write his name on your dance card for a waltz."

"Oh, no, never a waltz. Even when we were children, I was tongue-tied around him. I wouldn't know what to converse about during a waltz," Hester insisted. "If you are determined to pursue such foolishness, put his name down for a country dance, something where partners are exchanged during a promenade and no conversations are necessary."

"Absolutely not. You must be my spy and interrogate Kit for information," Letty said.

"What sort of information?"

"Why, everything he knows about Talmadge Hammond, of course! I've quite set my mind on putting my mother's teeth on edge by stealing his heart."

"Letty! He could be squat, smell of cheap cigars, and have warts."

"True, but we won't know how pleasing Mr. Hammond's appearance is until Kit drags him in the door. Even if he's a toad, I shall do my best to beam on him brightly," Letty vowed.

"Perhaps he won't come," Hester suggested.

Letty grinned at her friend. "Piffle," she said.

Until…

****

Talmadge Hammond was a most welcome surprise. He was immaculately turned out in an evening suit obviously tailored by one of Boston's best haberdashers, the white of his shirt, the gleam of the dark silk stock at his throat, and the sheen of his black coat, pantaloons, and weskit the equal of the other men in the room. He was also more conservatively turned out than Kit himself, but then her brother did prefer a more dashing style. Even in evening black, Dorian "Kit" Kittridge appeared slightly bohemian, since his fair hair was tousled and his jawline beginning to darken with a new growth of beard.

Mr. Hammond looked far more presentable, his jaw freshly shaven, his side whiskers neatly trimmed and unable to disguise the roguish dimple that danced into view when he smiled. His deep chestnut hair waved back from his brow and, unlike the other men in the room, his complexion reflected hours spent being warmed under the afternoon sun. An inch or two taller than her brother, he lacked Kit's slouch. Mr. Hammond held his shoulders straight, though not as stiffly as did Geoffrey Haversham, recently returned home after being expelled from West Point for reasons unknown but speculated on in whispered conversations in various corners.

Geoffrey's disgrace would hold court with the gossips, her mother among them, Letty knew, and the distraction would allow her to slip from the maternal eye to enchant Kit's new friend. Would he be a challenge, she wondered? Would he turn out to be a bore? She would know the answer by the end of a single dance. A waltz had already been reserved for him on her card, much to the consternation of gentlemen hoping to capture her for a second turn around the ballroom. If a second dance was to be granted, the yet unmet Talmadge Hammond had a better chance at securing it.

As they were, as expected, late arrivals, Kit entered the ballroom on the lookout for their hostess and heavily laid on apologies, roguish smiles, and forward hand kissing. Letty watched from a distance, losing track of the story her current prattling male companion related. Her fan fluttered near her face, cooling the flush that had arisen as the result of her partner's overenthusiastic polka gallop.

"Would you mind procuring me a glass of punch, Mr. Everly? Our dance has left me quite exhausted," she said, heartlessly interrupting his tale.

"It would be my pleasure, Miss Kittridge. Promise you won't disappear into another man's arms while I am gone," he pleaded smoothly.

Letty peered at him over the top of her open fan. "Mr. Everly! You will make me blush," she teased while promising no such thing.

The width of the smile he delivered before dashing off meant that if her brother hadn't beat the man back to her side, she would have to concoct another reason to slip free of his attentions. Surely, she wasn't the only young woman in the room who found most of the men tediously dull.

Perhaps that was Kit's fault though. She measured all men against her scandalously charming older brother, and very few were ever his equal. Would Mr. Hammond be roguish enough to hold her attention?

At first glance, he most definitely passed muster.

As Kit worked through the crowd, Hammond didn't so much trail behind him as appear to be politely finding his way across the room.

"Did I not gift you with a pocket watch on the last anniversary of your birth, brother dear?" she asked as Kit spilled past the last human obstacles that separated them.

"A dandy it was, too, Lett," he answered, brushing his lips in a quick peck of a kiss on her cheek.

"Now if you'd only learn to look at it occasionally, you might be on time for an affair," she said.

Kit's grin twitched. "Oh, I'm always on time for an *affair*, just not for frippery social functions."

Letty struck him with her folded fan, the blow glancing off an immaculate, though already rumpled, weskit. "Cad! Behave and introduce me to your companion."

Her brother chuckled. "I hasten to obey, dearest. You did order me to bring him along, after all."

She looked past him to where the stranger stood, the curve of his lips indicating amused enjoyment of their byplay. His eyes were the deep blue of a sapphire and sparkled like a cut and polished gemstone. It had always been one of her favorite stones, but henceforth she would remember this man's gaze when she chose to wear her own sapphires.

"Allow me to present Mr. Talmadge Hammond, late of some forgotten little hamlet to the northwest. Tal, my sister, the insidiously pertinent Miss Noletta Kittridge."

"Miss Kittridge," Hammond murmured, his voice deep and caressing as he took her hand and bowed over it.

"Mr. Hammond." She curtseyed briefly. "Dare I hope that your acquaintance with Kit is of sufficient duration that you recognize he frequently lies?"

"About your request that he foist me on our unsuspecting hostess, Miss Kittridge?"

"That I am insidiously pertinent," Letty corrected. "What I am at the moment is surprised to find your name has made it onto my dance card."

"Put there by elves?" Kit asked.

"By good fortune, I would hazard," Hammond said. "Dare I ask which dance I have been fortunate to be awarded?"

"A waltz," Letty said.

"Which by an amazing twist of fate is the very next dance," Kit murmured as he studied her card. "I don't see my name on this anywhere."

Letty took her brother's arm and turned him to face the dance floor. "That is because your name is on Hester's card for this dance. Don't flirt too much with her. You know it will leave her tongue-tied and incapable of following you in the figures."

Kit sighed, then set off to claim his partner.

Hammond was still smiling, not just with his lips but with his eyes. "You are quite the commander, Miss Kittridge. How did you know Kit and I would arrive in time for this particular dance? Do you have a lookout stationed?"

Letty took his proffered arm, letting him lead her to the center of the ballroom. "I simply know my brother very well, Mr. Hammond. He always arrives precisely ninety minutes late for a party. Well, a society party. Is he ever late for an evening of billiards or cards or whatever other entertainment you men have planned?"

This time Hammond laughed. She loved the deep rolling sound of it washing over her. "More often he's the first to arrive," he admitted.

"I'm not surprised," Letty said, moving into his arms as the musicians flowed into the opening stanza of a Schubert waltz. "He is a rapscallion. I'll actually miss that aspect of his personality when he grows old, conservative, and cranky."

"It's difficult to picture him that way, and yet…"

Letty laughed softly, then glanced over his shoulder to the edge of the ballroom where Mr. Everly stood, a cup of punch in his hand and an expression of stunned disbelief on his long face. "Oh, dear," she murmured. "I'm afraid I'm just as rapscallionly as Kit is. Be warned, sir. I've just left my last dance partner afloat on a sea of consternation."

"Fortunately, Miss Kittridge, I do know how to sail," Hammond said and swung her into the flowing movement of the dance.

****

Idaho Territory, 1863

Letty nearly cried when Obadiah Short wrestled the rickety dressing screen into her cell. Kit had made it for her. Inexpertly, yet it had held up well during those long months. Its shelter had been the only privacy measure she'd had in the rough cabin she and Kit had shared, and then in Rosser's back room. Now it would serve her here for a few last days.

"Thank you, Mr. Short," she said as the gangly youth backed up to see if it was solidly placed on the floor of the cell.

"Least ah could do, ma'am," 'Diah rumbled, obviously embarrassed.

Letty stared at him silently a moment. A long moment it must have seemed, for Short fidgeted under her gaze yet didn't turn away. "The least," Letty echoed.

'Diah backed toward the open cell door. "Mr. Cain'll be along shortly with the rest o' yer things. He stopped by Bergen's store ta aug… Well, ah cain't rightly 'member the word, but ta pick up a few things."

"Augment?" she asked.

"That's it," 'Diah agreed. "'Spect lawyers know lots o' fancy words like that."

"Yes," Letty said.

Under her steadfast gaze, he fidgeted more. "Ah'm right sorry ya landed here, ma'am. If'n ah could…"

"But you can't," she finished.

'Diah's head dropped, chin to calico-shirted chest. Scuffed a dilapidated boot toe against the flooring. "Ah cain't. Ah'll pray fer ya, Miz Pearl. Pray real hard."

"Thank you, Mr. Short." Obadiah Short could wear out the knees in those rough trousers and all the prayer in the world wouldn't make a difference. Even Tal Hammond was unlikely to make a difference despite the reputation he'd had back in Boston for ferreting out information the police had overlooked or ignored. Information that led to his client being pardoned and released. A scandal, as far as her father was concerned. Had that been the real reason he'd refused to countenance Tal as her chosen husband?

She would never know, though if it were possible to berate a parent on the other side of the veil, she would single her father out for inadvertently setting things in place that had brought her to a hangman's noose. Perhaps they wouldn't meet. For her sins, she'd be bound for Lucifer's court while her father's self-righteousness would have led him to the gates of Heaven. Had St. Peter let him in or left him to rot on the doorstep?

'Diah gave a courteous tug to the brim of his hat, a murmured "ma'am," and backed out the door. It had barely closed before Letty heard the broad piece of lumber drop into the brackets on either side, securing her wicked self from contaminating the God-fearing citizens eagerly awaiting the entertainment of her hanging.

Lacking the delicate lapel pin watch Kit had given her on her birthday three years ago, or the pocket watch she had presented to him on his—both of which had been sold to finance their ill-fated journey toward a golden future—Letty had no concept of how much time passed between 'Diah Short's departure and Tal's arrival. The gaps between the roughhewn logs were sealed too well to allow either breeze or gleam of sunlight into the cell. With the hatch in the door closed, she would live her final days in a suffocating darkness little eased by the lone lantern. While she now had the screen, it would give her little privacy if the flickering flame in the lamp threw the shadow of her silhouette against the thin patchwork of muslin stretched like a canvas between the posts. She had sacrificed a petticoat to the project the previous autumn when she and her brother had moved into the single-room cabin a quarter mile south of the camp.

She had danced more steps in a single evening than what she traveled between the cabin's rickety door and the general mercantile in the small gold-happy settlement. Once upon a time the local shopkeeper's wife had welcomed her as another *good* woman in camp. And then…

The sound of men's voices preceded the scrape of the cell's bar being removed. Daylight spilled into the room, a welcome reprieve, though blinding now that her eyes had adjusted to the dim shadows.

With his back to the sunlit front office, Tal's face was hidden, but she knew the way he held his shoulders, braced his feet, pausing briefly in the doorway to acclimate his sight to the twilight of the cell. His armor was righteousness, little dimmed by the sturdy, dung-colored clothing of a man living in, and off, the wilderness. His sword was the written law, his prowess with it feared by his courtroom opponents thousands of miles and what felt like lifetimes away. He'd been the knight to win her heart, once. This time she feared the dragon of circumstances would best him in the coming battle, then consume her.

"My apologies for lagging behind young 'Diah, ma'am," he drawled, his voice nearly unrecognizable with the stain of his New England antecedents stripped away. Taking a lone step into the cell, he dropped a familiar carpetbag on the foot of the narrow cot. At his back, the door to the room was closed and secured once more. Ah, but she was a dangerous woman. They believed she had killed a man. No doubt every male in town feared her.

All but Tal Hammond.

"Let me know if any of your things are missing," he said. "I might have overlooked something."

Letty doubted it was possible. She had so little left. "It will take but a moment to do a thorough inventory, Mr. Cain. Would you care to wait?"

"If you're willing to put up with me, Miss Pearl."

She'd once wanted to spend her life with him, but even shared minutes hurt now. She was a lost cause, and in attempting to clear her name of murder, Tal would be the one left to deal with failure.

He was right. She did know the identity of the murderer, but who would believe the word of a fallen woman? Her life had been destroyed when Kit died, and she had been unable to defend herself. Rosser's death had stripped what little protection had remained. Better that her existence end than another's life be lost due to a brief miscalculated display of passion.

Rather than open the carpetbag, she stared at the bundle beneath Tal's arm. A bundle that was quite clearly bedding. "Mr. Short informed me that you had stopped for supplies. I had not realized you intended to share my quarters. However, as I have no funds to pay for legal services, I am reduced to rendering other *tender* in its stead."

"The blankets are for you, not me," he said. "Those on the bed at the saloon were no longer tenable for use, and I prefer my clients not to contract an ague while in my care. Plus, if you recall, I am not expecting—nor will I accept—tender of any type while I represent you."

"I will not be treated as a pauper, Mr. Cain. I can and will pay for services rendered."

Tal moved past her to place the additional blankets on the cot. In doing so, he bent near her ear, his voice dropped to a whisper. "I'm not a man who accepts that sort of payment, Letty. Now go through the things I collected and make sure there is nothing missing. I thought perhaps you had something of Kit's, but if you kept it elsewhere—"

"Hidden, you mean," she clarified. "There was nothing. We sold off everything of worth to make it this far. As Kit left debts, whatever Rosser collected for my…time with various gentlemen went to alleviate them."

She thought he'd take a seat next to her, but Tal chose to settle on the floor once more, his back to the wall. The shadows thrown by the lantern showed lines in his face that hadn't been there two years ago in Boston. His skin was more weathered than it had been in the city, burned a darker shade by hours in the sun. When he swept the sweat-and-rain-stained felt hat from his head, waves of dark hair straggled over his brow. When he shoved his fingers through it, pushing it back from his eyes, her heart gave a jolt of fond remembrance. Of him doing the same thing, then rolling to his side after making love to her.

When they parted that day, she had known he was walking out of her life.

Yet here she was with Tal once more, though this time he was refusing her offer. He had stopped loving her. He had not stopped being the defender of those he felt needed saving. As Pearl, she fell into that category now.

Part of her accepted that. Another part cried for what might have been.

If her parents had not been inflexible.

If the war had not come.

If she had been brave enough to leave with him.

So many regrets, so many dreams crushed.

The sound of axes chipping away at timber in the forest behind the jail jarred her back to the present. To the lost cause she was.

To Tal where he sat as he waited, his feet braced against the floor, his wrists resting on his upraised knees. The jacket he wore had fallen open, allowing her to see both the empty holster on his belt and the knifeless sheath strapped to his thigh. The sheriff would have stripped him of their contents before allowing him past her door.

The man sitting patiently at her feet was not the man she knew. Dirt stained his fingers, wedged beneath his nails. She could smell his sweat, could recognize it as days old, now absorbed by his shirt. There was no sign of the dapper man she'd fallen in love with, in his countenance. He'd become a wanderer carrying as few possessions as she now owned. His weapons would be better cared for than his clothing. Hygiene had become just another word in a large vocabulary of unused terms.

Letty bent to the carpetbag and opened it.

"I'll warn you," Tal murmured quietly. "While most of your things escaped damage, there are a few drops of blood on the shawl. I would have replaced it, but Bergen didn't have merchandise of a feminine sort."

There was so little to go through, so little left of the things she had packed for the trip west. Despite the traces of Silas Rosser's blood, the shawl was a welcome addition. It would help keep the cold out, would give her fingers something to do by tangling in the fringe to hide the fact that it was difficult to keep them from shaking when she didn't have them clasped tightly together in her lap.

She would mount the scaffold wearing her

threadbare best and the only treasure she had left.

Lacking any way to hang her clothing in the cell, Letty carefully returned each item to the carpetbag and turned to the stained reticule. In Boston, there would have been a modest amount in newly printed greenbacks in the bag. In the camp, her only currency the past months had been her body. The only item she still possessed of value was worth more in sentiment than any amount of either coin or gold dust.

And it was not in the purse.

She turned the bag inside out, hoping the lining had developed a hitherto unnoticed hole through which the treasure had fallen.

Nothing met her search.

“Something’s missing,” Tal noted.

Letty closed her eyes against the tears that threatened. She bit her bottom lip to hold back a sob. She hadn’t lost her stoic control over the knowledge that the townspeople were going to murder her in a solemn ceremony in a few days’ time, but the theft of the only item she had clung to broke her.

The tears spilled over as she curled up on the bunk, her head bowed, her arms wrapped around herself. It was impossible to hold back the sobs now. The dam had been breached.

A moment later she was enveloped in strong arms. Arms that turned her quivering form into the comfort of a man’s hard, inflexible embrace. Unable to help herself, Letty burrowed against Tal, wrapped her arms around him, and cried silently, the hopelessness of her situation consuming her.

He let her exhaust the overwhelming grief. The strength of his grip never faltered. He stroked her hair, rubbing his cheek against it rather than breaking the embrace. When she felt him drop a tender kiss on her crown, she cried all the harder.

"What's missing, Letty?" he murmured as her sobs subsided.

Rather than move out of his arms, she kept her face pressed to his chest, listening to the steady thump of his heart. "My ring," she whispered. "The one you gave me the day we…"

She couldn't finish the sentence. She'd felt him go rigid at the reminder of the afternoon they'd made love.

"Lett," he said quietly.

She couldn't stop the wave of longing, of regret, from washing over her, making her tremble. He'd apologized for the modesty of the offering, knowing she owned far more impressive jewelry. The gold band was narrow, winnowed even more by the filigree design cut into it. The setting was simple, a single creamy pearl, the hue enhanced by the gold setting and tiny glints of twin miniscule emeralds on either side. Emeralds to match her eyes, he'd said. They had both known she would never be able to wear it in public, though it was a token of his love for her.

A final gift before he walked out of her life.

Tal's hand on the back of her head drew her closer. Her brow rested against him, feeling the scratch of his beard, feeling the beat of his pulse in his throat. "Hush," he murmured. "I haven't forgotten."

She'd already cried too many times over all she'd lost in the past. She would not give in to the need now. And yet…

Tal Hammond still knew her too well. But she couldn't allow him to support her. She was a Kittridge of Boston, even if that distinction meant nothing in the wilds of the Boise Basin.

Letty took a wavering deep breath and sat up, easing from his arms. It was time to regain control of herself. To show him that the past was dead, even if in doing so she was lying to him.

"It appears," she said, "that I will have to accept your offer to represent me *pro bono*, Mr. Cain. I have nothing of any value to offer in exchange for your services after all."

Chapter Four

When 'Diah arrived with a cracked bowl and a bucket of fresh water, Tal excused himself from Letty's cell. What she really needed was a relaxing soak in a deep tub, the water both pleasantly warm and fragrant, scented with scattered drops of perfume. Instead, she would make do with water still chilled by the melting snows farther up the mountain and the last sliver of the scented soap she had left Boston with a year ago. He'd have to ask around, see if there was civilized bathing available in the camp, even if it was just an easily transported shallow tin tub. Perhaps the madam at the brothel just outside of town had one and could be sweet-talked into lending it to Letty. There was probably little chance that consideration for a fellow soiled dove would grease the path, but a generous donation from his pocket would certainly make that consideration more likely to make an appearance.

It was too early to be paying calls to the whorehouse, though. He needed to locate a roof, and, if possible, a bed he could call his own for the duration of his stay, and a meal that could be washed down with halfway decent whiskey. Well, at least a glass of something that wouldn't kill him outright. After that, he had some questions to ask. Hopefully the answers wouldn't be delivered with a round of lead as a chaser.

'Diah was absent, having been sent off on an

errand by the sheriff. Lacking a local guide, Tal turned to Sheriff Linus Strand for recommendations on where to find a meal.

The lawman filled the room that served as his office and living quarters. Tal was left propping his shoulders against the open door while Strand shifted the positioning of his boot heels before the iron stove in the front room. “Might try the Friendly Gal Saloon across the way, though I’d augment their coffee with a dollop or two of alcohol. That way, neither one of them will eat your guts out,” the man drawled. “Least ways, not too bad. You want something more civilized, try the Gilded Moon. Foley’s wife throws together meals that are palatable, unlike what you get elsewhere in camp. Not what we’ll be serving your client, though.”

Tal kept his distaste for the lawman’s implication of the quality of meals Letty would be given from showing. Settling his hat in place, he tweaked the brim by way of thanks as he reclaimed his pistol and hunting knife from the table at the sheriff’s side. There was a coffeepot on the potbellied stove, but the scent emanating from the sheriff’s tin cup had only reached boiling point while making its way through the tubes of a still. “’Preciate the effort, Sheriff, but I’ll arrange for Miss Pearl’s vittles.”

Strand harrumphed. “Camp’s responsible to feed prisoners, Mr. Cain. Nothing says the meal has to be tasty.”

“Miss Pearl isn’t the guilty party. She’s innocent until proven guilty by the facts and a duly sworn-in jury,” Tal said.

The sheriff chuckled and lifted the cup of homebrew to his lips. “You honestly think there are twelve men in this camp that won't turn in a guilty verdict, Counselor?"

"When I prove Pearl wasn't the shooter…"

"Yeah," the lawman said, his mouth curving in amusement. "*When*. If you can."

Tal shut the door behind him quietly. It didn't matter how far a man got from a proper courtroom, the one thing that didn't change was the law officer's belief that the person arrested was far from innocent of the crime. Granted, he'd represented a few unlucky villains during his time before the bar, but Noletta Kittridge wasn't one of them. Still, if he hadn't recognized her, would he believe her guilty of Rosser's murder? She had been covered in the man's blood. Had been forced into a profession from which a good man would have protected her. Could she have killed Rosser? Letty insisted that the woman he'd known and courted back in Boston no longer existed. That in her place stood a woman whom life had beaten down. He knew beyond a doubt that Noletta Kittridge was incapable of taking anyone's life, but was Pearl?

Unfortunately, he thought she was, if pushed beyond reason.

He needed more facts. Needed to know what had happened to bring Letty to this juncture, one that had even him wondering what she was capable of doing.

His job was to save her from the hangman's noose. His Letty hadn't totally withdrawn. The way she strode down the street, head high and back straight, belied everything she wanted him to believe of her. Everything that Letty no longer believed of herself.

There was still a nip in the mountain air despite the arrival of spring, and yet the glare in the street as the sun reached its zenith seared a man's sight after the dim confines of the jail. Tal resettled his hat, tilting it low over his eyes. The forest had been pushed back, but it would take little more than an hour for the shadows to creep in again. Considering all he had to accomplish yet, Tal was all too conscious that the day was slipping away.

His horse waited patiently, hitched near a water trough before the sheriff's office, its tail flicking at the flies trying to make its acquaintance. Tal sized up the camp as he moseyed out to the hitching rail and unwound the reins. The settlement hadn't impressed him at first glance and had less to recommend it now. There were a few buildings that appeared more substantial than the others. One was the general store. But the most impressive structure in the camp proper was the Gilded Moon Saloon. It spanned two lots and boasted a partial second floor. Curtains at the windows argued that the upper region was the owner's living quarters and that he most definitely had a wife in tow.

The horse shoved its muzzle against his chest, regaining his attention. The nudge was also its way of insisting he owed it something. Aware that the demand would be made, he'd included a slightly withered apple among his purchases at the mercantile and now fished it from his jacket pocket.

"Satisfied?" he asked the horse. The crunch as it bit through the core was answer enough.

Waiting until the apple was history, Tal trailed his mount down a path behind the sheriff's office, drawn to the sound of a hammer striking iron.

The blacksmith's hammer raised and fell with precision as he beat a horseshoe into shape. A recently constructed lean-to housed a few animals, though it was unclear which would benefit from his labor. The scent of recently felled pine battled with that of heat rising from the forge and the dung of the stable. The man laboring at his anvil stopped long enough to agree to board Tal's mount for the duration of his stay for the trial, though he was of the opinion that having a trial at all was a waste of time and community funds when the gal had clearly killed her man.

It hadn't taken long for the community to tar Letty with guilt. Was it because men found the idea of a woman taking revenge on a man frightening? Or had Silas Rosser had a lot of friends? He needed to design the questions he asked to learn more about the man. A chore that would no doubt result in a sleepless night.

Unsaddling his horse and shouldering saddle bags and bedroll, Tal slipped his rifle free of the saddle holster and headed back to the wide path down the center of the camp.

Food was nearly as much a priority as information, but as he could combine the search for both, Tal decided in favor of the sheriff's suggestion and stopped at the Gilded Moon Saloon.

Like all the other buildings in town, it was a long structure, though wider since it sat on two lots rather than one. The glass paned windows that bracketed the main door gleamed. The door was propped open with a chair that featured gracefully curved legs and a back of carved spindles. Rather than makeshift boards laid across barrels or stumps, round tables surrounded by more elegantly crafted chairs were arranged on a freshly scrubbed plank floor. The place was in the process of emulating the establishments he'd enjoyed in

Virginia City.

Obviously, improvements were still in progress. Along the wall to Tal's right a bar with graceful lines held the attention of a man diligently rubbing stain into the top, giving it a richer though false mahogany color. The fellow looked up at the sound of Tal's heels echoing on the floorboards.

"Come on in, friend," the man called, straightening. He was a tall, gaunt man with a long narrow face and eyes deep set beneath an overhang of bristling dark brows etched with gray. If he'd opted for a chin-hugging beard, he could have been mistaken for a close cousin of President Lincoln. As he'd gone for being clean shaven, and had a watered-down Irish accent, the resemblance was fleeting. Though in dark trousers and pristine white shirt, the sleeves of which he'd rolled up, the fellow was the best-turned-out citizen Tal had come across yet in the camp.

"What can I get ye, lad?" the barkeep asked, putting the rag he'd been using to the side and grabbing another to wipe a trace of stain from his hand.

"The sheriff tells me the best meal in town can be found here," Tal said. "Would appreciate putting that to the test, unless I picked the wrong time of day to indulge."

"Not at all," the fellow said. "The wife keeps a pot on the boil for travelers such as yerself. Would ye be preferrin' coffee or a spot of whiskey ta wash it down?"

"Both," Tal decided.

"Make yerself at home, friend," the man urged and brushed aside a homey calico curtain gathered across an open doorway in the back wall. "Moira, I've a lad in search of a bowl and a bit o' bread. Be a lass, would ye?" he called, then dropped the makeshift door and turned to where tin cups rested on a shelf near a potbellied stove and filled one from a waiting coffeepot.

Tal settled at one of the round tables in the center of the room, draping his saddle bags over the back of a chair and resting the barrel of his rifle against them. The barkeep set the cup of steaming coffee down and returned to the shelves behind the bar to snag a bottle and two glass tumblers. "Mind if I join ye?" he asked, taking the chair across from Tal.

"Not in the least," Tal assured. "Nothing worse than drinking on your own when you don't have to. Company's always welcome."

The barkeep grinned as he poured medicinal doses of whiskey in the glasses. "Particularly when yer in need of…well, let's call it what it is—intelligence on the lay of the battlefield."

Tal chuckled. "You know who I am then."

"Not yer name, lad, but definitely what ye've set yerself ta accomplishin'. Fintan Foley at yer service, proprietor of this grand establishment." He offered his hand.

"Adam Cain," Tal said, shaking. "You are probably the first man I've met today who hasn't told me I'm on a fool's errand."

Foley lifted his whiskey glass, admiring the way the amber-toned liquid looked in the sunlight spilling through the open door from the street before taking a swig. "Not sayin' yer not on such an errand, lad, only that 'tis a battlefield yer facin'."

"Don't be discouraging the lad, Foley," a woman scolded as she pushed aside the curtain to the kitchen, a tray held before her. Nearly a foot shorter and plump where her husband was angular, Moira Foley's hair was brushed with a single streak of silver in an otherwise bright, gleaming copper shade and secured in a snood at her nape. A proper housekeeper's apron encircled a cinched waist and covered the dark blue woolen gown beneath it. "Ye'll be curdling the lad's good intentions," she said. "He's a hard-enough trail to travel without ye tossing stones in his path."

Before her husband could respond, Mrs. Foley set her tray on the table and transferred a bowl of stew to a place before Tal. "Eat up, laddie. Bread's fresh made, and we've some butter and cheese if ye'd like."

The offer was generous and tempting. Butter and cheese were rare commodities this far from civilization.

At Tal's hesitation, she took pity on him and patted his arm. "I make 'em myself, lad. We've a cow or two out back."

"Dig in," Foley urged. "Ask whatever ye'd like."

"Indeed," Moira agreed, settling into another of the spare chairs. "That poor lass has seen too much sorrow already. She may well have killed that Rosser, but she had good reason to do so if she did. The man took terrible advantage of her situation. If only she'd come to us, we'd have kept her safe, but Rosser'd stepped in a'fore we even realized her straits."

The scent rising from the bowl before him was too tantalizing to resist. Tal savored a spoonful and gave an immediate compliment to the cook seated next to him. Moira Foley beamed as she pushed the plate of neatly sliced bread toward him.

"You knew Pearl before she began working for Rosser?" he asked around a second mouthful.

A slight grimace of distaste flitted across Moira's face. "She didn't answer to that disgraceful name when she first arrived in the camp. Miss Noletta Kittridge, she was. A proper and good woman."

"No two people could have been farther apart in temperament than Miss Kittridge and her brother," Foley added. "Never could figure why she'd come to gold territory with him. She was a lady. He wasn't what I'd call a gentleman. More a wastrel. Worked his way from one card game to the next. Managed to win frequently enough to be suspected of dealin' underhanded but lost enough for the idea not to stick long."

Having sat at a table with Kit in the past, Tal agreed with Foley's observation. Kit might have known how to deal himself a better hand, even to doctor a deck. It didn't mean he was slick enough not to get caught cheating, so the likelihood of his manipulating cards was probably low. That didn't mean Kit hadn't known how to distract the other players with a constant flow of bonhomie.

Unless Kittridge had improved a hell of a lot during the journey to the gold camp.

"What happened to him?" Tal asked.

The Foleys exchanged a look. "There's a split opinion on that," Fintan allowed. "Some say he was drunk and passed out on his way back to the cabin where he and his sister were stayin'. Hell of a storm that night. In any case, Miss Kittridge found him the next day not far from their place. Frozen to death, apparently. Still others thought he was waylaid and killed. There wasn't a coin on him when he was found, which was odd considerin' he'd cleaned the pockets of half the men at the poker table the night before. Did it at that table there," he added, indicating a spot in the far corner with a tilt of his chin.

Letty had found her brother. Tal tried to imagine the depth of her despair. She'd already lost her parents, her home, her status. The loss of Kit not only left her on her own, it had left her to fend for herself in the wilderness.

There was more to be done than saving her from the noose. He needed to discover how his one-time friend had died. For himself as well as for Letty's sake.

"There were signs of foul play then?" Tal asked.

Foley shrugged. "Not that anyone could tell at a glance. Doubt there's a soul in camp would know what ta look fer. As it is, the closest thing to a doctor we've got is Pollard, the blacksmith, and he arrived 'bout a month or so ago, when the snows started meltin'."

"Sheriff Strand…"

Moira puffed in disgust. "Useless, like so many men in office in the territory."

"Now, lass, Linus Strand had the right qualifications needed when the camp voted him into office," Foley said, then turned back to Tal. "He'd been in the army durin' the war with Mexico and was the best shot in camp. He'd also stood up ta a couple ruffians that tried ta jump claims back when the strike was new."

"Those fellas stick around?" Claim jumpers could easily morph into riled card players willing to kill the man they thought had duped them.

"Yes and no," the saloon owner said, disrupting Tal's musing. "Became the first tenants of the buryin' ground after Strand put them down."

If the sheriff was of the fire first and ask questions later brand of lawman, Tal was surprised anyone had thought a jail was even necessary.

He turned to Moira Foley. "You said you wished Miss Kittridge had come to you after her brother died. Does that mean you were friends with her?"

The woman fidgeted with a fold in the skirt of her apron, not meeting his eyes. "I wish I could say yes, but the truth is we were rushing to get this building finished 'fore the weather turned. There really wasn't time to socialize, and Miss Kittridge kept to herself mostly as it was. We rarely saw her in camp. But perhaps Mrs. Bergen would know more. It's far more likely that Miss Kittridge would visit the mercantile for supplies."

"'Sides, the type of upbringin' Miss Kittridge's had wouldn't incline her to be visitin' a saloon," her husband added. "Still, we'd like to think she knew we ran a decent house here. Might be gamblin' at the tables of a night, but the lass here is dead set against the mattress trade."

"As others in this camp should be," Moira snapped. "Panning fer gold is a hard business. However, that's no reason these men can't be true to the wives and sweethearts waiting fer them back East."

Foley sighed. Tal couldn't decide whether it was over the prospect of his wife launching into what was obviously her personal crusade or the fact that the Gilded Moon wasn't cashing in on a service much in demand in the nearly all-male community.

"'Preciate the information and the meal," Tal said. "What do I owe you?"

Foley named a price that Tal found quite moderate considering the scarcity of supplies so far from civilization. When asked to supply meals to Letty, Moira agreed to do so and invited him back, mentioning that a peach cobbler was on the menu that evening. Tal asked for recommendations when it came to finding a bed and was directed to the bunkhouse accommodations.

Damn, but he missed the comforts of Virginia City.

****

Letty knew she'd finally fallen asleep and was dreaming when she heard a woman's voice ask to see Miss Kittridge. Although she'd answered to that name only a few months before, it seemed years since she'd actually *been* Noletta Kittridge.

"You'll have to get up from that chair, Linus Strand," the voice insisted. "I don't know what yer mother taught ye, but I'm sure it was that a gentleman always stands when a lady enters the room."

"Weren't no woman involved, Moira. Raised up myself. Did a durn good job of it, too," the sheriff drawled.

Letty stirred, realizing she hadn't been dreaming after all.

"That bowl for me? Smells mighty good," Strand said.

"If ye want to enjoy my cooking, ye know where to find it and what the Gilded Moon charges, sir," Moira returned.

"A sight too much, considering what the camp pays me."

"Then get off yer duff and stake a claim," Moira challenged. "It's what ye came here to do, isn't it? While yer thinking on that, open Miss Kittridge's cell and move that chair in there fer me to use. I've decided to visit with her while she enjoys today's special, and this tray is getting heavier by the moment."

Letty hastily got to her feet and slipped free of Tal's coat, folding it neatly at the end of the narrow cot. She'd donned it when she lay down rather than use one of the blankets he'd supplied, simply because it retained his scent. Having the weight of it draped over her was nearly as comforting as being buried in his embrace. Something she had no right to enjoy any longer.

The moment she was alone with the few possessions Tal had gathered and the pitcher of water and basin 'Diah had brought, she'd slipped behind the crude dressing screen and stripped away the blood-stained undergarments. All she'd had to replace them with was a lone petticoat, a spare chemise, and the simple gray calico dress. Scrubbing her skin clean had left the water a deep pink shade and nearly exhausted the last of her lavender-scented soap. Dressed in relatively clean clothing, she'd pulled the hairbrush through her tangled locks. Now they hung limp and free about her shoulders. So many hairpins had been lost along the way west, she had insufficient to hold even the most basic twisted knot in place; no ribbon to bind a braid. She'd made the effort to look less a drab for Tal rather than for herself. Now Letty was glad she had gone to the effort. She barely knew Moira Foley, but the woman had been friendly on the occasions they had met. At least someone in the camp might remember her as more than just the jade she'd been that morning, forced to walk through the crowd wearing little more than a blood-soaked corset.

Letty shook her creased calico skirts out hastily. Prior to her incarceration, she'd had no reason to visit the sheriff's office. Now she knew it intimately.

The building was merely two small rooms, the cell smaller than the larder had been at the Kittridge house in Boston. The main room barely managed to contain a cot for the sheriff, a potbellied stove, and the table he used in place of a desk. His spare clothing hung from nails, and an empty barrel served as the resting place for a wash basin. Mr. Strand would need to move his chair into the outer room just to have space to open the cell door wide enough for Moira Foley to maneuver her skirts through.

A moment later, the trap in the door opened, and Strand ordered her to stand against the far wall near the head of the bed where he could see her and not to make a move. Letty wondered what he thought she would do. Attack him like a wild animal? She had been raised in a gentleman's home, not by savages in a backwoods cabin in the wilderness.

And yet it was a cabin barely as large as the sheriff's office that had served as the roof over her head in the camp while Kit still lived. The four walls had reinforced the fact that she knew nothing of how to survive on her own.

Moira bustled in ahead of the sheriff, scolding him further about his lack of manners. "Gracious! A body can barely breathe in here," she declared of the cell. "You can just leave that door wide open, Linus."

"You'll have to be locked in, Moira," he countered. "It's the law."

The woman gave a ladylike snort. "Nonsense. We are just two defenseless women."

Strand pointed emphatically at Letty. "She killed a man. Shot him dead."

Moira shook her head slightly. The hair bundled in her snood quivered with the motion. "And who is in possession of a pistol right now? Not Miss Kittridge. Now bring that chair in here."

"If I do that, where the hell am I gonna sit?" he demanded.

"Such language in the presence of ladies, Linus. The chair? While I could perch next ta Miss Kittridge on that extremely uncomfortable-looking bed, this tray has to be set down someplace."

Swearing under his breath, the sheriff hefted the roughly built chair through the door and slammed it down adjacent to the inner wall. It was the same spot Tal had sat during his visit.

Moira slid the tray she carried onto the seat and turned to face Letty as the building's main door slammed shut behind the riled and temporarily exiled lawman.

"Oh, my dear Miss Kittridge. What can I say?" the older woman murmured.

"You've no need to say anything, Mrs. Foley," Letty answered. "It is kind of you to visit."

Moira waved a hand, dismissing the very idea that she was being kind. "I wish I could say it was my idea to supply ya with some o' my stew, but truth is, Mr. Cain arranged for yer meals. Yer quite fortunate he strolled into camp today."

"Yes," Letty agreed. "He's very…"

What could she say of Tal? That he was thoughtful? Kind? Charming? That once she'd wanted nothing more than to spend her life with him and yet had lacked the courage to go against her parents' wishes to do just that?

"Handsome," Moira Foley supplied, taking Letty's hands in hers. "Determined. He seems to be a good man, Miss Kittridge."

"On a fool's errand," Letty said, slipping free of the other woman's grasp. "Please, sit. The stew smells wonderful."

"I brought a cup of coffee along as well. My coffee is much better than anything Linus Strand would boil up. If he offered ye any, which I doubt he did," her guest replied as she perched at the end of the narrow cot.

He hadn't, but 'Diah Short had brought her a canteen of water when he'd come to take the tainted wash water away. There had been no glass and, while cool, the water tasted slightly of mud, no doubt stirred up by the panning of miners upstream from the creek 'Diah had visited, or from the bottom of the community well.

"If ye would prefer tea, I have a nice Ceylon tucked away and can bring it next time," Moira continued. "In fact, if there is anything ye need, just let me know."

It was a kind offer but one she would not take up. How many days would it be before the noose was slipped around her throat and she danced on air?

Letty settled on the edge of the bed and carefully lifted the sturdy napkin Moira had draped over the bowl. Immediately the scent of stewed meat, vegetables, and spices rose in a cloud of steam.

"Wrap the cloth around the crockery, dear," Moira recommended. "That way ye can lift the bowl and if ye balance it on yer knees, both yer skirt and yer hands will be protected from the heat."

Letty breathed deeply of the rising steam before carefully dipping the edge of the spoon into the rich gravy.

"Do ye recognize it?" Moira asked.

"The recipe?" Letty had no intention of learning what animal had found its way into Moira's cookpot.

The older woman smiled. "The cutlery, dear. It was yers. I bought it to supplement what Foley and I brought with us for the restaurant."

To the rest of the town, the Gilded Moon was a saloon, but Moira Foley always called it a restaurant. Perhaps one day it would be, once the camp grew into a town and proper people began taking up residences, building homes that were graceful and welcoming rather than little more than hovels. Would the newcomers wonder who the souls remembered with nothing but roughly carved markers in the cemetery had been?

"When yer brother died and the household goods were sold off, even though the set was incomplete, I insisted Foley bid on it. It rounds out what we already had nicely. The pattern is so lovely. Is it real silver?"

If it had been, they would have sold it long before reaching the camp, Letty knew. The Boston creditors had ensured that anything of worth in the Kittridge household was carted off to the auction house before either she or Kit could smuggle it away. She had been lucky to afford two place settings, a couple of tin plates and cups, a coffeepot, and a sturdy skillet for their adventure into the wilderness. She'd had no idea what to do with the skillet or how to brew coffee, though at first Kit had expected her to supply meals. His pistol and ammunition had been much more dear.

"Nickle plated," Letty said before slipping the spoon between her lips.

The stew was hearty, the seasoning dainty, but there was no disguising the gamey taint of the unidentifiable forest creature used in its creation. Letty dipped her spoon once more, steeling herself to eat.

As she ate, Moira Foley chatted, decrying how depleted her larder was, boasting of the canning she'd done the summer before, of the tinned goods they had secured. Of how difficult it was to be pleasant to the mercantile owner's wife. "She has never seen a play or read poetry, much less a novel," Moira declared. "I knew we would be roughing it when we set out, but I had hoped for a touch more connection to the arts. Ye know what I mean, Miss Kittridge."

"Yes," Letty said, wishing strongly that the good-intentioned woman would simply go away. She had lost everything she cared about: her home, her friends, her place in society. Tal. Then Kit had died, and she'd lost the will to live. Moira Foley had simply lost a theatre, a greengrocer, a library. As the camp grew, she'd regain every one of them.

When the bowl was empty and the cup drained, Letty thanked the saloonkeeper's wife for the meal politely, lying about enjoying it. Moira patted her arm as if consoling a hysteric, reiterating that if there was anything she could do, dear Miss Kittridge had only to ask. "If only I had been in my right mind when ye needed help before. When yer brother died. I just didn't think things through…"

No one had. Not her father in risking the entire family fortune. Not Kit in convincing her they could begin again in the West. He'd sold her on San

Francisco, then dragged her into the wilderness of gold country.

She had been just as blind. She had let Tal walk out the door believing she didn't truly love him.

A lifetime of lessons in deportment came to her rescue. Tamping down the rise of despair, Letty kept her face the mask of a lady. "I know Mr. Cain asked you to supply my meals, Mrs. Foley, but I'm afraid doing so would harm your sensibilities. I cannot accept your kindness knowing there was the chance that you would suffer rebuke from others in town," Letty said firmly.

"Oh, but it is no trouble, and…"

"Thank you, but if I'm given nothing but stale bread and water, it will suffice for the few days left."

"But Mr. Cain…"

"Mr. Cain will absolve you," Letty assured. "I'll speak to him."

When Sheriff Strand stomped back in the door to his office moments later, Letty issued the still-protesting saloon owner's wife out the door of her cell.

Moira Foley was barely gone before despair swept Letty into its caress. With the door barred again, she curled up in the far corner of the cell with Tal's coat wrapped around her once more and let the memories of every wrong step she had ever taken rush over her.

****

Burl Bergen looked up in surprise when Tal strolled around the corner of the mercantile. "Find yerself in need of somethin' more, Mr. Cain?" the man asked. He didn't bother to put down the adze he was using to craft boards from a seven-foot length of timber. "Wife can help ya inside. I got coffins ta build."

Tal dropped his kit to the ground and leaned both rifle and his shoulder against the building. “Coffins? As in more than one?”

The adze bit into the wood. “As in two specifically. One fer Rosser and one fer yer murderin’ filly.”

“She’s innocent,” Tal said. “You’ll have gone to the effort for nothing by making a coffin for her.”

Bergen chuckled. “Doubt it, Counselor. What’re ya here fer?”

“Rosser. I’d like to see his body.”

The shopkeeper spat a bit of tobacco juice into the dirt. “What the hell fer? He ain’t a pretty sight, I can tell ya that right now. Lookin’ at him could put a man off his feed fer a week ’er more.”

“All the same,” Tal insisted, “I’d like to see his body.”

Bergen swung the adze, burying the blade in a bit of untouched bark. “Damn strange request. Ya okay it with Strand?”

Tal pushed off the building. “Hell, the sheriff doesn’t care what happens to Rosser.”

“Other than ta see he gets planted fer he starts stinkin’ up the camp,” Bergen grumbled. He gestured toward what looked to be a hastily tossed together shack. There were gaps between the boards wide enough to slide kissing coins through. Some of the boards looked clawed rather than planed, but if this was where bodies had been stored over the winter when the ground was frozen, no doubt it had only barely kept wild animals from feasting on the departed.

It certainly would do nothing for the esthetics of the camp regarding scent. Although Rosser had only been dead a few hours, when Bergen threw the door open, the aroma of death that escaped nearly gagged Tal.

Despite the gaps in construction, it was too dark to examine the corpse inside the makeshift morgue, though.

"I need him dragged out in the sun," Tal said.

Bergen had been in the act of turning away, but the request stopped him cold. "Do what? Hell, ain't he already got 'nuff flies on him ta suit ya, Counselor?"

"I need to *see* him, Bergen. Unless you want to supply me with a couple lanterns…" Tal let the suggestion fester on its own.

"Gawd damn it!" the shopkeeper snarled. "Fine. Ya can take his shoulders. I'll get his feet."

Silas Rosser had been a big man and was a damn unwieldly weight as a dead one. In the close confines of the shed, the scent of blood and excrement draped his carcass. He'd been fully dressed but for his boots when gunned down, and the close quarters in which he'd been shot had left burn marks on his shirt as well as forced the cloth into the gaping wound in the center of his chest. Tal noted it all briefly before Bergen dropped the dead man's bare feet in the dirt and headed back to his interrupted work.

Tal lowered Rosser's shoulders to the ground and stepped back to catch a breath of less poignant air. A gentle breeze curled from the woods two hundred feet away, the scent of it hinting at pine needles and freshly felled lumber. It had been so long since he'd enjoyed the sight and sweet aroma of spring flowers, Tal wondered if he'd even recognize them anymore. If he'd appreciate them quite the same as he had in the past.

Bergen's adze wasn't the only tool cutting into

timber in the camp. The sound of axes, saws, and hammers rang throughout the clearing as new structures continued to go up. With the snows melted on the lower slopes of the mountains, more merchants would be arriving daily. Miners were already drifting through, stopping long enough to have a drink and ask after the location of the nearest gold-bearing stream. Within a few months, the nameless camp would grow to the size of a small town, acquire a moniker, and begin sending messages back to Fort Hall on the Snake River, demanding that the Shoshone and Bannock tribes be cleared from the area.

Before stopping by Bergen's, Tal had dug from his saddlebags the journal he'd long ago stopped using to record the stops on his journey, along with the stub of a well sharpened pencil. Now he slipped them from the inner pocket of his weskit and, returning to the remains of Silas Rosser, hunkered down to study the man who'd created the woman now calling herself Pearl.

Rosser hadn't been a comely man, his features brutish even in death, but he'd been a powerfully built one. The scent of sweat rose from him despite the cloying reminders of death that made it difficult to breathe near him. Turning away, Tal pulled his neckerchief up to cover both his mouth and nose. It didn't make Rosser any pleasanter to be around, but the mask made it possible to examine the corpse without gagging.

Tal carefully peeled the man's shirt from the wound. Matted with sticky, drying blood, the fabric clung before giving way entirely. The shot had taken him directly in the heart. Death would have been instantaneous. The burn marks on Rosser's shirt indicated the muzzle of the weapon had been either pressed to his chest or fired within inches of it. That indicated either an execution or a struggle with someone for control of the weapon. He doubted the sheriff would appreciate such insight. He hadn't impressed Tal with being the sort of man who cared about details.

Tal did. Even before hitting Boston he'd read about detection techniques the French and British police had begun using to solve crimes. It was day and night from previous crime investigation, which had been more of the fox-and-hound-chase variety.

No one in a gold camp was going to put any effort into solving murders when the most common types were hastily escalated arguments ending in an exchange of shots fired before spectators in the street, over a card table, or at a claim site.

Whose pistol had been used? Rosser's? Or someone else's? It was still an unknown on his list of need-to-knows, something to query Sheriff Strand about. Tal shelved it for the nonce.

Why the hell wouldn't Letty supply the name of the killer? Was she protecting someone? And if she was, who, and why was she doing it?

Rosser had gone to his death barefooted but with his braces. He hadn't pulled them into place yet that morning. They drooped in loops down from where they attached to his trousers. Trousers that sported outturned pockets.

Tal glanced over to where the sometime undertaker was sending wood chips flying. "Who checked Rosser's pockets?"

Bergen wiped at the sweat on his brow with his

arm, adding a damp mark on the sleeve of his shirt. "Don't know 'bout what others might 'a done, but I had a look. Had jest 'nuff on him ta pay fer his own buryin'."

And likely a bit more, Tal thought, but it was long gone now. "Was he wearing a holster when he arrived here?"

"A holster? What would he have that on fer? He was a man who favored a knife."

"Then he didn't own a pistol?"

"Didn't say that," Bergen insisted. "Jest that a handgun weren't his weapon o' choice."

Tal turned his attention back to the body at his feet. There was something he hadn't consciously noted earlier. Rosser's shirt buttons weren't entirely done up. The first fastened lay just below the bloody gap in his chest. Another button might well have been blown to bits by the shot. Or it could have been missing entirely.

Tal flipped open his journal and jotted a few notes. Rather than tuck the notebook away immediately, he laid it on the ground and bent closer to Rosser's body.

The man had cultivated a flowing mustache but otherwise seemed to have a nodding acquaintance with a razor, though not a regular one. A couple days' growth of dark beard bristled along his jaw, cheeks, and throat. It nearly obscured the scratch marks. He'd seen similar marks on both men and women in the past, in Boston. Three long marks that started near Rosser's left ear before nearly disappearing into the scruff along his jaw. Marks made by an attacker's nails. The gouges were deep enough to draw blood, but easily overlooked considering blood coated his clothing.

Had Letty been fighting him off with nails drawn?

If so, why had she felt the need to defend herself?

"Ya gonna keep him out here all day?" Bergen demanded. "Flies are bad 'nuff without lurin' 'em in with a rottin' corpse."

"Nearly done," Tal said staring at the outturned trouser pockets. Had Rosser carried a pocket watch? A whetting stone to sharpen the knife that also wasn't on his body?

The items in his own pockets were few, Tal realized: the watch and chain his parents had given him before he left for what they had expected to be a stellar career in law in Boston, a compass, a folded selection of greenbacks, and a few coins in various denominations. The only thing he would miss was the watch because, when he opened the case cover, the photograph of Noletta Kittridge smiled back at him.

Tal pushed back to his feet and pulled his neckerchief down again. "Think I've seen all I need to," he told Bergen. "We can put him back where he was."

"*Ya* can drag him back in on yer own, Counselor," the shopkeeper said. "He'll keep jest fine wherever ya drop him."

Tal took a grip on Rosser's shoulders and backed toward the open door of the crude morgue, his teeth gritted with the effort. He'd have to make a note in his journal to remind himself not to die in this damn, unfeeling, Godforsaken camp. And he sure as hell wasn't going to let Letty be killed in it either!

Chapter Five

His reputation had preceded Tal at all three of the long, narrow boarding houses. Despite the fact that the furnishings consisted of tiers of bunk beds wedged head to toe with barely enough room for a man to move between the rows or lift his head without encountering the mattress of the fellow above him or a ceiling joist, none claimed to have a vacant bed for a fellow passing through long enough to attempt robbing them of the entertainment of hanging a woman.

He shouldn't have been surprised, Tal told himself, but that didn't help one damn bit when it came to getting a roof over his head for the night. It had been hellishly cold the evening before when he'd tossed a blanket down by the campfire. Maybe he could sweet-talk the mayor or the sheriff—or anyone else who poked their nose into the conversation—into letting him use the saloon proper at Rosser's place as temporary lodging. He had some searching to do for Letty's ring. The cabin the Kittridge siblings had shared was another option.

'Diah had told him the mayor was one of the first gold fanciers to arrive at the strike the summer before. That meant not only could he ask about the Kittridge cabin or Rosser's as a place to drop his saddlebag and kit, he could pump the man for information about when the Boston-bred siblings had ridden into town.

He ran Ebner Melton to ground in the Friendly Gal Saloon.

The name promised more than it delivered, for there wasn't a woman in sight, friendly or otherwise, when he stepped past the sturdy plank door. It was propped open, a wedge rammed beneath the bottom edge to keep it in place. Tal had to dip his head to avoid a lintel set so low only a man a full head shorter could have passed beneath it without incurring a head wound. He'd have to be shorter still to keep his hat in place.

The premises were a step up from Rosser's but not by much. The bar stretched the length of the building and had been upgraded from barrel-and-board construction to a long narrow table with boards nailed across the front. Like at the Gilded Moon, they'd installed an actual floor rather than make do with packed earth. Square tables took up most of that floor room, surrounded by less-than-grand chairs on each side.

Seated at a table near the back, his body hunched forward over the hand of solitaire he'd dealt on the surface, was the man he'd met earlier in the day, the mayor.

Tal moseyed straight to the bar where a man was engaged in filling bottles from a tapped keg. "Afternoon," Tal greeted him. "How far away am I from getting a decent glass of beer?"

The barkeep barely glanced up from his work. "'Round fifteen hundred miles if ya head back to Saint Louie, or six hundred ta Frisco," he answered. "Ya want an almost tolerable one, stand right there and I'll draw a mug."

Melton chuckled. "You'd do better with Trask's

whiskey," he advised. "It'll burn your gut out but won't poison you otherwise."

"It's not that bad, Ebner," the bartender insisted.

"You whittled the spirits of that beer down so often over the winter, Trask, there is no longer enough alcohol in it to kill the taste of bad water," the mayor countered.

"A whiskey then," Tal said. "And you can get a damn fine beer closer than Frisco."

Trask looked dubious. "Where?"

"Virginia City, down in Nevada Territory. Wintered there. Stayed nicely drunk most of the time, too," Tal admitted, stretching the truth.

"Easier to keep warm that way," Melton said.

"Damn right," Tal agreed. "Mind if I join you, Mr. Mayor?"

For answer, Melton abandoned his game and nudged his foot against a chair leg to kick the seat a sociable distance from the table. "Welcome the company, Mr. Cain. How's your case coming along? The lovely Miss Pearl tell you why she did it?"

Tal settled into place at the table, grinning. "Innocent until proven guilty. That's what the law says, which means until proven otherwise, Miss Kittridge is innocent of the charge of murder."

"Kittridge," the older man mused. "Haven't heard her called that in a good bit. She tell you her name?"

Since he'd known it before and wanted to keep that fact secret, Tal took a moment to sample the shot of whiskey that Trask set down before him. "No, but Mrs. Foley did when I stopped at the Gilded Moon to eat."

"Hell, if you've already enjoyed Moira's cooking, you're finding your way around camp just fine,"

Melton declared. "I'd steal that woman away from Fin if she hadn't already broken my heart. Said she'd just got Fin trained up the way she wanted for a husband and wasn't interested in starting from scratch."

Tal smiled while the mayor himself chuckled as though the woman's response still amused the hell out of him.

"It's a bit difficult to get lost in a camp this size," Tal said. "Unfortunately, it's still too small to accommodate some needs."

"Madam June's just up…"

Tal cut the man off before he could wax poetic on any of the prostitutes' attributes or talents. "I'm still looking for a roof to bunk under," he explained. "As I've been told there's no available bed to be had, I wanted to ask you about possible places that came to mind. I understand Miss Kittridge and her brother had a cabin. Is it currently inhabited?"

"Burned down," Trask contributed from the bar. "Door was left open and some critters went in. Knocked over the stove. Were just 'nuff coals still warm to start a fire."

"That isn't what happened," Melton said. "Rosser destroyed the place so Miss Kittridge had no place else to go but his saloon."

Tal tapped a forefinger against the jigger of whiskey. "And no one said or did anything to give her an option?"

"She was damaged goods by then. Doubt it's escaped your notice, Counselor, but we got more than a hundred men and only a handful of women, and most of those are in the same business that welcomed Miss Kittridge. As to other choices…well, not a one of the good ladies were interested in taking her in. Neither Bergen nor the couple of wives who followed their gold-happy spouses had room for a guest who lacked talents in the way of cooking or scrubbing. Your client's a pretty little gal brought up like she was royalty, or the Eastern equivalent. Moira might a put up with that, but Foley had an eye for shapely gals back East, so she wouldn't have held the door open for an armful like Kittridge's sister," the mayor explained. "Without housekeeping skills, no man would take her on as a wife either. Was only one thing she could do, and she did it to survive."

Beneath the table, Tal's hand had curled into a fist the moment Melton called Letty "damaged goods." Now he had it clenched so tight his nails cut into the palm. He forced it open. Ordered it not to shake with suppressed fury as he moved it back to the tabletop and lifted the shot glass between forefinger and thumb, tossing the remaining whiskey back before carefully replacing the empty jigger on the tabletop.

It still took another moment to unclench his locked jaw. A performance to show he was ignorant of some facts was necessary, though. In Boston, friends insisted that when he had taken up law the stage had lost a great actor.

Tal pushed the brim of his hat back. "What did you mean by 'she was already damaged goods'?"

Melton had leaned back in his chair, but now he hunched over the table again, his forearms braced on the top. "It's a mighty thirsty tale," he said.

Tal called to the bartender, who had retreated behind the bar to continue preparing for his evening custom. "The mayor is parched. Maybe we'd better have a bottle over here."

"The mayor is always parched," Trask said, but he brought one of the freshly filled bottles over. "Considering he ain't out dippin' a pan at his claim much, he's also usually shy on the wherewithal ta quench that thirst. Ya got the price of a bottle on ya?"

Tal dropped a greenback on the table.

"That'll do it," the barkeep murmured. He swept it up and returned to what he'd been doing.

Melton waited for Tal to refill both their glasses, then downed half of his. "Might be best to go back a bit further, to the day the Kittridges trailed into town."

Considering he'd planned to ask about that, Tal nodded and topped the mayor's glass off.

"It was just before the weather turned," Melton began.

****

The problem wasn't that the camp planned to hang her, it was waiting for them to do so that was at fault. It gave Letty far too much time to contemplate all the steps taken to reach this point in her life. She should have gone against her parents' will and run off with Talmadge Hammond. In being a dutiful daughter, she'd chosen a martyrdom that had now swelled to ungodly proportions.

The sound of axes biting into tree trunks was far too close to be ignored. The timber might be slated for the new constructions in progress. But it could also be felled and hewn to build the scaffold. Listening to the bark of blade to wood chipped away at her resolve to be strong. Kit had used alcohol to numb his crumbling sense of self-worth. If she requested it, would the sheriff supply a bottle of the poisonous brew the miners downed? If she could force herself to drink it, would she cease to care about what the inevitable losing of her case would do to Tal?

He would take it hard, she knew. Would blame himself when the fault lay entirely with her. With her lack of will to go on.

She heard him arrive, heard the outer door crash back against the wall.

"I need to speak with my client," he insisted. He sounded like the man she'd fallen in love with, like he'd gotten the bit between his teeth and had no intention of letting anyone break his spirit.

"Jeezus," the sheriff snarled. "I'd just nodded off. You can't just barrel in here demanding things, Cain."

"Then I'll demand them, Linus," another man said. Letty was surprised to recognize the voice. It wasn't as slurred as she'd frequently heard it as the mayor cadged drinks off men at Rosser's saloon. "Open the door so we can speak with Miss Kittridge."

Miss Kittridge. Tal had been in the camp but a few hours and he'd already trained two residents to call her by that name once more. The thought alone brought a sad smile to her face.

"Hell, let yourself in then," Strand snapped. "What're you here for, Ebner?"

The mayor chuckled. "A treasure hunt," he said, excitement ringing in his rough voice.

The bar securing her cell was thrust aside, the door flung wide. Then Tal was there, at her feet, one knee to the floor, the other acting as a support for his arm as he took both her hands in his. She saw her name ready to spill from his lips. The wrong name.

"Yes, Mr. Cain?" she said hurriedly.

He caught the slip before it tumbled free. "The mayor believes a search of Mr. Rosser's premises is in order. We have your missing ring to find but also his cache of funds and gold dust. 'Diah and I ran into a fellow named Gately at the saloon earlier claiming he was looking for the cash box to acquire his wages."

"Rather to make off with whatever he could find," she murmured, knowing Tal would recognize in her clipped tone how much she despised the bartender.

"Like your ring?"

Letty shook her head slightly. "I never wore it there. He wouldn't have known it existed, and I doubt he thought any of my things worth the trouble to pilfer. They have not held up well to the rigors of travel or life in this camp."

Since Gately knew she was still engaged in paying off the debts Kit had left behind, the only value he would have seen when he looked at her was the tender paid out to use her body.

"Silas didn't trust him," she told Tal. "He paid him nightly. But there was no cash box. Silas liked keeping his money close. He wore a money belt."

Tal's grip on her hands tightened slightly. "He wasn't wearing one this morning. If he had been, I doubt his shirt would still have been tucked in his trousers, considering his pockets were turned out when I visited the mortuary shack."

She knew Tal felt her start in shock, for his grip on her hands tightened gently. "You went to see…" she whispered before regaining control. Of course, he would have. He was determined to prove her innocence. It wouldn't have been merely the scene of Rosser's death he would wish to investigate, but the state of the victim as well.

Letty took a deep breath. “Then he simply hadn’t donned it yet. It would still be where he hid it after the saloon closed.”

“Was it the same place every night?”

“No, but I know a couple spots where it might be,” she admitted.

He pushed to his feet. Cupped her upturned face between his hands and dropped a kiss on her brow.

“Sheriff? It’s your decision. Either the mayor goes with me to look for Rosser’s funds, or you leave him here to protect Miss Kittridge,” he said. Then he was kneeling before her again. “Now where exactly should we be looking, darlin’?”

****

Unlike the other saloons in camp—or those Tal had noted in other towns—there was no grandly painted name across the front of Rosser’s building. Everyone he talked to simply called it Rosser’s place, and that sufficed. At least now that the sun had crested and begun its slow dip to the west, light would spill through the open door. Once they threw back the barred shutters in the rear room, a lamp would be needed only to see in any particularly shadowed corners, should they need to extend the search. Letty had warned that Rosser might have a hiding place of which she was unaware. As there were already quite a few on the list she’d given them, Rosser hadn’t been a man willing to trust others. The fact that he had trusted Letty with the locations where the money belt might be kept seemed to indicate that whether the man had cared for her or not, he knew she wouldn’t betray his secret.

When it came to trust where currency was

involved, the sheriff hadn't been willing to extend it to Ebner Melton. Tal figured he had good reason. The man obviously aspired to the title of town drunk in addition to that of mayor. Instead, they'd left Melton to watch over Letty rather than leave the jail without a jailor.

"Damn but I wish I hadn't sent 'Diah hot-footing after the judge. I trust that lad more than the mayor," Strand said as he opened the now-abandoned saloon's door, pushing it wide. He turned slightly to look back at Tal and never saw the stripped-down branch swung from the shadows inside. It took him across the ribs, thrusting him back into Tal's arms.

Tal dropped the lawman in the dust and barreled through the door, taking down the man inside with a tackle before he could use the rough quarterstaff again. The weapon flew from Gately's hand, clattering against the far wall. Tal was rolling back to his feet when Rosser's former bartender grabbed his leg and yanked him to the hard-packed floor. His breath left him in a rush, but Tal managed to smash the heel of his boot into the barkeep's face, the rowel of his spur nicking the man's jaw. The howl of surprise and pain that followed was briefly heartening, but he hadn't put the behemoth out, just made him mad.

Gately got to his feet and spit blood to the floor. "Yer trespassin', mister."

"Rosser leave you the saloon in his will, Gately?" Tal demanded. He used the wall as a support as he climbed back to his feet. One trick he'd quickly learned on the streets of Boston was to look more beaten than he actually was. Considering the neighborhoods where many of his clients resided, it was a well-honed ploy.

He'd fallen back on it so often over the past two years of roaming it had become a habit. A very handy one if a man wanted to stay alive.

Now that he'd found Letty again, that was the condition in which he wanted to remain. A dead lawyer helped no one, particularly not the innocent.

"Si's gone, so why shouldn't it be mine?" Gately snarled, as he settled into a wrestling stance, legs braced apart, arms spread, elbows bent. "I earned the right ta it."

"Wages are what you are owed, nothing more," Tal countered. "But as I have testimony stating that Rosser paid you every evening, including last night, there are no outstanding wages owed."

The bartender shifted to the side, feigning an attack before stepping back in place near the open door. "Suppose Pearl told ya that und thinks she earned the rest."

"I think she worked damn harder than you ever did," Tal said. He moved back, putting more distance between himself and Gately. As he hoped, the dumb ox moved in sync, putting his back to the door.

Gately spat on the floor again. Tal jumped back as though attempting to avoid the spittle. The larger man followed again, a thin smile of anticipation on his lips. Tal pulled his fist back, purposefully telegraphing a punch.

The barkeep leaned to the side.

Behind him the sheriff brought the grip of his pistol down solidly against the back of Gately's head. The big man stumbled forward, losing his balance. Tal swept up the quarterstaff his opponent had lost and brought it down across Gately's back. There was a resounding crack as the branch splintered. The bartender sprawled unconscious at Sheriff Strand's feet.

"That went well," Tal said, gasping for breath. He tossed the ragged piece of wood away and sank down on the nearest bench.

Strand leaned weakly against the door jamb. "We need a bigger jail," he said. "What the hell am I supposed to do with him with Pearl in the only cell?"

"Release her on her own recognizance?" Tal suggested.

The sheriff snorted. "Release a murderess so I can jail someone who didn't like your face, Counselor? That's not the way it plays out."

"Was worth a try," Tal said. "But if you did release her, she'd have the same problem I have. No place to stay. Not unless you're willing to let me toss my bedroll down right here."

"At the scene of the crime?"

"Hell, no. That room isn't fit for habitation. I mean, right here where I'm sitting. The mayor seemed to think it was a good idea."

Strand dropped his Remington revolver back in the holster at his belt. "The mayor is like to think anything is a grand idea. 'Specially if you happen to be paying for his libations."

"I might have asked for a bottle," Tal admitted, then looked around. The only table and bench that hadn't been overturned during the search they had obviously interrupted were those at which he sat. The plank that had served as a bar rested tipsily against the cast iron stove, while the barrels it had rested across had been overturned. Timber cut to slip through the stove's door was flung aside as though an irate child had kicked building blocks while in a fury. Bottles lay on their side, some leaking whiskey into the thirsty dirt floor. “It appears Gately might have had a few ideas on where Rosser tucked his hoarded income. Think he found it?”

“Nope,” the sheriff said. “I can search him, but if he had found it, when he heard us, he would have hightailed it out the rear door or the window in the bedroom. Unholster that Colt of yours and keep it trained on him while I get some rope to tie him up.” He pressed his forearm against his stomach. “Then again, maybe I should just shoot him for walloping an officer of the law.”

“Self-defense, without a doubt,” Tal said, smiling in amusement at the suggestion. Strand might irritate the hell out of him, but the man had good intentions when it came to upholding the law in the camp. Tal couldn’t fault him for that, even if Strand and the rest of them were dead wrong when it came to Letty.

Slipping the intimidating eight-inch-long barrel of his Model 1860 six-shooter free of the holster at his belt, Tal checked the chamber, then cocked the hammer back. “How long will you be?”

“Not long at all,” Strand said and, though he was bent over fighting pain, headed back toward his office.

Chapter Six

They found the money belt, hidden deep in the shadows of the rafters above the bed. They hadn't found her ring.

"Is there another cache where Rosser might have tucked promissory notes away?" Tal asked Letty as he sat on the floor once more, his back to the wall next to her narrow bed this time. He'd shown up with a tray of Moira Foley's latest offering. This time there had been enough for two. Letty wondered whether he realized it was the first time they'd ever eaten together.

While her friends had ensured his name appeared on the guest lists for balls and evenings of music, it had been absent from those invited to partake of dinner before the entertainment or supper after it. Society's hostesses drawing ranks against any romantic dreams their daughters might fancy about unsuitable matches. It was one thing to have enough gentlemen for debutantes to dance with, but quite another to feed them.

Despite the far from salubrious accommodations of her cell—particularly as Strand had insisted upon barring the door while he found his own supper, though he had left the small window in the door open—having Tal's companionship during a meal altered the very air between them. They were no longer the couple who had courted clandestinely in Boston, but they were more than merely client and counselor in this brief niche of time.

Events had changed them both too much to not have made them strangers once more. This time, however, they were strangers who shared a bittersweet past.

And souls who had been lonely for far too long.

Letty doubted he'd spent as many hours thinking about her as she had spent contemplating memories of him. Wondering where he was, how he was. Whether another woman had been wiser than she and now called him her own. She hadn't dared to ask him if he had another sweetheart elsewhere. Soon it wouldn't matter.

The tray with its empty plates awaited the time when he would leave her once more. Earlier in the day she had done her best to push him away. Now she dreaded being left alone with her thoughts. They turned too often to what she had lost in not following him into exile. He thought she had given up hope in the wilderness of Idaho Territory. He had no inkling that she had abandoned it the day he walked away from her in Boston.

Having taken her hand in his, Tal touch-traced the contours of her fingers. With his gaze intent on the occupation, his face was alternately bathed in light or cloaked in shadow as the flame in the lantern danced with every stray draft. Whether dark or light caressed it, she found the lean angles of his face little disguised by his ragged beard. Angles she didn't remember memorizing in the past. Had she merely not seen them, or had the two years they'd been apart sculpted them in his beloved countenance? And if they had, how worn and hollow did she look to him now?

"I don't remember Silas collecting actual

promissory notes. He did keep a tally of outstanding debts, though," she said. "His preference was for gold dust. Did you locate the bag he kept it in, as well?"

"We did indeed secure it. Now we trust the sheriff not to make off with Rosser's profits," Tal said.

"I don't know him well, but I believe he is considered trustworthy," Letty murmured. "Gold is the real wealth in camp. It was why Silas ensured that he profited from the finds. He had a scale that added an extra quarter ounce for his coffers."

"Thus giving every man he gulled a reason to kill him," Tal pointed out.

"But they didn't," she countered and waited for him to ask her again who had pulled the trigger. When he didn't, Letty wondered whether he'd given up on getting an answer or merely bided his time on when to pose the question again.

"Mostly I'm curious about the amount Kit owed, the markers you were paying off, Letty. It would be nice to know whether the debt was cleared or still in play."

Letty. He was taking advantage of the absence of either sheriff or mayor. As if she ceased to be *Pearl* when they were alone.

She shrugged. "If there is still an amount outstanding, whoever Kit owed must be satisfied with what they have been paid already, Mr. Cain." Her sanity required that she not call him by any other name. It was too painful. "I am no longer receiving any monies of any sort."

"But if there are no markers, then perhaps they were paid in full and Rosser was gulling you, Lett," Tal said quietly. "If so, you were being constrained against your will at his saloon."

"Even if that were so, where would I go?" she asked knowing the hopelessness she felt echoed in her voice. "The wagon road to Oregon is days away on horseback, and I not only have no horse, I have no provisions, no way to protect myself on the trail. If a Shoshone or Bannock hunting party didn't fall on me, road agents would. Probably road agents from this very camp."

"You aren't hearing what I'm saying," he insisted. "*Constrained against your will* could be construed as Rosser's death being self-defense."

She turned her hand, entwining her fingers with his. "It wasn't self-defense. It was an accident."

Tal sat up straighter. "You never said that before."

"It doesn't matter," Letty said. "Silas died, and I have the blood-soaked garments to prove I was with him when he did."

Tal sighed. "I know you didn't do it. Why not tell me who did?"

"Because it's better this way."

"No, it isn't," he insisted, but he didn't press her further. "Did you ask our ever-considerate sheriff to burn those blood-soaked garments?"

Letty shook her head slowly. "I wanted to, but someone I used to know complained quite often about clients destroying evidence without a thought to the outcome."

"That someone should have been quoting poetry instead of griping about his day," Tal said, obviously recognizing the reference was to himself.

"He would have been as endlessly tedious as the men who did, had he followed their example."

"You still have them, or does Strand?"

She laughed softly. "If he had them, they would be feeding the fire. I bound them in a tight bundle and shoved them into the shadows beneath the bunk. You may have them if you wish. I certainly have no use for them any longer."

"When we leave this godforsaken place, I'll buy you new ones," he promised.

She would never leave the camp. She'd simply take up residence in the small cemetery. Rather than voice that all-too-real eventuality, Letty held her own counsel. She didn't want to deal with Tal's rebuttal, just take comfort in his presence for a while longer. All too soon he'd be pushing to his feet and seeking his own bed elsewhere.

Instead, she gestured with her free hand toward the tray he'd brought from the Gilded Moon. "It was kind of you to join me for dinner, Mr. Cain."

Tal gave a male grunt of amusement. "I was under the impression that, had I not forced my company upon you, you'd be served whatever inedible concoction with which Strand puts up, Miss Kittridge."

"Mrs. Foley tattled, then."

"I prefer *informed*."

"Tattled," Letty insisted firmly. "She'll wish to have her crockery back before she retires. As soon as the sheriff returns, you'd best be on your way with it."

His grip on her hand tightened. She was just as loath to release him, but allowing him to linger wore at her resolve.

In the outer room, she heard the door open as Strand returned from his meal. "You ready to hightail it, Counselor?" he called.

Tal sighed and, without releasing her hand, got to his feet. This time the sheriff had stripped him of his spurs as well as his weapons. She'd only realized that when she missed the jingling sound of the barbed rowels when he moved. A sound that helped remind her that this man was not the one she'd fallen in love with oh-so-long ago. Gentlemen in Boston carried walking sticks rather than buckling spurs to their boot heels.

Tal was comfortable in his new role. She saw it in the way he moved more than in the way he dressed, though that had little in common with how he'd once been groomed. Tal had become the frontiersman. Kit had resisted embracing the designation, continuing to sport his elaborately figured weskits, fitted frock coat, and silk stock even though the items hadn't held up well on their journey. Only his derby hat was a tip to the working-class man, and perhaps because of that it had survived their wilderness foray in much better condition. The winter winds had caught it up, pressing it into the snow-covered branches of a bush near their hovel of a cabin in January. Its presence had sent her searching for her brother, only to find him frozen along the side of the path from the camp.

In the outer room, the stomp of Sheriff Strand's boots reminded that they were no longer alone.

"I'll be here with breakfast in the morning," Tal said. The way in which he released her hand seemed as reluctant as she was to release his. "See if you can remember who your brother might have owed money to, so I can find out if Rosser was paying the debts as he said."

"Other than to the Bergens' mercantile, it would probably be gambling debts Kit accrued, and he wouldn’t have told me of them, Mr. Cain,” Letty cautioned. “But I will cast my mind back to see if I recall the names of his local cronies.”

“’Preciate it, ma’am,” Tal murmured as he settled his weather-worn felt hat in place. He knocked on the door to let Strand know he was ready to leave before gathering Moira Foley’s tray of empty plates and cups up from the floor. “Have a good night’s rest, Miss Kittridge. Things will be brighter in the morning.”

She doubted it. “Sleep well, Mr. Cain. I appreciate the effort you’re going to on my behalf.”

The sound of the sheriff hefting the restraining board from before the cell door robbed them of further privacy. As Tal stepped past him, Strand lingered in the portal. “If you’re ready to call it a night, miss, I’ll take the lantern back, if you don’t mind.”

“I don’t mind, Mr. Strand,” she said, staying where she’d sat at the head of her rough, narrow bed during Tal’s visit.

Strand reclaimed the lamp without needing to cross the threshold. A moment more and the barricade was back in place on the door. His face appeared in the observation gap. “If I leave this unlatched, you’ll have a bit of light and slightly fresher air, miss,” he told her.

“Thank you, sir. I would enjoy the respite.”

The sheriff grunted and tromped back to the front, where she heard him returning Tal’s possessions to him.

All but the great coat he’d left with her. Letty slipped into the heavy garment once more and hugged it, and Tal’s scent, close. In the little-relieved dark, regrets temporarily nudged the hovering despair from the forefront of her mind.

****

“Did Kit Kittridge die owing you anything?” Tal asked Fintan Foley. He leaned on the bar, a shot of fairly decent whiskey in his hand, one boot heel hooked on the foot rail that had been installed since his visit earlier in the day.

“Oddly enough, no, he didn’t. Night before he was found frozen ta death he’d been the luckiest cuss at the table. Before the rest of the players left, Kittridge took care of payin’ off markers ta me and ta Bergen. Even gave Bergen some extra on account so his sister could get fresh supplies.”

Tal straightened up. “You telling me that Bergen owes Miss Kittridge cash since she hasn’t used it for merchandise?”

Foley finished polishing the glass in his hand. “Guess I am.”

“Know how much she’s got on account?”

“Been a while since that night,” the barkeep cautioned. “Might a been twenty.”

“Dollars?”

Foley nodded. “With prices for goods over the winter, twenty cents wouldn’t a bought her a damn thing.”

Things weren’t that much cheaper in the spring, Tal thought, wishing he’d brought more of the funds cached at the Bank of California branch in Virginia City with him. But he hadn’t planned on anything more than basic supplies, convivial shots of whiskey, and a few nights in accommodations that kept him out of the weather and possibly supplied a bed to stretch out on.

Tal downed a swallow of whiskey, savoring the burn a moment. “If Kittridge struck it big that night and died on his way home, you think Bergen ever mentioned to Miss Kittridge that he had funds for her discretionary use?"

"Never thought about it," Foley said, "but if ye knew Bergen well, ye'd know that was a damn unlikely situation. The bugger adds the weight of his thumb to the scales when measurin' out flour un such if ye don't keep an eye peeled his way."

"So she doesn't know," Tal pursued.

"Might be ye could get her ta sign it over ta ye fer takin' her side in this," the bartender suggested. "Not like she'd find much use fer it now, is there?"

"Could get herself enough basic fixings for meals to see her way out of this camp once Strand releases her," Tal said.

"Could if she knew how ta cook 'em up," Foley agreed, then added, "and if the sheriff ain't escortin' her ta the gallows."

"Miss Kittridge is innocent."

Foley folded his bar towel and set it aside on a shelf beneath the counter. "All right, say she is. How's she gonna get out of camp? Walkin'? And where's she gonna head?"

Tal knew exactly where Letty would be going. Anywhere she wanted as long as she let him tag along with her.

"I'll have to suggest she put some thought into what she wishes to do after the trial is behind her."

Foley shook his head, no doubt over the foibles of damned fools—a classification he clearly felt Tal fit—and snorted for good measure. "Yer really somethin', Cain. *What* I ain't exactly sure, but somethin'."

In response, Tal downed the rest of the whiskey in

his glass and tapped the rim for a refill.

****

Why was it still so difficult to find sleep, Letty wondered as she gave up attempting to find a comfortable position on the hard, narrow plank surface of the rough bed. She couldn't blame the lack of warmth, for lacking proper nightwear, she had not removed her dress but merely let Tal's great coat enfold her and the blankets he had supplied soften the bunk somewhat. She couldn't blame her restlessness on Sheriff Strand's snoring in the outer room. Rosser's had been much worse, and there had been no escape from the noise while forced to lie next to him. She couldn't even blame her forthcoming walk to the scaffold as the reason slumber avoided her.

But she could blame Tal Hammond.

Damn him for stirring up even more memories, ones best forgotten. When he looked at her, she knew he was seeing the Honorable Noletta Kittridge, not the woman she was now. She was no longer honorable, merely a woman who had done what was necessary to survive after her brother died. She had taken the only route offered and become Rosser's property. It had been the height of winter in the mountains and even the occasional supply train of laden mules had been unable to make it through the snows. Yet even if Kit's death had occurred once the snows melted, there would have been no other choice than the one she had made. She was a woman alone, a woman whom the trail west had proven was incompetent at the most basic chores. Even if she still possessed the rifle and pistol Kit had purchased and lavished with care, she hadn't the least idea of how to load either and had proven to be a hopeless shot when he attempted to teach her to use them.

The weapons were long gone. Rosser had claimed them before another scavenger raided the Kittridge cabin. The horse, mule, and saddle she and Kit had arrived on had gone in exchange for the meager shelter they had shared outside of town. She couldn't even trade the cabin back for a single horse and saddle since it had been destroyed by fire shortly after she'd left it for Rosser's place.

She knew Tal wanted her to think about where she wished to go once the trial was over, but how could she possibly make such a decision when she knew she wouldn't be leaving. A noose awaited her. "Innocent until proven guilty," he would remind her, but the reality was that she needed to be proven innocent because circumstances insisted she was guilty.

Which she was. She might not have pulled the trigger of the weapon that had killed Silas Rosser, but she had wished him dead every hour of every day she'd been under his control.

But Tal…

She shouldn't think of him, of what failure would do to him. He had lost other cases, but the clients had been strangers, not someone he cared about.

And he did still care about her. About Noletta Kittridge. If only she could make him see that she was Pearl now. That Noletta Kittridge was already long dead.

Even if Noletta Kittridge's dreams and memories lived on in this shell of the woman she had become.

Chapter Seven

It was late, but the men around the table at the Gilded Moon hadn't shown any interest in heading for their various lodgings. Tal wondered whether any would get the inclination if he essayed a few little disguised yawns. He'd dealt with far more problems than a day should hold. And he'd only been in camp since nine that morning.

If there was someone still plump enough in the pocket to toss cash in the center of the table or pay to replenish the bottle of whiskey passed around, the local businessmen were content to play on. That they had included him in their inner circle merely meant they sensed he had money to lose.

Which he did, if in doing so information was forthcoming.

It didn't hurt that the whiskey served at the Gilded Moon was steps ahead of what he'd downed at the Friendly Gal earlier. But, as he understood things, Foley brewed his own with input from his wife about the ingredients and packaging. Each bottle Foley presented had a hand-painted label featuring a gold-toned full harvest moon front and center. There was also a good chance the liquor within wouldn't make him go blind as fast as drinking what was served elsewhere, either.

Tal considered the cards he'd been dealt. A hand

that could go either way depending on what he threw and what he drew. Hold on to the mismatched royals or toss them in the event at least one of the new cards would be a third seven?

“Take one,” he said, destroying the pair in his hand as he tossed a card aside.

Ebner Melton, the current dealer, slid a replacement his way. “One card? You’re either holding an impressive hand there or absolute rubbish, Cain.”

“Yup,” Tal agreed and reached for the glass at his side. Someone had added another dollop or so to it recently and he hadn’t even noticed. Yeah, he needed sleep badly. Whether he’d get any depended on whether his brain could shake loose of Letty’s predicament. He doubted it could. “You fellas planning on plucking me clean in a single night or leave me enough to live on until the trial ends?”

“Could always leave afore the trial, Cain,” Bergen said. “Gal’s guilty.”

“If that turns out to be the case, then perhaps you’d hand over that twenty dollars I understand her brother left on account with you,” Tal suggested. “Least ways she could pass it along to me as payment for my services.”

The shopkeeper’s eyes widened in surprise. “Twenty dollars! I ain’t—”

“Sure you do,” the mayor said. “Sat right here and watched Kittridge hand it over to you. ’Course, events after that might a knocked it clean out of your head, but I’m damn sure his sister hasn’t drawn on the funds, considering Rosser swooped her up faster than you do your winnings.”

Bergen concentrated on rearranging the cards in his

hand. "I'll have ta look at ma books."

"'Preciate it," Tal drawled. "I'll be by around ten tomorrow morning to collect for my client."

When Bergen frowned again, Foley chuckled. "Hell, Burl, Miss Kittridge might not know yer holdin' it, but the rest of us fine upstandin' citizens know ye are. 'Sides, ye hand it over ta Cain here, and chances are he'll have it ta lose back to ye—"

"Or one of us," Ebner inserted.

"…at this very table tomorrow night."

"Just out of curiosity," Tal murmured, "was there any interest accruing on it? Seeing as the camp lacks a bank—"

"Lacks a lot o' things," Foley said.

"…I wondered how financial transactions were handled around here," Tal finished. "Now that the pans are back at work on the claims, there must be more gold dust used than legal tender. There've been assayers in other camps I've drifted through."

"Had one here at first," Ebner said. "Died just before the snows came. You haven't said whether you want any new cards, Burl. You holding on to those or what?"

Bergen tossed three down. "I'd a kept more if'n ya dealt better hands," he grumbled.

"Who says I don't?" the mayor demanded with a chuckle as he tossed the shopkeeper a trio of new cards. "Okay, gents, who's in and who's out?"

"What did the assayer die of?" Tal asked as he tossed another donation to the middle of the table.

"A nasty cut," Ebner answered. "Right across his throat. Damn effective, too. Killed him instantly, or close enough to that."

“Served him right fer usin’ false weights,” Bergen contributed.

“That’s the pot callin’ the kettle black if I ever heard it,” Foley said. “Ye ever not weigh a bit of yer thumb along with the flour and sugar at yer counter?”

“Flour and sugar ain’t gold dust,” Bergen said. He met Tal’s bet but didn’t raise the stake.

“Who killed the assayer?” Tal asked.

“Rosser,” Ebner said.

“And you didn’t hang him?”

The mayor shrugged. “Why do so? He’d done the community a favor.”

“Plus, he still had his Bowie knife in hand,” Foley added. “Strand might be handy with his pistol, but even he wasn’t about to go up against Rosser and that hungry blade.”

And yet, considering it sounded like the camp thought Rosser dangerous, not a one of them was willing to term his murder a well-deserved comeuppance.

“What happened to the assayer’s property?” Tal asked.

“You mean his ill-gotten gains? We held a camp meeting and decided to use them for the camp’s benefit,” Ebner said. “Built the jail, put in hitching posts and horse troughs. Rest of it takes care of paying the sheriff and any deputies when he needs them, or to feed prisoners. Even I get a small stipend as mayor.”

The assayer’s death had definitely been a windfall. It had kept the residents free from contributing to the camp’s welfare or, God forbid, pay taxes, Tal decided.

It had also, apparently, supplied Rosser with the assay scales Letty had mentioned.

"Ya volunteered yer name fer the position, Melton, and got it 'cause nobody else wanted ta be mayor," Bergen snarled.

"True," Ebner said. "Something I thank the good Lord for every day."

"Or would if we had us a church," Bergen added.

"Or weren't struck down by lightnin' on the steps fer ye could get ta the door," Foley contributed as he matched the bets on the table.

Melton chuckled as he tossed another greenback into the pot. "True again. I think we're back to you on the betting, Cain."

Tal checked the revision to his hand, then raised the wager as expected. "Who's the last mark you gents gulled regularly at the table?" he demanded, letting a touch of irritation enter his voice.

The mayor laughed. "Oh, Kittridge, without a doubt."

Bergen raised the bet, then nodded in agreement. "He was a slapdash player. Either keen as an eagle er easily distracted. Took us all by surprise when he walked away the big winner the night he died."

"Was he cheating then?"

Foley folded from the game before shaking his head. "Don't think he had the talent ta do so."

Bergen grunted. "Drank too much ta have a clear 'nuff head fer cullin'. Wasn't drinkin' as much that night. Surprised as hell that he turned up froze ta death the next day. Must a passed out along the track, though. The shack he und his sister was usin' warn't in the direction most folks traveled between the camp und winter lodgin's, so it's not surprisin' that he warn't found 'til it was too late."

Tal put his cards face down on the table before him and leaned back in his chair. "I heard Kittridge was reclaiming his markers that night, paying off his debts, but Miss Kittridge was under the impression that her brother still owed a lot of folks money when he died."

"How'd she figure that?" the mayor asked.

"It's what Rosser told her, and he was keeping back her share on those services she offered to whittle the debts down," Tal said.

"Well, considering the sheriff and you didn't find any markers for Kittridge or for anybody else in the camp when you searched for Rosser's ill-gotten gains earlier, Si either didn't have any at all or they're still tucked away tidy-like somewhere," Melton said.

"Ye owe him anythin', Ebner? Of all of us here, yer the one most likely ta have unpaid debts," Foley pointed out.

"Ya owe me some outstandin' funds fer a new shirt und some tins of beef," Bergen reminded.

"I'm a bit suspicious over whether the contents of those tins were beef, Burl," the mayor growled, "but the cost of the shirt should be picked up by the camp, considering I only wear it on special civic occasions."

Tal reclaimed his cards and studied them idly. "From what you're all telling me, it is unlikely that Kit Kittridge had any outstanding debts, which means Rosser held back Miss Pearl's wages to pay off phantom markers. He was cheating her."

"Guess so," Bergen said with a nod.

"And further, that Rosser killed a man in cold blood before winter hit for gouging miners out of their hard-earned dust with a crooked scale and was considered as having performed a service to the community for doing so."

"Yep," Ebner Melton agreed.

"So why is everyone so het up to hang her when, if she did kill Rosser, it could be construed as a community service to rid the camp of the man who not only was lying to her and cheating her of coin well earned, but also because he was using the same scales the assayer had and was skimming more than his fair share from every gold-toting miner to walk in his door?" Tal asked.

The men about the table stared at him.

"He what?" Bergen demanded.

"How do ye know he was usin' the assayer's scale?" Foley asked. "She tell ye that?"

"She did," Tal admitted, "and I see no reason why she should lie about it. What happened to the scales after Rosser dispatched its owner?"

"Hell if I know," the mayor said. "Sounds like the sheriff needs to turn Rosser's place inside out a bit more thoroughly."

Tal picked up his glass of whiskey and swirled the remaining liquid around in the glass. "Doubt it's there. That Gately character turned the saloon proper over pretty well before Strand and I got there this afternoon. Chances are he made off with it."

"Then Strand can start with Gate," Foley declared. "We still playin' this same hand o' cards, or are ye all ready ta clear out and let me close up fer the night?"

"Hell, we got money on the table, Fin," Bergen snarled. "A man don't walk away from that. Whose turn was it?"

"I tossed in my bet," Tal said before finishing off the whiskey in his glass. "Bergen?"

The shopkeeper studied his hand a last time, then folded.

"I folded a while back," Foley reminded. "It's up to ye, Ebner."

The mayor looked at the modest pile of money in the center of the table, then at Tal. "Considering you only took one card, I must have dealt you one hell of a hand, Cain. I fold. Take it."

Tal leaned forward to sweep his winnings closer. "Thank you kindly, gents. My horse, my client, and I will all eat well tomorrow."

Bergen and Foley pushed back their chairs, but the mayor lingered. "Just out of curiosity, Cain, what kind of hand were you holding?"

Tal chuckled and flipped the cards over to display his original mismatched royals, the remaining seven plus the final card he'd been dealt: a three of hearts. "Rubbish," he said. "Absolute rubbish."

****

Rosser's saloon lacked every comfort a man wished for but the roof was sturdy enough to keep the rain off, Tal admitted as he lay on his bedroll on the dirt floor listening to the storm sweep in over the mountains. It sounded as though the wind outside was hurling bullets of water. An entire barrage of them beat overhead, but they weren't what kept him awake and restless. No, those twin problems were the result of Noletta Kittridge's reentry into his life.

Twenty-four hours ago, he'd thought her well-relegated to the past. A memory that slid back into his mind only when melancholy had him in its grip. Something that didn't happen often. He'd made his bed with a decision that had nothing to do with Letty but everything to do with the man he was. A man who thought peace and compromise should be sought between the different political factions of Union and Confederacy and who was considered a traitor by war hawks on either side of the question because of it. His personal compromise had been to slip away to Canada and avoid the war. In doing so, he'd lost Letty.

Some would have considered her lost to him before that. Her family had refused to consider his request for her hand. Even his once close friend Kit had turned away, though he'd confessed that it had more to do with having the healthy size of his allowance dissipate if the cut wasn't made.

Until she'd stumbled out the saloon door into the street that morning, the last time he'd seen Letty had been the afternoon before he boarded a train north, away from Boston.

The afternoon she'd given herself to him but had watched him walk away with dry eyes.

She was planning to do so again. Mount whatever number of steps the good citizens of this sorry excuse for a settlement built on the scaffold and, with that damned Kittridge pride keeping her shoulders squared, her back straight, and her chin high, would be dry eyed as she let them kill her.

He couldn't let it happen. Couldn't let her slip away from him again.

Tal twisted in his blankets, turning over. Damn her stubbornness. Why the hell wouldn't she tell him who had pulled the trigger on Rosser? She'd been less Pearl and more the Letty he remembered during their shared meal that evening, even though the tête-à-tête was held perforce behind a secured cell door. Perhaps she would weaken. Would finally see that all it would take was one name voiced and the Sword of Damocles currently hanging over her head would vanish.

As much as he longed to share her life, he'd be content simply to save it if that was her wish. This time her life wouldn't be constrained by the expectations of her parents; it could be anything she chose to make it. She'd been stripped of the life she knew, subjected to unexpected poverty, failed by the men in her family. Was that why she had given up? Why she blocked his efforts to clear her of the murder charge?

He'd been on the job only one day and already had uncovered lies she'd been told and omissions made by men greedy for every coin that came their way.

Overhead a crack of thunder sounded. Tal threw aside the bedding. Even in the cave-like dark of the empty saloon he easily found the lantern he'd placed on the lone surviving table. The spark he struck with flints caught the lamp wick on his first try.

His was the only shadow thrown against the wall. If Rosser's shade still hung around, it hadn't appeared. The only ghosts in the building were those of the past, and Tal had brought them in the door with him.

His journal lay where he'd left it. It was time to give Letty a reason to want to live. Show her there was a way to do so.

Lacking pen and ink, Tal set his knife to sharpening the well-used pencil and began drafting the first legal document he'd put his hand to in two years.

****

"I need you to sign a couple things," Tal said as he entered Letty's cell the next morning.

He'd caught her brushing her hair, a chore that in

the past she'd found soothing. It hadn't been the day before and wasn't now.

"What sort of documents?" she asked, putting the brush aside.

He had a tray in hand, the surface crowded by two plates featuring rashers of bacon, a dollop of oatmeal—though it appeared to have the consistency of wallpaper paste—and still steaming biscuits. Proper teacups half filled with coffee and a tea-table-sized cream pitcher filled with molasses were wedged in the remaining space.

Tal set the tray on the floor. "Requests for the release of funds," he said, pulling two sheets of folded paper from his trouser pocket.

"What funds?"

Rather than pass her the documents, he set them on the floor at her feet, then handed her a fork and one of the plates. "One authorizes me to take possession for you of either money your brother had on account or its equivalent in merchandise from Bergen's mercantile."

Letty moved over on the bunk to leave room for him to take a seat next to her. "Did Silas somehow overpay our debt with the Bergens?" she asked.

He took up his own plate and passed her a spoon. "Rosser didn't pay anyone anything. Kit took care of all outstanding debts the night he died. According to the men who sat at the table with him that night, he cleared them out at cards. He was still plump in the pocket after reclaiming all his markers. They assumed that included those he owed Rosser, considering that's where he was bound when he left the Gilded Moon that night."

The night he…

Letty tried to push the memory back. She didn't

want to relive that horrible day in January. It rushed at her all the same.

It had been a terrible one, the wind howling around the eaves and rearranging the overnight snowdrifts high against the small cabin's walls. To reach the noxious, narrow shed that served as a garderobe she had to fight her way out the door through sheer force, repeatedly gaining an inch or less at a time by battering the door against the barricade of snow. The moment there was enough room to squeeze through the opening, she'd done so, only to lose her balance and tumble into the drift. With snow clinging to her lashes and burning her cheeks, she faced the wicked wind rushing down the mountainside and soon felt covered in ice. With thoughts centered on the weak but warming tea that awaited her return to the cabin, she had scrambled to her feet. Had rewrapped the shawl and blanket about her shoulders and gathered her skirts, prepared to stomp a trail to the necessary.

And stopped when she realized the only disturbance in the snow was from her own struggle.

Her heart had frozen the moment she realized there were no half-covered footsteps leading to or from the cabin. Kit hadn't returned late and left early as she'd supposed. He hadn't returned, the evening before, at all.

She found his bowler first, half covered in snow but caught in the denuded branches of scrub bush. He'd been another fifty feet down the trail toward the camp.

Frantic to get him to respond, she'd rushed back to the cabin, gathered up every blanket and quilt they'd acquired and wrapped them around him before running, sliding, falling, her way to the only outpost of civilization in this wilderness. Someone had wrapped her in blankets, forced her to sit near a stove, and handed her a glass of whiskey. After that, the day faded into desolation. She'd no idea how she made it back to the cabin. Grief had her in its grip.

And then the three men had forced their way past the door and made her deep despair far darker.

The plate lay in her lap. She could feel a modicum of heat from the oatmeal through the stoneware and the thin layer of her skirt and lone petticoat.

Letty forced herself away from the past, focusing on the food before her. Rather than lift the spoon she gripped it tightly. "That can't be right," she said, amazed that her voice sounded calm, considering her heart pounded rapidly yet with remembered terror. "I was told Kit's pockets were empty when the men took his body to the Bergens' shed."

Unaware that it was a lifetime of having what it meant to be a Kittridge of Boston drummed into her that gave her a modicum of control, Tal bent to pick up the cream pitcher. "Molasses?" he asked, offering it to her first. "Sounds like I'll have to put a few more questions to the camp undertaker about your brother's personal possessions."

If she lifted the spoon and tried to eat, would her hand tremble, giving lie to her control? It was too dangerous to risk it. If he noticed, there would be further questions. Ones she did not want to answer. She concentrated on the surprising information he had learned. "But Silas told me…" she began.

Since she appeared blind to the offer of molasses, Tal poured a generous spill over the lump of oatmeal on her plate, then did the same to his. "Which brings us to the second document," he said. "It formally requests that you be compensated for unpaid wages from the monies and raw gold in Rosser's possession at the time of his death, with the addition of interest, considering he lied to you about Kit's debts. There was over a thousand dollars in his belt, Pearl, and probably far more than that in the poke of gold dust. The mayor is willing to back up your statement that Gately was paid in full every night and thus has no claim to the funds. Says he witnessed the transaction many times. That leaves you as the only claimant. The document requests that the camp hand over the full amount to you."

She stared at him in astonishment. There were funds due her, and not merely from Bergen's mercantile? With over a thousand dollars, she could…

Do nothing. She was still accused of killing a man.

"It doesn't matter, Mr. Cain. It changes nothing. It does add another document for you to draw up, however," Letty said. "A will in which I assign all my worldly goods to you. After all, according to many of the sermons I listened to in Boston, it is impossible for a person to pay their way out of Hell with any amount of legal tender. I have no need of the funds but am sure you will put them to good use. It should be a relief that this will not, after all, be a *pro bono* case for you."

He had a laden spoon part way to his mouth but, at her pronouncement, let it drift back to rest on his plate. "Lett," he said softly.

She raised her hand, palm out to halt whatever protest he intended to make. "Don't argue with me over this, Mr. Cain. A modest windfall will do me no good in a very few days. Simply draft the third document if you wish me to sign the two you've brought with you today."

Rather than answer her, he sighed deeply. It was answer enough. He would do as she asked, Letty knew. Talmadge Hammond had always been a most honorable man.

It was she who had not been the least bit honorable. She had sent him away. Forsaken a future shared with the man she loved. For that sin Fate had punished her, had set her on the path that led to this cell. Would lead to an inglorious death. All that might save her soul now was the vow she had made to protect another.

Would it be a sufficient penance for her shortcomings? For the only crime that she had consciously committed? That of lacking the courage to follow her heart that day long past in Boston.

Chapter Eight

Tal hadn't stayed with Letty long. She seemed distracted. Was it over the idea that she'd been lied to, or had the mention of what might have gone missing from Kit's pockets after his death caused her to look off into space? He hated to have her relive that day—particularly since the mayor had left him in no doubt of what she had endured to be labeled as "damaged goods"—but he needed the information to win her away from the noose. They didn't have the leisure to indulge in an extended investigation. Her life was at stake and the clock was ticking.

Since she refused to sign the documents he had already drafted until a will was added, he headed back to what equated to his humble office as well as lodgings in the saloon proper at Rosser's.

What passed for a street had become more mire than pathway, thanks to the violence of the storm the night before. The day had dawned clear and pleasant though, so he propped the door open to supply extra light and freshen the air in the room, shoving a wedge of pine beneath it. It was all he'd found to secure the door with the evening before. If the camp intended to grow, a locksmith was most definitely needed.

With the lamp lit at his side, it didn't take long to honor Letty's request, but before he could return to the jail to get her signature on all three documents, Ebner

Melton's generous form paused in the open portal to block the light.

The mayor rapped knuckles against the wood before offering a bright greeting. "Hard at work, I see," he said. "Good, lad. Don't let me disturb you. I'm just here to look the place over."

Tal folded the latest bit of legal work in half, then in half again, and slipped it into the inner pocket of his vest. "Not disturbing me at all. Strand know you're here?"

Ebner Melton tsked the idea away. "Noticed he let the previously hogtied Mr. Gately loose from the hitching post last night, so no doubt Linus is currently limiting his duties to making sure Miss Kittridge stays corralled. Besides, no call to get his permission, Cain. As mayor of this fine camp, I believe it's my duty to make best use of the buildings we have. Don't you think this place would make a dandy town hall?"

Although new miners were drifting into town daily to size up the yields in the surrounding creeks, Tal wasn't willing to bet the camp would ever reach "town" status, much less require a town hall. While the mountains rising around them were beautiful and the forests rich with bird song and timber, he personally couldn't wait to ride out of the place. It hadn't taken him long to consider the area tainted. It was filled with people determined to hang an innocent woman.

"Speaking as one who has sheltered beneath this particular roof, I'd say it's damn dark and stinks of spilled whiskey and tobacco—both smoke and badly aimed juice. Attributes that might discourage a less visionary man," Tal said.

Melton chuckled. "Could be that's what I like

about the place. Grant you, it could use some windows punched out, but otherwise it's large enough to hold meetings in and offers a dandy room in the back for a man to rest his mind."

Or sleep off a hangover, which seemed far more likely in the mayor's case. Obviously, Melton wouldn't mind sleeping in the heart of a crime scene either. "You been back there since they carted Rosser out?"

"It's what I'm here to check out," Ebner said. "Are you implying that it might need a spruce up?"

"Bit more than that," Tal allowed as he picked up the still-lit lamp. "I need to give the place another look around to ensure I've collected all of Miss Kittridge's possessions. You can act as Strand's surety that I don't make off with anything else."

"Like those missing markers or that essayer's scale?" the mayor asked. "Might as well see what can stay and what needs to go."

The saloon proper was barely twenty feet deep, with the room beyond coming in at less than ten. It took less time to cross to the closed back room door than it had for Melton to make his pronouncements.

The lamplight barely penetrated, but either the scene inside or the smell of blood and death caused Ebner to fall back a step. "There's a window, isn't there?"

"Indeed, there is," Tal agreed and handed the lantern to the man. Because he'd spent time at the scene the day before as he and 'Diah had gathered Letty's things and again when he'd accompanied the sheriff in the search for Rosser's money belt and gold poke, he managed in the dim light to detour around the bed and take down the board that secured the shutters. Since his eyes had become accustomed to the building's shadows, when sunshine spilled in, Tal immediately squinted in the glare. He took a further moment to breathe deeply of the pine-scented breeze that wafted in before turning back to the scene of Rosser's death.

Melton had gotten control of himself and was surveying the now visible evidence of a violent demise. "Mattress is a loss," he said. "Bedding, too. Not surprising, I suppose, but I have endured less salubrious accommodations in the past."

"Less salubrious than these? Hard to believe." Tal leaned back against the window, letting the sun warm his shoulders.

"Obviously, you have not been engaged to drum knowledge into the heads of unappreciative rural youngsters nor endured the accommodations supplied to those making the attempt. Both students and accompanying board are not only the reasons I gave in to the siren call of gold, but why I drink," Ebner said.

"That explains a lot," Tal murmured.

The mayor studied the room. "I suppose the bedding can be burned and replaced. Otherwise, it shouldn't take much to remove the blood on the floor. A strong back and a shovel should do it. 'Diah's just the lad to handle that. Afterwards, boards for a proper floor."

"Goes without saying that a town hall requires a proper floor," Tal said.

Melton hadn't entered the room, preferring to stay where he was in the open doorway. "When you searched the place with Strand, there was no sign of those markers then?"

Tal figured reclamation of the building for town

purposes came in lower on the mayor's list of priorities than previously advertised.

"You think we didn't look hard enough?"

"Merely that you might have ceased searching once the gold and money belt were found," the mayor said. "Maybe we should turn over a few more things before leaving."

"Could," Tal said. "And if or when we find those supposedly missing markers?"

Ebner's eyes darted about the room but managed to avoid resting on the bloodstains. When they lit back on his form, Tal found himself presented with a broad smile. "If or when," the older man repeated. "Damn but I like the way you think, Cain."

"Keeping the options open," Tal allowed. "You seem to have known Silas Rosser fairly well."

Now that sunlight flooded the room, the mayor set the lantern aside in the saloon proper and, stripping off his coat, dropped it outside the room as well. "No more than any other man in camp," he insisted as he eyed the bed. "You look under that mattress?"

"Rope supports," Tal said, glad that he'd had the forethought to shift Rosser's modest cache of Gilded Moon whiskey from beneath the bed and into his own saddlebags. Only the empty bottles remained behind. "Markers would have fallen to the floor unless they were confined in something, and the sheriff came away empty-handed when he searched." He folded his arms across his chest but didn't move to help the mayor when the man flipped the trailing blanket back onto the bed.

"Could have tucked them away inside the mattress," Melton suggested. "Simple slit done up with a bit of cord. Used to hide the whiskey bottle away from the righteous that way in my previous occupation."

"Then search away," Tal said, maintaining his stance against the wall. "Tell me about our dead man. The stories I've heard about Rosser don't seem to fit. He offers Miss Kittridge his protection *after* she's been molested by three miners and then proceeds to cheat and lie to her about her brother's debts. He also burns down her cabin to ensure she has no option but to stay here. He kills an essayer for using a crooked scale, then acquires the same scale to use when weighing the dust he's paid for drinks and wagers. The camp applauds him for the one and turns a blind eye to the other. It doesn't make sense."

Melton was engaged in shifting the thin, stiff mattress off the bed. "Does if you knew Rosser. He was a fine fellow unless you crossed him, then he was a damn dangerous one. We told you about that Bowie knife, didn't we?"

Tal glanced down at the pile of Rosser's clothing not far from where he stood. There had been neither knife sheath nor knife at the scene, nor on Rosser's body at the pseudo morgue. He hadn't noticed one at the sheriff's office either. Where *was* that notorious Bowie knife? He'd have to ask Sheriff Strand if it had been appropriated for someone else's use.

"What was the attraction of this saloon over the others?" Tal asked. "I've been to both the Gilded Moon and the Friendly Gal, but not the remaining one yet."

"The Spent Bullet," Ebner supplied. "Now there's a tale to tell on how it got its name."

Before the mayor could wax poetic, Tal cut him

off. "Rosser serve cheaper drinks?"

"Naw, and before you ask, the liquor here was the worst rot gut in camp," Melton admitted. "Not bad once you got used to it, and far better than no spirits to warm a man. Place was wide open, though. More fellows were shot or stabbed on the premises than at any other saloon in camp. Games of chance going as long as all the players hadn't passed out, and when they did, Si just tossed them out in the street."

There had been similar places in Boston. He'd been forced to visit them when running a client to earth, in the stretch along what had once been Ann Street, and hadn't understood the attraction then, much less now. "And men still returned? Why?" Tal demanded.

"Matter of courage, I suppose. Rubbing shoulders with dangerous fellows probably made some of the youngsters feel more like men. You want to help me with this thing?" Melton suggested, indicating the mattress. He'd managed to make it hang off the bed frame at an awkward angle, but not to flip it over.

"Doubt Strand would appreciate my touching it," Tal said. "Why did you include Rosser's in your rounds of the bars, Mr. Mayor?"

"Simply going where my constituents drink," Melton declared, continuing his wrestling match with the unwieldy bulk of the mattress.

"So, wherever there was a chance of a free drink?"

"Man needs to do whatever it takes to keep moving once the snows come," Melton insisted as he straightened from his struggle and put a hand to the small of his back. "Any idea where 'Diah's gone off to? Haven't seen him around today, and there's no one better suited to clearing this place out than that boy."

"I believe Strand sent him to alert the local judge that his services are required. For a kid who hasn't been in town long, Short seems to be in great demand."

"For a very good reason," the mayor said. "Seems when he parted company with his brothers, they kept the picks, shovels, and pans needed to ferret gold from the mountain streams. Young 'Diah is willing to do just about anything to scrape together a grubstake. Has even offered to do laundry—not that it's in great demand among miners. I believe Rosser was going to avail himself of such services. Last week he was grumbling that Miss Kittridge had requested the bedding either be replaced or bleached to Hell and back."

Melton smiled as though in fond remembrance. "Si might have tricked her into working for him, but he did keep her safe and would occasionally do something to please her."

"Other than considering an alteration to the bedding, what else did he do?" Tal asked.

Ebner took a moment to consider his answer. "Well, he brought June in to check her over after she was molested and to explain what she needed to do after entertaining of an evening."

Mentally, Tal added a visit to Madam June's parlor house to his search for information. "Anything else?" he asked.

Melton scratched the back of his neck as he studied the uncooperative mattress. "Yep. Got rid of the men who broke into her cabin."

The mayor was finally getting around to telling him something of real interest. It took an effort to appear as unconcerned and relaxed as he had been, but Tal stayed where he was.

"Rosser kill them?" he asked.

"No!" The question had taken Melton by surprise but then he seemed to reconsider. "Maybe one," he conceded, "though his death could have been an accident, too."

Tal raised a questioning brow, waiting to hear the details.

"It wasn't long after the turn of the year when Kittridge met his end. Middle of winter, which meant no one was working their claims. That makes for a hell of a lot of bored men all getting on each other's nerves. Nothing much to do but keep exchanging the same batch of dollars and coin back and forth across a table over a hand of cards."

Tal could well believe it. He'd done much the same the past two winters himself. What had cabin fever to do with the events that had played out in January, though? "Not following you," he said.

The mayor probed about the unbloodied sections of the mattress. "We'd all heard the same stories, had taken the measure of the men we sat across from at the tables or bent an elbow with. Kittridge's demise was a seven-day wonder when it came to a topic to rehash. Was not surprised when these three first let slip that they'd visited Miss Kittridge the day after. A few more drinks and they progressed to bragging. That's when Si marched off and brought her back to his place. She had a front row seat to his physically tossing them out and his promise to kill them if they ever came back. They'd been regular customers of his, too. Of course, they just moved their custom down to the Spent Bullet where they complained about Rosser's attitude while emptying a bottle. Si heard about it, but since they weren't coming near this place, he let it be. Which was surprising. Usually everyone took care not to rile him. Hell, he was the most dangerous man in camp."

Tal had only seen Rosser dead but could well believe he'd been a force with which to be reckoned. Big, broad, and muscled. Why anyone in camp could think Letty capable of killing him was a bit of a mystery.

Unless the man had been taken off guard. The killer had come armed with a pistol at a time when Silas Rosser obviously hadn't been close to his knife.

"You think Rosser felt his reputation would keep men from ambushing him?" Tal asked.

Melton shrugged.

"A man who's able to convince an entire camp that it's dangerous to cross him isn't, in my experience, stupid," Tal said.

The mayor sighed. Leaned heavily on the rough lumber at the foot of the bed. "He wasn't an educated man, but you're right, Cain, Si wasn't stupid. I think he was letting them work up steam to make a move on him. That way, when he killed them, it would be in self-defense."

"And yet you just told me that one died in an accident," Tal reminded. "The other two still alive?"

Melton scratched his ear. "Cleared out despite the weather after finding their friend. He'd gone hunting, and it looked like he'd been brought down by a wolf pack. Wasn't pretty. He'd put up a hell of a fight before they made a meal of him."

The forest was a dangerous place at the best of times, Tal knew, but during the months when food was difficult for every creature abroad in it to find…

"Then what makes you say Rosser might have had a hand in the man's death?"

The mayor tested the sturdiness of the shelf attached to the wall. Ran his fingers around the rim of the abandoned wash bowl. "When Bergen collected the remains, he noticed there was a deep gash on the man's thigh that looked nothing like teeth marks. Figured the fellow had cut himself by accident, since he carried a knife, and the scent of his blood had drawn the beasts down on him. But then again, that might simply have been a fortunate happenchance to disguise something much more dire. Still, it's hearsay. No accusation was made."

Considering Rosser's reputation in camp, Tal doubted anyone was brave enough to make one. The only reason Melton mentioned it now was that Silas Rosser was safely dead.

"But the other two men skedaddled shortly afterwards?" Tal asked to clarify the pattern events had taken.

"Didn't even wait for their friend to be brought down out of the woods," the mayor said. "Probably had the right idea. Whether they made it elsewhere, though, is pure speculation."

Tal found he was tapping his forefinger against his biceps in thought. Three men who patronized Rosser's saloon had broken into the Kittridge cabin after Kit's death and raped Letty, who had then been whisked off to Rosser's, supposedly for her own protection. Rosser then bans the men from his premises, shrugs off the idea that they've got a grudge against him, and then one of them dies in uncommon circumstances with what appears to be a knife wound that would have announced his presence to every wild predator within scent of it.

Rosser had one hell of a subtle way of getting his point across. Had he targeted Letty as property to be claimed all along? Kit had been on his way to make good on his debt to Rosser the night he'd died. Had Rosser killed him and then sent three of his customers to ensure that Letty would accept his offer of protection even though it meant prostituting herself? It seemed too convenient that he should come to Letty's rescue only after she'd been raped by a trio who knew him well.

The more questions he asked, the more complicated the case became. He'd been in the camp barely twenty-four hours and had progressed from Rosser's death to Kit Kittridge's and at least two murders for which Rosser himself was responsible. None of it had moved him any closer to proving Letty's innocence, yet his gut told him it was all connected. But how?

"You have some place other than under the mattress you'd like to look for those markers, Mayor?" Tal asked.

"I think the effort has left me with a strong desire to wet my whistle," Melton said. "If I recall, Si has a barrel or two that would do that quite well. Shall we…"

Tal pushed away from the open window. "Nope. Any remaining alcohol stock is about to become the property of my client, and I think she'd prefer to sell it off rather than have free samples distributed."

Melton swept his coat up from where he'd dropped it on the packed dirt of the saloon floor. "Anyone ever tell you you're a pain in the nether regions, Cain?" he grumbled.

"More than once, Mr. Mayor," Tal murmured.

"More than once."

****

It was too dark to read in the cell, even with the lantern, but the book of Shakespearean sonnets served quite well as a small but firm desk upon which to rest each of the documents Tal wished her to sign. He'd asked Fintan Foley to serve as witness to her signature, which meant her cell briefly had been very crowded with tall men. Once Foley returned to the Gilded Moon, the sheriff left the cell door open rather than bar it again. Letty wondered whether Tal had requested the respite or whether Strand wanted to overhear their conversation.

"Happy now?" Tal asked as he folded the documents and stuck them in the inner pocket of his vest once more.

"Perhaps 'happy' isn't the appropriate word. 'Satisfied' suits much better," Letty said.

"I've got a few new questions for you," he warned. "Spent some interesting moments with the mayor. He seems to think the late Mr. Rosser had an eye out for your welfare."

"Mr. Melton is the worst gossip in camp, Mr. Cain. I would take what he says with a grain of salt," she answered. "However, as I do enjoy the respite your visits offer in my day, please ask what you will."

Tal settled on the floor, his back resting against the wall once more. His lips tipped upward at one corner in amusement. "If that was a compliment, ma'am, it was downright left-handed in the delivery."

"I suppose it was," she agreed. "Your questions?"

"Tell me about Rosser. Were you acquainted with him before your brother's death?"

Letty shook her head. "Not acquainted. It is a small camp, and I saw him occasionally lounging outside of his building. It is located near the mercantile, which I visited every few days."

"He made no overtures to speak with you?"

"Not until the day he came to the cabin to offer condolences and the safety of his saloon," she said. "Safety was a relative word, though. I had little choice in the matter. It was accept his generosity or risk a repetition of…"

When her voice trailed off, he reached for her hand. "There were other options."

"Yes," Letty agreed. "I could simply have walked out into the night and fallen asleep one last time under a blanket of snow. The other option was to starve to death. A braver woman, a truly honorable woman, would not have entertained much less thanked Silas Rosser for what he offered."

She slipped her hand free from Tal's grasp. "And I did thank him, Mr. Cain. If you think I was unaware of what I was walking into, please disabuse yourself of that notion. It was foolish to tell him I would willingly do anything required in exchange, but I kept to my word."

"The bond of a Kittridge," he murmured.

"The only specie I possessed," she said.

"Now, that's a lie," Tal insisted. "Rosser sold you to any man who had sufficient funds or dust to meet the price he asked."

Letty twisted her hands together in her lap, preferring not to meet his eyes. "Yes. There was no other option."

Tal was quiet once her confession had been made.

He watched her hands, she realized, and tried to rest them quietly. Wringing them gave lie to her insistence that the rope was her due.

It had been since the day before, when she'd been covered in Silas's blood. Today…

Letty took a deep breath. Today she was suffering from a bombardment of memories, most of them tied to how she had loved Talmadge Hammond.

To the admission that she would make only to herself—that she loved him still.

Tal shifted position, drawing one leg up to rest his arm against it. "What of Rosser himself? Melton seems to think the man was taking care of you in his own way."

"A very strange way, then," Letty said.

"According to the mayor, he'd hired 'Diah to do laundry."

"Laundry," she repeated.

"Bedding, to be precise."

"I'd no idea," she said. "Was there anything else Mr. Melton equated to kindness on Silas's part?"

"That he might have killed a man."

"Killed a man!"

"Personally, I'm inclined to believe he killed more than one. Not one of the three men who accosted you in your cabin were camp residents for long after the deed," Tal said. "He ever mention having taken care that they wouldn't be a problem any longer?"

Letty got to her feet. It was no longer possible to maintain a calm pose. She took two steps, all the room there was to pace in the cell, then turned, her skirt brushing over the toe of Tal's boot. Had Silas Rosser killed the men? She'd witnessed his ejection of them from his saloon, but since she no longer had anywhere to visit in the small settlement, she hadn't realized they were no longer residents.

"You said he killed at least one of them?" she asked, crossing back to her bunk.

Tal remained where he was. Tilted his head back against the wall and sighed. "I've no evidence that he had anything to do with the man's death. Just hearsay from the mayor, but Melton says it was termed an accident, death by misadventure in the woods while hunting, though there was reason to suspect he had help on his way to Hell."

She'd always known Rosser was a brute. She had agreed to allow him to sell her favors, but it had been the only way she could pay off Kit's debts.

Except that Kit hadn't any debts.

She'd been lied to, held ransom by her own blindness, used and cheated. How could Rosser or anyone else think that in arranging for bedding to be laundered and killing a man, Silas was looking after her interests?

Letty sat down again. There simply wasn't enough pacing room to help her mind deal with these things.

Tal pulled his pocket watch free and clicked it open. "I told Bergen I'd be by at ten to reclaim the unused monies in your account. Unless there is something you'd like in merchandise instead, that is."

"I am already in your debt for items purchased for my comfort yesterday, Mr. Cain," she reminded. "Please reimburse yourself and use the remainder as you will. You have given me quite a lot to think about, but do you feel the questions you had for me have been sufficiently answered now?"

Tal got to his feet. “I’m sure to come up with more in the future, Miss Kittridge. For now, I have just one remaining.”

She looked up at him, his tall, roughly dressed form, longer hair and unshaven jaw both unfamiliar and yet comfortingly dear. “And it is?” she asked.

“Isn’t it about time you told me who really killed Rosser, Pearl?”

Chapter Nine

Burl Bergen placed the final coin in Tal's hand, the entire transaction one heavily laden with resentment.

"Hope yer happy now, Counselor," the merchant growled.

"Indeed, I am," Tal said as he pocketed the money. "To ensure there is no doubt that the account is now closed, I made a duplicate of the request for payment and, as you can see, am now indicating that monies have been paid in full, that I served as Miss Kittridge's agent in the transaction, and that it occurred on today's date."

He'd been scribbling away on both copies, finalizing the legalities as he explained them to Bergen. When finished, he presented one to the man by simply pushing it across the well-scrubbed counter. "Miss Kittridge thanks you, as do I."

Bergen gave a harrumphed grunt as he closed his account book with the document between its pages.

"Now," Tal said. He tossed one of the newly acquired coins in the air and snagged it back with a quick catch. "I have some questions and am ready to pay for your time in answering them."

When he tossed the coin in the air again, Bergen grabbed it, looked at the denomination, then pocketed it. "Yer full o' questions, Cain. Ever run dry on 'em?"

"Not so far," Tal admitted. "Questions are like

weeds, they propagate easily."

"Well, I don't know nothin' more 'bout Rosser's death than ya already been told," Bergen announced, "so ya jest lost yer money."

Tal leaned a hip against the counter. "These questions haven't anything to do with Silas Rosser's death. I'm more interested in Kit Kittridge's death and the man who was killed by the wolf pack."

"What the hell have those ta do with Si's death? Ya think Miz Kittridge kilt her own kin as well?"

Tal sighed. "Miss Kittridge hasn't killed anyone. She's innocent."

Bergen smirked. "Sure she is. Ask yer question."

"*Questions.*" Tal emphasized the plural. "You dealt with both Kittridge's and the miner's bodies."

"Yeah, I tucked both her brother und Vindry's corpses in ma shed 'til the ground warn't froze up no more."

Vindry. It was nice to have the name under which the miner had checked into Hell. "The mayor tells me that while Vindry was savaged by wolves, he also had a knife wound."

"Yeah. Probably cut hisself while tryin' ta fight off the pack."

"Were there any other injuries that he might have incurred while doing so?"

Bergen screwed his face up in thought. Tal waited, tramping down on his impatience. "Gash on the back o' his head," Bergen said. "Might a hit a rock when one o' the animals knocked him down. Plenty of rocks layin' 'bout in that area."

"Could it also have come from a man clubbing him from behind?" Tal asked.

"Why would a man want Vindry dead? Only one reason miners try ta do each other in, und it's always a claim dispute. Nobody was arguing 'bout claim boundaries durin' the winter. Only souls even near their claims were ones that had tossed up cabins at the sites, und there were few o' those."

"Perhaps it wasn't another miner who wanted him dead," Tal suggested.

Bergen folded his arms across his broad chest. "I'm guessin' yer hopin' I name a particular fella."

"A woman had been accosted not long before Vindry's death."

"Miz Kittridge, ya mean."

"I understand Vindry bragged about taking his pleasure with her," Tal said.

Bergen shrugged. "He weren't one o' ma associates, so I never heard one way 'er t'other. Considerin' her brother was dead, who ya think woulda minded what he said?"

"Rosser comes to mind. He did offer her his protection."

"Took her in, ya mean. But why wish another man dead because he'd enjoyed her first?" Bergen demanded. "Ya ain't thinkin' straight, man. She's got ya drownin' in them pretty eyes o' hers, ain't she? 'Cause o' the way she talks, got ya thinkin' she's still a fine lady, und that's reason 'nuff ta believe she didn't do fer Si. Yer wrong, though. She took ta bein' a whore like a duck ta water."

It took all of Tal's self-control to keep from striking the man. After all, Letty had allowed Silas Rosser to sell her favors. Bergen was only wrong in that she had sought the profession out rather than be constrained to it. “My client is innocent until proven guilty,” he said through gritted teeth. “That’s how the law reads.”

“’Course it does,” Bergen agreed. “Back East. This here is the Territory, gold territory. We ain’t got rules written down. We ain’t got government watchin’ out fer us. If’n we did, there wouldn’t be a one of them damn injuns eyein’ our scalps.”

Tal had heard enough of Bergen’s tirades over the poker table the evening before to not want a rehash. It was time to draw the man back to the point at hand. “You would swear in a court of law that at least two wounds on Vindry’s body could have been the result of human intervention rather than a result of the wolf attack, though?”

“What court o’ law? Ya mean when old Brevard gets dragged inta camp fer that trial yer het up ta have? Yeah, I suppose. Not that I think the marks was anythin’ other than related ta them wolves gettin’ him.”

He was going to have to cut Bergen off before the man delivered his own opinion at the trial. If the identity of Rosser’s true assailant hadn’t been found by then, the only way he might be able to save Letty was to paint Rosser as a man who collected enemies through his own deeds. Enemies who wanted revenge.

“Let’s move to Kit Kittridge,” Tal said. “Were there any wounds on his body that could have resulted in his losing consciousness and subsequently freezing to death that night or possibly even have killed him outright before he froze?”

Bergen looked down at his counter, shook his head in wonder. “Ya are the most curious cuss I’ve ever run up agin, Cain. Ya think every man what dies in this camp was helped along by another man's hand?"

"You believe a slip of a woman killed a man who could easily have overpowered her," Tal insisted. "But no, I don't think every death occurred through human agency, just these specific deaths."

"Fer what reason would anybody want ta do in Kittridge? He didn't rile no one. Didn't cheat at cards—mostly 'cause he warn't slick 'nuff ta pull it off und knew it," Bergen said.

"He'd won a large sum of money that night and was visiting creditors to collect his markers," Tal reminded. "When he left the Gilded Moon, it was to visit Rosser's to pay his debts there. He could have been followed, taken unaware, and robbed. When you collected his body, did you find any of his winnings in his pockets? Anything of value at all?"

"Nope. He'd been cleaned out. I thought, seein' as how his sister found him, she'd gathered up what he had."

"If she had, do you honestly believe she would have agreed to Rosser's offer of protection and all that it entailed?"

"Don't claim ta know how a woman's mind works," Bergen said. "Could a had her own reasons fer movin' in with Si. Could a fancied herself in love. That's prob'ly the way it was, und when she know'd he didn't return the feelin', she kilt him. Plenty o' those sorts o' killin's in the papers back home."

Tal admitted to himself that there were numerous cases in the newssheets of women having killed husbands or sweethearts who strayed or treated them badly, but nothing about Letty's situation within Rosser's saloon indicated she entertained romantic notions regarding the dead man. Perhaps, to be thorough in his investigation, he should ask her what her feelings toward Rosser had been.

"You agree then that, if Miss Kittridge did not remove items from her brother's possession, Kittridge could have been robbed the night he died?" Tal summarized.

"Suppose so," Bergen allowed.

"Then let's go back to the state of his body, other than it being frozen when found," Tal suggested. "Were there any wounds that could be construed as inflicted by an attacker?"

Bergen sighed. "Not a wound so much but a curiosity," he said.

"A curiosity," Tal repeated. "What was it?"

"The scarf 'round his neck. Wasn't knotted like most folks do 'em, but double wrapped und trailin' behind his head. But that weren't the only odd thing."

Tal waited for what he knew would be the true kernel of worth to spill free.

Bergen unwove his crossed arms, placed the heels of his hands on the counter's edge, and leaned forward. "After the game broke up at the Moon, when we all left, Kittridge warn't wearin' a scarf. Fact is, he didn't even have one with him."

****

Letty was startled awake when she heard Tal's voice in Sheriff Strand's office. She'd been dozing, but fretfully. The dreams that visited her efforts to sleep were as bad as her thoughts when awake. The small mirror she'd made do with for so many long months wasn't large enough to show her much of her face, but what it did show looked haggard. There would be dark circles beneath her eyes when the trial commenced. When they hanged her.

She swung her legs off the bunk. Planted her booted feet on the floor once more. A hand went to her hair from old habit. Very old habit. She doubted she'd taken much care of her appearance in months. Now she wished to at least resemble the shadow of the woman she'd been as Noletta Kittridge, the spoiled society darling who daringly strolled Boston Common on the arm of a man who made waves in the staid halls of the local judicial system. She had reveled in the whispers about them that made the rounds at afternoon teas. How foolishly naïve she'd been.

How foolish now to even wish to be a reflection of that young woman.

Just yesterday she'd been resigned to being Pearl, the soiled dove accused of murder. The woman the camp would hang for the crime. When had she begun slipping back into Noletta Kittridge's skin? Had it been that moment when her Kittridge heritage had reasserted itself in response to the jeers of the camp after her arrest?

Or had it been the moment she recognized Talmadge Hammond's voice?

The cell door was closed, but Linus Strand had left the observation hatch open again, allowing her a modicum of fresh air. It still required the lantern to supply light, but as she had no occupation but to await her trial and subsequent execution, it was the sweetness of the pine-and-spruce-scented breeze wafting through the open door of the sheriff's office that she appreciated the most.

"Sheriff," she heard Tal greet the man in the outer

room. "Mind if I have a moment with my client?"

"Again? Already?" Strand sputtered. "You only left a short while ago."

"Can't stop discovering I have more questions to ask," Tal said. "You gonna open the door, or should I just do it myself?"

Letty heard the creak of Strand's chair. He was probably tilting it back against the wall again. "Hell," he snarled. "Do it yourself. I just got comfortable."

"Don't get too comfortable," Tal warned. "I've got a few questions for you as well."

Then he was at the door to her cell, removing the makeshift barricade. By the time he entered the cramped room, Letty was on her feet, hands pressed against her calico skirt.

"In what manner can I help you this time, Mr. Cain?" she asked.

He pulled up short in the open doorway. "You may not feel inclined to answer these questions, Miss Kittridge. I don't mean to remind you of a very sad occasion, but…"

Letty raised her chin. Met his eyes. Read concern in his face. "There are many sad occasions in my past, sir. I believe I am strong enough to face them in your pursuit of information."

"Perhaps you'd like to sit down…"

She'd done little else but sit or lie on the cot. It was best to face life and whatever Tal had brought to her door this time while on her feet.

"Ask," she murmured, steeling herself for yet a new bout of memories. There were so few that she considered happy ones anymore.

"Your brother," Tal said. "When you found him,

did you happen to notice whether there were traces of any footprints other than his, that there was a disturbance in the snow that might indicate a struggle?"

Letty closed her eyes tight at the thought of Kit, of his devil-may-care attitude and how, when things had gone terribly wrong for them, his once-cocky nature resurfaced only because he forced it back to life. Had he known the joie de vivre rang false to her? When tears threatened, Letty bit down on her bottom lip to fight them back. She sensed Tal's nearness. He had taken a step into the cell. Was he preparing to catch her if she swooned? Even Noletta Kittridge was a stronger woman than that, she thought. Pearl was made of even sterner stock. Or perhaps he was as tempted to take her in his arms as she was to throw herself there.

Her lashes were damp, but her voice had no quaver when she gave him his answer. "I'm afraid I was too concerned with keeping Kit alive. I'd no notion that it was already too late. I covered him with blankets and ran to the camp for help."

Tal turned slightly, looked back into the front room. "Sheriff, I know you heard what I just asked. When you reached the scene, what did you see?"

"A well disturbed trail through the night's accumulation," Strand said. "I wasn't among the first to arrive, so the snow around Kittridge was a trampled pack as men milled about. How the hell is this connected with Si Rosser's murder?"

Tal grinned. "That's what Bergen wanted to know, too. Right now, I'm undecided, but it is beginning to appear to me that you had one hell of a crime spree in this camp before the thaw."

Then he was facing her again, and so lost in sorting

things out that he forgot who they were. That he was a drifter who just happened to have been a lawyer and that she was a whore who just happened to have been something better. The backs of Tal's fingers brushed lovingly along her cheek. Captured a rogue tear that had escaped her lashes. Brushed it out of existence.

"Did you or anyone else empty your brother's pockets before they took him away?" he asked.

"I don't believe so. The thought never entered my mind," Letty admitted. "Is that important?"

"It is if he still had a pocket full of greenbacks after paying off everyone he owed," Tal said. "Bergen told me your brother's pockets were empty when he…"

It was endearing that he stopped short of reminding her just what Bergen had done with those who died over the winter months. "When he stored Kit's body," she finished for him. "The same Mr. Bergen who didn't tell me there were funds on the Kittridge account at his mercantile?"

"Yup, and I agree that if there had been even a stray nickel, Bergen would have palmed it for himself," Tal said.

"Well, I did check your brother's pockets, Miss Kittridge," Strand volunteered, "and there wasn't a thing in them."

"You didn't think that strange?" Tal asked. He turned slightly, leaving her facing the sheriff. "I believe you were one of the men at the table the night Kittridge walked away with a tidy grubstake."

"I was," the law man agreed, "but there was no way of knowing how much or to whom he owed anything. Could have distributed every cent to clear debts."

Tal glanced her way. "Would your brother have paid everyone off and left himself with nothing to wager the next night?"

Letty's hand flew to her mouth as she realized what his questions implied. "No," she whispered. "He would not. I was too upset to realize that at the time. He knew the larder was nearly empty. While we were not indulging in feasts, Kit never let our tally with the Bergens run very high. He was quite aware that we needed to eat if we were to survive the winter."

He had also promised her that as soon as the snows melted, they would retrace their path to the California trail and journey on toward the promised land of San Francisco. In a vow made just days before his death, Kit swore he would give her part of whatever he won, when he won, to finance the rest of the trip. With a forced laugh, he'd insisted the money would be safer with her than if left in his pocket. She doubted those details had anything to do with his death. Or with what Tal's questions suggested—that Kit had been accosted and robbed.

"Sounds like we need to talk to everyone in camp and find out who Kittridge paid off that night," Tal said.

Strand frowned. "What do you mean *we* need to do any such thing?"

Tal gave him a half grin. "Because, while I'm solving the mystery of who actually killed Rosser, *you* need to find out who robbed and murdered Kit Kittridge. It did happen on your watch, and the chances are the man who did so is still in camp."

"Hell," Strand snarled. "You been nothing but a pain in my backside since you waltzed into camp, Cain. You better lose heavily if I ever play a hand of cards with you, which ain't likely, considering I heard you bluffed the mayor out of a tidy pot last night."

"But you will look into it?"

"Even after you've left town, Counselor," the sheriff said. Letty was surprised when the lawman turned to her. "That's a promise, ma'am. My word on it."

****

There was stunned confusion in Letty's eyes when Strand returned to his meager quarters in the front room. From his lounging position in the doorway of the open cell Tal watched as the sheriff slammed his hat on his head and checked the rounds in his pistol before shoving it in his holster.

"I'm trusting you not to sashay out of camp with your client, Cain. Soon as I stumble over the mayor, I'll send him over on temporary deputy duty, so you can be about your business," Strand said.

"Appreciate the vote of confidence, Sheriff. Neither of us will budge from the building," Tal assured him.

Rather than leave the main door open as it had been, Strand shut it firmly behind him as he left.

"Best get comfortable, Letty. There is no telling how long it will take to run down Melton. Last I saw him he was looking for libations of a fiery nature."

Her skirt swayed slightly as she returned to the poor excuse for a cot and took a seat once more. "At least we will be entertained until then by further questions that you wish answered, Mr. Cain."

"*Mr. Cain*?" he repeated, following her, taking the place she left vacant next to her on the bed. "Lett, there's no one to overhear us. Can't you call me by my first name even now?"

She shook her head sadly. "I wouldn't know which one to use. Besides, it is best not to forget who we are now."

"And that isn't Noletta Kittridge and Tal Hammond?"

"No," she said. "Neither of us have been those people in a long time."

Her voice held both resignation and conviction. It hurt him to hear either. "We could go back to being them," Tal offered. "Could leave this place and start over again in California or go south to Santa Fe or Tucson. No one in any of those places ever heard of the Kittridges or of Talmadge Hammond. There would be no reason for us to answer to assumed names. We could be Mr. and Mrs. Hammond of points east and have a future worth a fig again."

Perhaps because they were temporarily alone, she rested her head on his shoulder. "A lovely dream, but that's all it can ever be."

He slipped his arm around her waist, allowed his cheek to brush against her hair. "Lett, I'm going to get the charges against you dropped. They aren't going to hang you."

"You have been very diligent," she agreed, "but only a miracle will save me."

"You're wrong. All you have to do is tell me who pulled the trigger and ended Silas Rosser's life."

Although it was the truth, the one bit of information that he had been trying to shake free, the repeated demand led her to draw away from him once more.

She raised her head from where it felt so right

against his shoulder, turned to face him. "Tal," she whispered. Hearing his name on her lips once more hurt. Her tone had been so sad.

Letty put a hand to his face, her palm cupping his bearded cheek. "I don't like the woman I was forced to become. It doesn't matter that you've now got several camp residents calling me *Miss Kittridge* again. I'm not her any longer. I'm not Pearl either, even though it is Pearl they will walk to the scaffold. I can't allow myself the comfort of a dream that has little chance of coming true. I must be resigned to what is to come."

"So you don't want to marry me any longer?" he asked, attempting to lighten the atmosphere. To hide his pain at her lack of faith in his talents to set her free.

A smile curved her lips. "I would marry you this very moment if it were possible, Talmadge Hammond, but it isn't."

"Damn this place for its lack of a preacher," he said, and then he kissed her.

At first, she didn't respond. *Damn that Kittridge pride!* Yet even as he thought it, her lips parted, and she kissed him back with remembered fervor. He drew her in, crushing her slight form in his arms as hers slipped around him.

"Lord, I've missed you," he said before kissing her again.

Letty gasped for breath, her hands in his hair. "I never should…" she began before he cut her off again. It felt too good to hold her, to taste her once more.

"I should have kidnapped you, stolen you away," he murmured.

She arched her throat, though there was little of it on display above the modest collar of her dress. He sampled that available. “I was a damned fool,” he said returning to her lips.

“No, I was,” she insisted, drawing away from him. “Now I am doubly damned.”

There it was again, that resignation, acceptance of a fate she didn’t deserve. “Hell, Letty, don’t you have any faith in my abilities at all?” Tal snarled.

Her breath shuddered as she drew it in. “I know your capabilities very well. I deserve this fate. I prayed for Silas Rosser’s death and that prayer was granted. I despised him, but I accepted his proposition with my eyes open and no coercion involved. Yes, I am everything that Noletta Kittridge was, but I am also the woman known as Pearl. You are too good a man to be saddled with the creature I have become.”

Tal took her hand in his. “Is that a long-winded way to tell me you don’t love me any longer? If so, I’d like to put evidence before this court that moments ago you said you’d marry me right now if it were possible, *and* that the way you subsequently kissed me also puts lie to the deposition you just tried to make. I know who kissed me, and it was Noletta Kittridge, not some hired dab called Pearl.”

She sighed. “You are impossible.”

“I know who you are. I don’t care what you had to become. I love you, Lett. I never stopped,” he said. “Don’t you see that we’re being given a second chance to get things right? Stop protecting whoever pulled that trigger. Tell me who killed Rosser.”

He was sure the name would slip free when her teeth caught the bottom corner of her lip in thought.

And then she looked beyond him to where the street door was swinging open once more to let Strand

and Ebner Melton enter the building. Their time alone had run out.

The name he needed would continue to be held hostage.

Which meant it fell to him to discover the culprit on his own.

Tal left the sheriff's office. The taste of Letty's skin was still fresh on his lips, the feel of her in his arms a lingering, if bittersweet, pleasure.

Feeling the way he did, there was only one place he and his questions needed to head. Stopping the first man he encountered on the street, Tal asked to be pointed in the direction of Madam June's parlor house.

Chapter Ten

Had it been 'Diah who told him Madam June lived in a proper house? If so, the boy had been damned right. Tal rounded the stand of conifers just north of the camp and felt he'd left Idaho Territory far behind.

While the rest of the camp structures resembled stacks of neatly piled logs, the parlor house boasted siding that gleamed with whitewash in the sun. The building was two stories tall with dormers set into a roof of slate shingles, which indicated the attic had also been sectioned into rooms. Unlike the buildings in camp, Madam June's establishment had a proper stone foundation, wide steps leading to a covered porch that ran the width of the house, and a front door with a metal knocker set into it dead center. From the number of chimneys sprouting from the roof, it appeared the warmth available in the parlor house didn't come just from the embrace of a comely woman's arms.

Every window featured glass panes, evidence that Madam June did not believe in lowering her standards simply because she had hied into the wilderness. The only rustic touches Tal could see belonged to the porch furniture, mostly two-seat-wide settees and a sprinkling of chairs composed of tied together twigs affixed to sawed-off three-foot lengths of new-growth deciduous trees.

As he mounted the porch steps, the front door

swung open and a petite middle-aged woman stepped from the house.

"Like what ya see, stranger?" she asked, her voice a throaty seductive purr.

Tal took his hat off. "Feeling like I took a wrong turn and ended up back in Omaha, ma'am. You hogtie a tornado to get the house this far west?"

The woman chuckled. "Would have been a damn sight less costly than lugging the materials along those rut-infested trails they call roads out this way. Was a wagon train unto myself, but I think it was worth the effort."

"Can't fault you on that," Tal said. "Name's Adam Cain, ma'am, and I've come burdened with questions concerning Miss Kittridge. Do you have the time to spare?"

In answer, the woman crossed the porch, her hand offered in a man's greeting. "June Gilchrist. Fortunately for you, Mr. Cain, this is the best time of day to deal with men bearing questions. I knew you'd get around to visiting me before too long. Word is you're a downright thorough sort of fella."

"Curse of my profession," Tal said as he shook her hand.

June Gilchrist's accent indicated she'd grown up east of the Mississippi but not far east. While bound into a fashionable gown that emphasized a narrow waist and lush bosom, there was still something cornfed in her speech. Although the day was still early, her dark hair was already fashioned into a knot high on her crown from which sausage curls dangled, brushing her partially bared shoulders.

"Can I offer you something to wet the whistle?

Asking questions can be a thirsty business."

"I wouldn't turn down a cup of coffee," Tal admitted.

"Nothing stronger? My personal liquor cabinet is a hell of a leap up from what you can get in the camp."

"Too early in the day for me, Mrs. Gilchrist."

"A man of moderation. We don't see many of those out this way," she said, then turned back toward the still-open front door. "You hear the man, Dorthea? Bring out my regular, would you, dearest? The day's nice, so why don't we enjoy it out here?" She swept a hand toward the sitting arrangement on the porch.

"After you, ma'am," Tal murmured.

She gathered her skirts to make room for him next to her on one of the settees, but Tal chose an adjacent chair. The choice seemed to amuse the madam. He was barely seated when a younger woman arrived with china cups and saucers in hand. Tal began to get politely back to his feet at her entrance, but his hostess waved him back in his seat, then shooed the younger woman back into the house.

"Ah, Mr. Cain, you will spoil us with your manners," June Gilchrist admonished.

Tal grinned at her. "I've found keeping them well-oiled also greases wheels when it comes to getting questions answered."

She laughed. "Yes, you are indeed a lawyer, sir. That tongue could charm a snake from beneath a rock, I have no doubt."

This time he laughed but delayed broaching his first question by sampling the newly delivered coffee.

His hostess set her own cup and saucer aside on a table. "You don't believe that Miss Kittridge pulled the trigger," she said matter-of-factly. "Frankly, I don't either. She's got mettle, but she's too soft to kill a man. Even a fella like Si Rosser. Trouble is, if she didn't do it, who did? If you've come to ask me for the names of possible suspects, I'm afraid I can't help you, Mr. Cain. And considering I probably know the men in this camp better than anyone, that doesn't leave things looking very good for your client."

Tal leaned back in his chair and hooked an ankle over his knee. "Melton told me Rosser asked you to administer to Miss Kittridge after the rape and to instruct her on certain…how shall I say this?"

"Si didn't so much ask as drag me to his place," the madam said. "Miss Kittridge's backbone was all that was holding her together that day. I did the doctoring and told her how best to keep clean. Left her a bottle of stuff I stir up to keep the midwife from the door and saw to regular deliveries of it after that. Did what I could, but only saw her the once."

"And yet you don't believe her capable of killing Rosser," Tal murmured.

"Honey, it doesn't take but a minute to size a person up when you've been in this business as long as I have. Take you, for instance."

"Me?"

June Gilchrist grinned at him. "She's not just a client to you. You're in love with her."

When he didn't answer, she leaned forward in her seat. "My guess is you knew each other in another life."

Tal chuckled. "In another life," he repeated and took another swallow of coffee. It was far better than what the Gilded Moon served, which surprised him.

"Back east," she said. "I'm even willing to bet you

went by another name at the time. Hell, so did I. Don't worry, I'm not about to mention it to anyone. We've all got damn good reasons for changing our names. Now, you got any more questions?"

"One," he admitted. "When you saw to her, did it ever occur to you that she'd be better off here than at Rosser's?"

June patted his knee familiarly. "You're letting appearances—this place…" She waved her hand to indicate the house. "…give you the wrong impression. I sank everything I had into coming here with my girls. Even brought along the men to build the house, promising them whatever equipment they needed to file claims once my building was finished. I'm playing the long game here, Mr. Cain, waiting for the time when the pans aren't pulling the gold out, but machines are. That's when my bet on this place will pay out. Until then, it's all I can do to keep my girls fed and safe. There was no room to add a stray, especially one who wasn't, and would never be, a professional dove. Besides, the moment she agreed to Si's terms, she was his property. I did what I could for her, but crossing Si Rosser was never in the cards."

Tal finished his coffee and set the delicate china aside. "Thank you for your honesty and your hospitality. I think you've told me what I needed, and perhaps a bit more." He pushed to his feet.

"Wish I could have given you names of men with far more reason to kill Si than Miss Kittridge had," she said. "The dress we were making for her is finished. Since it's paid for, would you like to take it along for her to wear? I know the things she has aren't at their best any longer."

“A dress?” he asked, feeling a bit thunderstruck. First a house that had no right to be in the area and now a much-needed addition to Letty’s wardrobe.

“Si’s idea. He knew that some of my seamstresses once were actual seamstresses and requested something be made up for Pearl, as he called her. It was supposed to be a surprise. For her birthday, perhaps?”

His hostess bounced to her feet, headed for the open door once more. “Maisie, bring Pearl’s new dress down, will you? Mr. Cain will be taking it back to her.”

It took no time at all before the clatter of female heels on an uncarpeted staircase echoed out to the porch. Then a buxom redhead burst from the house, a gown very like those Letty had worn of an afternoon back in Boston draped over her arms.

On her little finger a gold filigree band inset with a single creamy pearl bracketed by tiny emeralds caught the light.

****

When Tal returned to the sheriff's office, he had two well-dressed women in tow. Ebner Melton took one glance at the elder and hastily leapt to his feet to offer her the lone chair.

“Dear lady,” he murmured, capturing her hand to place a kiss in the gloved palm.

The woman chuckled, the sound low and sensual. Not the laugh of any lady of her acquaintance, Letty mused, but that of a woman used to manipulating men.

Tal stepped around Mrs. Gilchrist’s stylishly robed figure and the fawning mayor, guiding the second, and much younger, woman toward the open door of her cell. “We come bearing gifts,” Tal announced. “Miss Kittridge, may I present Miss Maisie Flagler?”

Miss Flagler looked flustered at the introduction. Her arms clutched a neatly bound bandbox, which made her curtsey awkward in its execution. The concoction of feathers, lace, and ribbons above her snood-captured copper curls quivered at the movement. “Miss Kittridge,” she whispered, the apparent awe in her voice rather embarrassing. “I am *so* pleased to meet you.”

At a loss over why Tal had dragged either of the women to visit her, Letty smiled faintly. “Miss Flagler,” she returned.

“The ladies have more than merely gifts to deliver,” Tal explained, “but we need Sheriff Strand on hand for the presentation of one of the items. Think you can find him, Mr. Mayor?”

Melton released the madam’s hand, which he had retained within his grasp, and swept up his hat from where he’d tossed it on Strand’s desk earlier. “Shouldn’t take long. If he’s not at the Friendly Gal, he’ll be at the Spent Bullet.” The outer door closed behind him a moment later.

“While we wait, Miss Kittridge can open her package,” June Gilchrist suggested. “Go on, Maisie. Don’t keep crushing it to your chest. Give it to her.”

The younger woman beamed happily as she thrust the bandbox at Letty. “I do hope it meets with your pleasure, miss,” she said. “Alice—Miss Purdue, she is—and I put our heads together over the design, but Madam June chose the fabric.”

Now quite curious, Letty set the flimsy box on her cot, but she glanced at Tal before moving to open it.

“No, this isn’t something I had anything to do with,” he murmured. “I do think you’ll be most pleasantly surprised though."

There was no option. She untied the cord that held the top in place and opened the package.

Inside lay a carefully folded spill of deep lavender silk. Real silk. She hadn't felt the cool luxury of such fabric since…

It hurt to even think of the last time one of the household maids had fastened her into a silk gown.

Of their own accord, her hands dipped into the bandbox, her fingers closed over the shoulders of the garment inside.

She felt more than witnessed Tal move into the cell to retrieve the lantern and hold it high so that light fell over the gift.

"Silas Rosser was going to present this to you," he said quietly.

Letty drew the gown from its nest. For it was a gown, not a dress like the serviceable drab gray calico she wore, but a confection worthy of entertaining ladies with impeccable bloodlines in her mother's parlor. "Impossible," she whispered.

June Gilchrist spread her own expensive skirts as she perched lightly on Linus Strand's chair just outside the cell door. "Unlikely, but not impossible," she corrected. "Silas did indeed request my girls make up something we thought a lady would wear in the city. That—" She flipped a hand toward the shimmering silk. "—is what they came up with. I think they chose well."

They had indeed, Letty decided—if she had still been able to entertain at an afternoon tea. There was absolutely no place she could wear such a gown in the camp. In the rough quarters at Silas's saloon the exquisite fabric would have snagged on the furnishings or doorways within minutes. The skirt would have soon been ruined further as it swept through the dust of the beaten dirt floor.

Maisie had stepped outside the cell to allow room to open the bandbox, but she now bustled back into the narrow space and around Tal's tall form to help Letty lift the gown free of protective tissue paper. "We had to guess at your measurements," she said. "Si wanted to surprise you, so he pawed each of us a bit and announced that Dorthea was about the right height, that we should use Florrie's bosom and my tiny waist for the rest. Still, we guessed at the shoulder width and length from nape to waist."

Letty barely heard the chattered details. The gown was a reminder of all she had lost. All that she would never have again.

"Had the bolt put away for a special occasion," June Gilchrist contributed. "Not only was the fabric right for what Si wanted, the color was good for a woman in half mourning, which you most definitely are for your brother."

For Kit, yes. No one, least of all herself, mourned Silas Rosser's passing.

With Maisie holding the gown's skirt so that it didn't brush against the floor or risk damage against either the rough cot or walls of the cell, it was possible to see that the bodice was modest, a ruffle trimmed in black lace serving as a collar, the same trim reappearing at the sleeves as cuffs. The elegance lay not only in the choice of fabric but in the cut and careful stitching. The women who had slaved over its construction had been more than mere seamstresses. At least one of them had clearly trained under a modiste.

"It is beyond lovely," Letty whispered before straightening her backbone and stepping back, away from the temptation. "But I cannot accept this, Mrs. Gilchrist."

The madam chortled. "My dear Miss Kittridge, it is not a gift of my giving. Si paid in full for its creation weeks ago. It is yours to do with as you please, but I believe everyone in this room, as well as the ladies back at my house, would like to see you take pleasure in wearing it."

"Wear it where?"

"To your trial if nowhere else," Tal suggested.

Letty turned to stare at him over her shoulder. "You jest, Mr. Cain."

"No, I'm actually rather emphatic that you do wear it. The judge and the men chosen for the jury need to see Miss Noletta Kittridge on the stand."

"I totally agree," June Gilchrist said. "Although I don't believe for one moment that *Pearl* pulled that trigger, the idea that Miss Kittridge of high and mighty Boston could have done so is clearly asinine. Not a one of the fellas getting a gander of you in that dress should find it possible, either."

"I would so like to see you in it," Maisie contributed. "We did so enjoy making it for you."

Tal set the lamp back on the floor but far from where any spill of silk might flutter near the warm glass enclosing the flame. With his broad shoulders propped against the wall, he looked quite at his ease despite being surrounded by women. Her father had only been comfortable around men and, though he was always ready to flirt with a blushing debutante, even Kit had tended to surround himself with male friends, avoiding the marriage-minded maidens of society. She had always known Talmadge Hammond was an uncommon man. Why was it only now that she realized he had no equal? That he never would.

"I think the fact that Rosser contracted for this type of gift to be constructed hints at something more than an effort to please you, Miss Kittridge," he said. "I believe it implies that he was making plans to leave the area and take you with him. From the stipulations he made about the gown, it seems likely that the destination he had in mind was a city. Had he made any mention of San Francisco, St. Louis, Chicago?"

"I can't imagine him considering leaving the camp unless the gold was playing out," Letty said.

June Gilchrist shifted in her chair. "It's showing no sign of doing that for years to come. Believe me, I keep close tabs on what's being pulled out and make a point of personally entertaining any miner who studied up on his geology before making the trip out here."

"Then why would Rosser suddenly decide to pull up stakes when fortunes were about to be made?" Tal asked.

"If he was even contemplating doing so," Letty cautioned.

"Maybe he was just going to send Miss Kittridge home," Maisie suggested. "He wouldn't know what sort of clothing she'd need for traveling. Probably thought the suit she arrived in was fine for the journey."

"Which it is no longer," June contributed.

With the lovely new gown spilling over the blankets on her cot, there was nowhere to sit but plenty of rough wall to lean against. Mimicking Tal's stance, Letty rested her shoulders on the barely planed timbers.

"It takes money to travel," she said, "and even with that found at the saloon, there still isn't sufficient to support myself long, much less return to Boston or refurbish my wardrobe."

"Again, I agree," Tal murmured, "which is why I still think Rosser himself was planning to leave the camp with you in tow. It also argues that we haven't found everything he had tucked away. Once Strand gets here and we can move on to the next item of business, I believe another treasure hunt at the saloon is on the docket. Whatever he was planning, there has to be some evidence to tell us what it was."

"And how he was planning to afford to do whatever it was," June said. "No matter how rich the nuggets and dust being pulled out of the creeks was prior to winter, Silas Rosser could not have acquired sufficient to set himself up as a gent a hell of a long way from this Territory. Either he acquired an extraordinarily large nugget, or he had another way of making money than that poor excuse for a saloon."

"You think that's possible?" Tal asked.

"The nugget's the most likely answer, but if he had one, it means the man who found it has been lying dead somewhere and no one's found him or filed on a very rich abandoned claim," the madam said.

Her mind spinning at the mere suggestion that she might have been on the cusp of leaving the camp, Letty stared unseeingly at the gown Maisie Flagler carefully tucked back into the protective bandbox. Had Silas said or done anything that could be construed as a plan to abandon the gold fields? Were there hints that she had missed? Admittedly, she had lived in a fog, preferring not to look deeply into what occurred at the saloon. So much that happened within its walls had been lewd, crude, violent, and so distant from her life in polite society that she had simply considered herself trapped in one of Dante's levels of Hell.

Tal's questions for her would soon resume, aimed at finding a possible connection between whatever Silas had been planning and whom he might have killed and robbed. Only she knew Rosser's death was unconnected to such things.

Only she knew how difficult it was becoming to withhold the name of his killer. Dreams of a life with Tal whittled away at her resolve. The lovely silk gown pricked at it further. And yet…

"There someone who keeps track of the various claims?" Tal asked. "Could be possible to match the records with the men panning currently, see if anyone is missing, check the yield of any claims that have been abandoned."

"Ebner Melton took over that office when we lost the assayer," June Gilchrist supplied. "He may appear to be the worst wastrel in camp, but he is also the most diversified."

Tal pushed off the wall. "The mayor? How so? I've heard that he has a claim but isn't working it."

"Isn't working it *himself*," the madam corrected. "If it wasn't worked at all, he'd lose it, so Ebner hired the men with adjacent claims to work his half a day each week. Whatever the yield is, he splits it with them. I've heard the deal was for fifty-fifty, but a man isn't going to work another man's claim for so little. I'm more inclined to think it's seventy-thirty. He probably doesn't charge them for writing letters home like he does everyone else."

Letty nodded. "I believe I heard something similar."

"It's the filing fees on the claims that are his true bread and butter now that new men are streaming into camp once more," June said. "I believe that, lacking a proper assay office, Ebner makes do with a table in the Spent Bullet where he has a map of the area's claims posted on the wall. If he isn't available—a very rare occurrence—the map has each claim owner's name noted."

"'Preciate the information, ma'am," Tal drawled, tipping his head by way of thanks.

He'd become the consummate westerner, Letty mused. Not only had he succeeded in shrugging off the echo of Massachusetts in his voice, he sounded like a man who had never crossed the Mississippi in either direction. Tal dressed differently, the gun holstered at his belt and knife sheath strapped to his leg as much a part of him as the spurs at his boot heels. He held himself differently. He'd become a stranger.

If circumstances had been different, *this* was the man who could have saved her, not the counterpart he'd been back in Boston.

The gown was safely packed away once more. Madam June suggested, now that she'd seen conditions at the sheriff's office, it return to her parlor house, where it could be hung in one of the garment presses until needed. Letty expected her visitors to now leave, but the two women stayed where they were, Mrs. Gilchrist in the chair and Maisie Flagler perched on the edge of the cot, the bandbox resting on the ground by her feet.

It was only when the sound of men's voices was

heard outside the building that Letty recalled they were waiting for the sheriff's return.

"…at that damn lawyer's beck and call," Linus Strand growled as he stepped back into his office.

Tal, Letty noticed, grinned at the man's snarl.

"Don't shoot the messenger, Strand," Ebner Melton snapped back. "It's not my fault you're doing a slapdash job when it comes to running a peaceful camp."

"What rock were you hiding under, Linus?" June Gilchrist demanded. "I was beginning to think Ebner had to traipse all the way to the Mormon lands to find you."

Strand swept his hat off, tossing it toward his makeshift desk without bothering to look where it might land. "I'm beginning to think that might be a damn fine idea," he declared, leveling a scowl at Tal. His eyes flicked to the pistol and knife still evident on the lawyer's person but kept his counsel on the advisability of entering a prisoner's cell armed.

"This won't take long," Tal assured him, "though it will cause a slight problem."

"Everything you're connected to causes me a problem, Cain," Strand said. "Go on, what is it this time?"

Rather than answer, Tal offered his hand to Maisie Flagler as she rose to her feet. She cleared her throat and glanced toward June Gilchrist.

"Go on, dear," the madam urged softly.

Maisie dipped her fingers into her exposed cleavage and retrieved a small drawstring bag. Pulling it open, she shook a small trinket from hiding.

When Tal lifted the lantern once more, casting light

on the item in Maisie's hand, Letty's breath caught in her throat.

Her lost ring glinted faintly in the soiled dove's palm.

Chapter Eleven

"Nice bauble," Strand said.

"It's Miss Kittridge's," Maisie explained, a hint of remorse in her voice. "Mos Gately gave it to me last night."

To Tal, the ring was a token of love—his for Letty. What had Gately seen it as? Payment for an evening with Maisie he could not afford in other circumstances? Or had he wanted to show the young dove she was more than merely a whore to him?

Strand fixed Letty in his stare. "You give it to Gate?"

"No," she said simply.

The sheriff's interrogative glare turned back to Maisie Flagler. "How do you know it belongs to Miss Kittridge? Could be a Gately family heirloom. I heard he was courting you."

Tal half expected June Gilchrist to disabuse Strand of the notion, but it was Maisie herself who scoffed. "When he was paying for time with me? 'Sides, I wouldn't have a fella the likes of him." She tossed her head at the mere idea. "This ain't…isn't an old piece of jewelry, neither. It's modern, and Madam tells me those little stones are real emeralds, not some colored bit of paste. Gately helped himself to it, Sheriff."

"We stopped by Bergen's place on our way here," June Gilchrist added. "Irene Bergen identified it as

Miss Kittridge's as well. She'd admired it on many occasions prior to the change in Miss Kittridge's circumstances. Actually, she said she'd been hoping that it would be offered in exchange for goods one day."

It would have been a logical move for a woman in dire straits to contemplate, Tal knew, but Letty gasped in surprise at the audacity of the shopkeeper's wife. Apparently, she had not considered such an option.

"Never!" she declared. "It has sentimental value far beyond its market worth."

"Just as well you didn't," June said. "Neither of the Bergens would have given you the equal of the ring in goods."

The mayor peered over the sheriff's shoulder. "I recall Miss Kittridge sporting the ring when she and her brother first arrived in camp," he added. "Believe I told her how attractive it was at the time."

Strand turned an eye to where Tal stood. "You got nothing to say in the matter, Counselor?"

"The list of personal items Miss Kittridge sent me to collect included a pearl ring," he said, although it hadn't. Strand didn't need to know he'd known the piece, had purchased it in the past with her in mind. "It was not among the items I removed from Silas Rosser's saloon. 'Diah can attest to that if need be."

"Hell," the sheriff snarled. "Gately was there when you arrived, too. 'Diah told me it looked like he'd been tossing the place."

"It gives him motive, means, and opportunity. He wished to give Miss Maisie a lover's token, there was evidence he'd been searching for anything of value at the saloon, and he was alone at the murder scene after

Rosser's death," Tal said. "I believe we have a case of theft to add to Mr. Gately's growing list of crimes."

Strand frowned. "I still have the problem of no place to jail him, Cain, but I'll bet you've got a solution brewed up on that slippery tongue of yours."

Tal grinned at him. "I believe Miss Kittridge might be willing to overlook the illegal appropriation of her valuables if, rather than hold them as evidence of the crime, the ring is returned to her now."

The sheriff switched his glare to Letty. "That just your counselor jawing, or you agreeing to what he said?"

Letty's back was straight, and her chin was raised. She met Strand's eyes with determination written in hers. "Yes," she said. "It is. As it is the only item of value that I own, it will go to Mr. Cain as compensation for his services at the conclusion of the trial."

"Which is no doubt why he's been so determined to find the damn thing," Strand declared, clearly exasperated. He flicked a hand at Maisie. "Go on, give it to her. For this you pulled me away from inquiries on that other matter?"

Since the demand was clearly directed at him, Tal nodded as the dove placed the ring in the palm of Letty's hand. "Just keeping everything legal, Sheriff, as is my duty as a duly admitted member of the bar."

"Of the bar where?" Strand snapped.

"As this part of the Territory lacks a judicial setup, it must be the one I was sworn into back East," Tal said.

"No further details, like *where* back East?"

"The where is immaterial, surely," Tal murmured.

The mayor chuckled. "Hell, Linus, all you have to do is listen to the man spout all those high-sounding words to know he's got every letter of the law memorized better than you ever will."

"Never would have thought a man could beat you at that game, Ebner, but damned if he hasn't," the lawman agreed as he turned away to reclaim his discarded hat. "If you'll all excuse me, I've got problems to solve."

As the door closed behind him, Tal placed the lantern on the floor once more. "Can I impose on you to see the ladies back to the parlor house, Mr. Mayor? I have a few new questions for my client."

Melton executed a bow that Tal doubted any man in his right mind had given a woman in nearly two hundred years. All he lacked was the plumed hat of a Restoration dandy. "I would be delighted, my boy. It isn't often a man has a chance to escort two lovely damsels to their abode."

Madam June swatted his arm fondly as she got to her feet. "You've been reading those romances of Walter Scott again, haven't you? I can always tell when you do. The actor in you attempts to take the stage."

Maisie hopped back to her feet, swooping up the bandbox in her arms once more. "Mr. Melton is the only man alive who would pack trunks full of books with him to a mining camp rather than a pick and shovel," she said with a grin. "He often comes out and reads to us."

"For a fee," June Gilchrist clarified.

"For the pleasure of your company, dear lady," the mayor insisted.

"Of course," she agreed, though there was a strong hint of sarcasm in the words. "We'll take excellent care of the gown until you require it, Miss Kittridge. As I trust in Mr. Cain's abilities, I'm sure you will have many occasions to wear it in the future."

"Just not in this camp," Maisie added. "It was lovely to briefly enjoy your ring as my own, Miss Kittridge, but I knew Mos Gately hadn't come by it legally. I'm glad you have it to wear once more."

"Thank you, Miss Flagler, and for the exquisite needlework on the gown," Letty said.

Maisie Flagler blushed with pleasure. "That was more Alice than me," she admitted, "but I'll tell her you was properly pleased with it." Then she, too, had maneuvered through the open cell door and issued from the sheriff's office, giggling over something the mayor said.

Tal watched as Letty opened her hand. It had been clenched tight over the ring since Maisie Flagler had handed it to her. Now they were alone, he expected her to slip it on her finger once more, and yet she let it rest in her palm.

"Did you really wear it when you first came to camp?" he asked.

"Every day," she whispered turning to look up at him. "When Kit and I learned the estate and every item of jewelry either Mother or I possessed would be sold off to pay Father's debts, I hid it beneath my weeds so they couldn't claim it as well. The day we boarded the train for Chicago, I slipped it back on my finger again, but it went back into hiding when we joined the wagon train west."

Her lips curved in self-derision. "Even ladies don't wear love tokens when gathering dried buffalo dung to fuel the campfire."

When he didn't say anything, she closed her

fingers over the ring once more. "You had more questions for me?"

Tal closed the distance between them in a single step. Taking her hand in his, he drew her fist open and lifted the ring free.

"I remember every moment of the day you gave it to me," Letty whispered. "Every precious moment."

Carefully, he slid the ring back in place on her finger. Lifted her hand to his lips, brushing them over her knuckles. "As do I, Lett," Tal murmured. "As do I."

****

Boston, Spring 1861

The message arrived at his office shortly after he'd returned from court. A sealed missive with his name scrawled across the front in a clearly feminine hand.

The house on Cedar Street. Back door will be open, the message instructed. It wasn't signed, but he didn't need a signature to recognize the script.

Although the partners at the law firm were unaware that this would be his final day in their service, Letty knew that in the morning he would board the Boston and Maine rail line for the first leg of his journey back to Methuen. He'd be home only long enough to say his farewells to his family before crossing into Canada.

The most painful goodbye was the one he would say that afternoon to Noletta Kittridge.

How long would they have? he wondered. The house on Cedar Street meant Letty had drawn her friend Hester Moorehouse into the plot. With her marriage to the pompous Carlisle Parry approaching, Miss Moorehouse spent most of her time at the home she would return to as a bride. Using her friend as an excuse, Letty had circumvented her parents' refusal to allow him entrance to the Kittridge home, stealing away for far-too-brief moments with him.

Conscious of the need to avoid being seen together, she would arrive at a rendezvous in a hired carriage. He would slip inside, taking his place next to her on the upholstered seat. With the curtains drawn for privacy, she melted into his arms, her mouth warm and welcoming even before the hack resumed its journey. One that ended all too soon back at the same corner at which he had stepped up into it.

Today, apparently, was to be different. *Back door will be open.*

Tal pressed his hand to his weskit pocket, ensuring that his parting gift was secure. Tucked the folded missive into the inner pocket of his suit jacket.

It took less than a minute to sweep the paperwork on his desk into a drawer. Someone else would be dealing with the clients he was abandoning. How long would it be before the firm realized he had resigned without notice?

Tal left the office.

Outside on the street, rather than give in to the temptation to hail a cab, he chose caution and hopped on one of the horse-drawn streetcars. It took him within a few blocks of Cedar Street, but finding his way to the rear of Miss Moorehouse's future home made him feel as though his life had become one of cloak-and-dagger escapes.

"Get used to it, Hammond," he growled beneath his breath. As a man soon to be without a country, invisibility would soon be his goal.

The rear door was indeed unlocked. It opened on well-oiled, silent hinges. The door led directly into a kitchen. Or what would undoubtedly be a kitchen soon. A sink was in place, but the room lacked sideboards, table, chairs, or stove. The whisper of skirts on the narrow rear staircase caught his attention a moment before Letty slipped into sight. She paused when she saw him, smiled timidly and held out her hand.

Tal took the few steps to her side. Before he could greet her, she pressed a finger to his lips, cautioning him to be silent. Robbed of words, he kissed her.

“Upstairs,” she breathed against his lips.

A strip of patterned carpet spilled down the hallway before them. He barely glanced at it, simply relieved that it softened the sound of their footsteps as Letty led him toward an open door. The nearer they drew to it, the more hesitant her step became. He knew why the moment they reached the entryway.

Unlike the kitchen, the room was already furnished. Not as a parlor, as he had expected, but as a bedroom.

Her timid smile and hesitant step should have been clue enough.

“Lett,” he whispered.

Then she was in his arms, her mouth against his. Her hunger for him the equal of his for her.

The hallway of another man’s home—even if it did not actually belong to Parry yet—was not the place to be found alone with the woman he could never claim. Tal drew Letty across the threshold into the room neither should enter, unable to stop himself from following the path of common sense.

A bare three strides left her standing at the foot of the bed—a bed built for two. Tall, gracefully spiraled mahogany posts rose from the four corners. Sheets so white they looked sun-bleached dripped toward a rug dark with jewel-toned flower shapes. Plump pillows worthy of a seraglio awaited the moment when heads would rest against them. There was neither quilt nor coverlet. Burgundy brocade drapes had been hung at the lone window, but the dressing table's mirror rested against the wall, still to be dealt with. A clock sat alone on the mantel above a hearth that lacked an andiron. Against the inner wall a selection of framed paintings awaited attention. It was a room yet in the making. Was it the bridal bower or the room of a bride who would sleep more often alone?

At least for an hour, it would serve as an escape from the world for fate-begotten lovers. He and Letty would, in the end, endure a future as unfortunate as that awaiting Hester Moorehouse, the young woman resigned to an arranged marriage with a man who valued her wealth but little else.

Tal closed the door to the hall and took Letty in his arms once more. "You are insane," he said.

"If by that you mean desperate, yes," she murmured.

"We risk…"

"I know the risk. Should a…a complication arise, I care not. I would welcome such a token, a reminder of the love of which they strip me." She met his eyes, gazing deeply into them. Was she memorizing the moment as he was? "My courage is fleeting. I lack sufficient to follow you. Instead, I harbor such as I have for the future. No matter what lies ahead, I will never be anything but yours, Talmadge Hammond. Yours until—"

He swallowed what she had yet to voice. *Until...*

As long as a limit was not placed and that spot in time where love dissipated into nothingness remained unnamed, there was a breath of hope, wasn't there? He needed to believe that even as logic told him it was foolish to dream it. Come tomorrow, he would vanish from her life. She from his.

It was for the best.

Surely, it was for the best.

Letty's mouth against his held a like desperation. He cupped her precious face between his hands, feasted on the need that drove them both. Her fingers were locked on his lapels, holding him as physically captured as he was emotionally. When his lips moved from her mouth to savor the creamy purity of her throat, she arched it, allowing him further territory for exploration.

Unlike the gowns she wore to society's evening fêtes, the day dress buttoned to her neck, covering her too well. With an effort, he put space between them. Space which enabled him to carefully free each small, close-set button that marched down her bodice. It would not do to rush, to inadvertently tear one free, though if they had been allowed to wed such considerations would never have entered his mind. Urgency drove them both. Their time together was limited. Each click of the clock on the mantel whittled away minutes they dared not waste.

There were far too many buttons for a man who heard a lonely future galloping toward him at a rakehell pace. When Letty murmured, "Let me," and pushed his hands away, Tal hastily stripped off his jacket and made short shrift of his waistcoat, tie, collar, and shirt. His eyes never left Letty as the dress gaped open to reveal creamy lace-and-ribbon-trimmed corset and chemise.

She pushed free of the sleeves, let the skirt drop, clinging in cascading folds over the fine lawn petticoats and the accompanying cage of her crinoline. Moments later, she was free of them all, stepping over the puddle of fabric at her feet. If only he'd been granted a lifetime in which to savor her…

No longer concentrated on shedding outer layers of clothing, her attention returned to him. Her eyes widened as her gaze dropped to his bared chest. Tal wondered whether she had ever seen a half-dressed man before, whether seeing him now would frighten her, make her reconsider what would occur in the bed at her back.

Letty raised her hand. Placed it gently over his heart. Slid her fingers up through the mat of dark hair that spread across his chest and angled down toward the waistband of his trousers. She closed the space between them. He felt the cool textures of ribbons and silk on her corset cover, and beneath it the hard spines of whalebone that confined her torso as she pressed against him, raising her parted lips to his.

"We must hurry, my love," she whispered. "Hester is both skittish and envious of our brief time together."

Although left unsaid, he knew Letty also needed to account for her time. If her family even suspected she was in his arms…

"I don't want to scare you," Tal murmured.

She touched his cheek, cupping it in her palm. Her lips twitched in amusement. "I'm not scared. Has it escaped your notice that *I* was the one who arranged this tryst, Mr. Hammond?"

He smiled. Rested his hands around her tiny, cinched-in waist. "No, Miss Kittridge, it has not. I'd no idea I was in love with such a forward minx."

"Then allow me to be even more forward," she purred and released the topmost fastening on her corset.

When it fell away to join the growing pile of clothes on the carpet, Tal lifted her in his arms. It felt so right to hold her close, but even righter when he laid her on the waiting sheets. He knelt then and slowly slipped each of her heeled shoes off. Slid his hand up the silky texture of her stocking to where it was secured in place by a beribboned virginal white garter. Above the garter, warm ivory flesh awaited his touch. The graceful flow of her chemise fell to her knees, but she had not worn pantalets beneath it.

With time of the essence, he peeled the chemise up and over her head, leaving her in nothing but stockings and garters.

The corset's boning had left marks on her blushing skin, but it had not lied about the narrowness of her waist. Even without the lacing, his hands easily spanned it. Her hips swelled in pleasant proportion beneath it; her breasts rose in twin swells, the tips already pointed—with the slight chill of the room now that they were exposed, or with anticipation?

Letty's eyes were huge, her breathing rapid. With fear or with desire? He prayed it was the latter and moved to lie next to her on the bed, needing to touch her.

But when his hand brushed over the hollow of her stomach, Letty caught at it, kept him from finishing the contact. "Now you," she said.

The rush of fear and anticipation was his now. All too conscious of her delectable form beside him, Tal sat up. Removed his boots, his socks. Fumbled with the fastening of his trousers, then removed them and his drawers in a single step. Would seeing him already armed to rend her maidenhood cause Letty to rescind her offer of it?

"Oh, Tal," Letty breathed.

He joined her on the mattress. Scooped her naked form tight against his and kissed her deeply. He ran his hand down her back, tracing the curve of her from nape on past her waist. Her fingers mimicked his, exploring along the broad expanse of his shoulders, inching downward but losing courage as they reached his waist.

Her timidity didn't matter. He was content to explore her, taste the delicate flavor of her skin. When he cupped her breast, and lifted it, her breath was a soft gasp of pleasure. She verged on madness when his lips settled on the poised tip and sucked gently, her fingers biting into the muscles of his back. When she arched naturally, offering him even more, Tal knew he was branded as hers for life.

If only they had a lifetime to savor together.

The incessant tick of the clock reminded that it was too dangerous to linger in each other's arms that day.

His hand trailed slowly down over the silken softness of her skin, moving from her rib cage to slide over her hip, to follow the line of her thigh toward the ultimate destination. Letty gulped at the air, inhaling deeply, holding her breath when his fingers reached and then slid along her most intimate folds. When the pad of his thumb teased the nub between her legs, she shivered.

Tal reclaimed her mouth, kissing her deeply, knowing desperation as well as desire was present in the nearly oppressive hunger he felt for her. She breathed his name, clutched at him as he taught her the ways of love.

And then she turned the tables on him. Was it curiosity, courage, or unconscious need to know him as well as he was learning her? Her fingers were tentative when they brushed his staff. Tal thought he'd lose control. Blood pulsed, preparing him for an explosive release. He closed his hand around hers and helped her guide him to the already damp entrance. Slowly he slid within her. Felt the thin barricade that proclaimed her virginity. Despoiling maidens had not been part of his amorous past.

Poised above her, he paused. "You're sure, Lett? There's no going back after this."

"I'm sure."

"It's probably going to hurt like hell," he warned.

She stared up at him. Brushed the backs of her fingers along his cheek. "Let it. I love you, Talmadge Hammond," she said.

"As I love you, Noletta Kittridge," he murmured and, kissing her deeply to swallow any cry she might make, completed the act.

She froze, her body rigid with the pain as he broke the delicate membrane that proclaimed her innocence. Her nails bit into his shoulders. But Letty didn't cry out, didn't pull away in distress as he slid back down the tight channel.

"Lett?"

She released a pent-up sigh. It was cloaked in relief. "I'm fine. Is there more?" she asked. The simple question pulsed with hope that, yes, there would be further joy to come with their joining.

"The damage is behind us. What follows should be

agreeable to you, ma'am," he teased, though he didn't move, waiting, giving her a chance to end their scandalous madness if she so chose.

Letty smiled happily up at him. "Teach me more," she requested quietly.

So teach her he did. Turning the incessant tick of the clock on the mantel to their benefit, he matched each stroke to it with metronome precision. Slide into her, withdraw. *Tick tock.*

Letty arched her back, her long delicate neck. Her breath came in open-mouthed gasps now, nearly matching his rhythm. Forward, back. *Tick tock.*

It was too difficult to be patient. Tal increased the tempo of his strokes, his own breathing now labored, his teeth gritted to hold his own pleasure trapped.

And then she convulsed around him, her body no longer hers to control. Tal drank her cry of ecstasy in, his mouth crushed against hers. When Letty rose to close the distance, to incite a still-deeper kiss, he lost the fine grip he had on sanity. Plunging deeply into her a final time, he was engulfed in sensation, in a torrent of delicious pain, in regret.

Tal collapsed on his side, rolling Letty so that their bodies remained linked. "You're mine now, Lett," he whispered, holding her close.

"I always have been," she said. "No matter what the future brings, I will always be yours, Talmadge Hammond."

"And I yours," he vowed.

It was only when they were dressed once more that he produced the ring from his waistcoat pocket and slid it into place. Although he knew she couldn't continue to wear it there, he chose the ring finger on her left hand.

The place where he would have preferred to slip a wedding band.

****

Idaho Territory, 1863

When the mayor returned to the sheriff's office, Tal excused himself, citing further inquiries he needed to make. Ebner Melton was agreeable when Letty claimed the unexpected excitement of the day had left her weary. She wasn't sleeping well at night, she told him. Melton noted that in her circumstances he doubted he would either and merely asked if she'd prefer the cell door be left wide open or closed. Although it was a wish for privacy that led her choice, Letty said she was sure the sheriff would prefer the door be secured. The mayor closed it but neglected to drop the bar on the outside. Odd how only yesterday she'd been deemed too dangerous to not be so constrained.

She handed the lantern into the mayor's care, making do with the modicum of light that found its way through the small hatch he left open in the door. It was enough by which to contemplate the ring that once more rested in place on her left hand. The only place she'd ever worn it. It had nearly broken her heart to remove it that day in Boston, but it was impossible to wear a token of Tal's love while under her parents' eyes, or the scrutiny of society.

Beyond the cell's walls the sound of axes, saws and hammering continued unabated. Some near, some farther away. Which belonged to the scaffold being built to hang her, she wondered. At which end of the camp would they execute her? At the southernmost end near where she and Kit had lived their barren life? Or to the north where the path led toward June Gilchrist's house and farther on to the myriad claims staked on the banks of the creek?

Probably to the south, Letty decided. They would leave the scaffold up once she had been executed, as a warning to newcomers. Tales would be told in the three remaining saloons and repeated in those that would undoubtedly spring up as the camp flourished and grew. Tales of that most dangerous of creatures, the drab who murdered her man.

Not that Silas Rosser had ever been that to her. He'd simply been the only thing standing between her and brutality and starvation. She had more than paid her debt to him.

Was Tal right, though? Could Silas have been planning to leave the camp, taking her with him? Nice as the idea of him setting her free sounded, she doubted he would ever have released her. She was a prize, one he'd never thought to possess. He liked the sound of her voice, of her upper-class accent, frequently ordering her to recite something remembered from her schooling while he used her for pleasure.

He had never attempted to improve his own diction. If he had been planning to leave camp with her properly gowned to appear in polite society, wouldn't he have tried to learn how best to fit in?

Or had his sights merely been set on opening an illegal house of gambling in San Francisco or one of the other cities Tal had named, installing her as the drawing card to entice men of wealth through his doors?

It would remain a mystery never to be solved. Silas was no longer available to answer questions, and despite Tal's efforts, within a few days she would hang. With the comings and goings of visitors to her cell claiming they knew her to be innocent, it was tempting to forget that most of the camp believed her guilty. Those were the men who would sit on the jury and condemn her.

It no longer mattered what plots Silas might have been hatching. He was dead and nothing about his death related to phantom plans for the future. In his determination to see her free, Tal was grasping at any oddity that wisped into view. But the only way she would be saved from the rope was if the true murderer stepped forward and confessed.

It would not happen. Self preservation would keep those lips sealed.

Letty sighed. Touched the ring that rested once more where it had always belonged. Miracles did happen. She could spend her final days with Talmadge Hammond at her side. Once upon a time she had hoped to vow to love and care for him until death parted them. She made the vow now, hoping that the money Tal had requisitioned from Silas's hoard would suffice as a gesture of caring. She would indeed love him until her final breath.

Would he see it as a release, as a chance to find love again in the arms of another woman? Or would he continue to love her until…

Chapter Twelve

Tal left the sheriff's office reluctantly, hating to leave Letty's side yet knowing once again their lives were measured by the ticking of a clock. When 'Diah returned to camp, would he have the man who served as judge in the gold camps in tow, or would the fellow follow a day or possibly two later? It was impossible to know, which meant he had to work on the assumption that the judge's arrival could be imminent.

Unfortunately, he had more questions than answers, and the answers he had did not relate to Rosser's death. Which simply meant he hadn't asked questions of the right people yet or hadn't formulated the question in the best way to learn what he needed to know.

Mentally, Tal ran through various scenarios to sway a jury that, while not chosen yet, was going to be heavily in favor of a hanging—for the entertainment of the occasion, if not to see justice done. Not that he himself wasn't in favor of a hanging. All they had to do was hang the right party. Which wasn't Letty.

With her stubbornly refusing to name the person who had sent Silas Rosser to Hell, his best defense was to shower the court with a host of possibilities for the role. Letty had let slip that the shooting had been an accident. Had she told him she'd been holding the revolver, though? Or was he just going on his belief that her weapon of choice was a scathing dressing down delivered in those succinct upper-class tones? In Boston, Kit had fancied himself a shootist. Had he taught her how to handle a pistol or rifle during their journey west? Despite Letty being at pains to tell him she was no longer Noletta Kittridge, Tal didn't believe she'd become a gun-toting frontierswoman, either.

He needed names of men who were in debt to Silas Rosser. He needed the markers or Rosser's ledger, if the man had kept such a thing. It didn't matter if a fellow was in this backwoods camp or in a town or city, if he was floating in financial debt and thought threatening the man he owed would ease up on demands for payment, the debtor just might pull a gun. If a struggle ensued and the man he owed was killed, the debt vanished. But the man would not wish to swing for the death, accidental or not. He'd keep quiet, even if it meant an innocent woman took his place on the scaffold.

One who, for some harebrained reason, wasn't supplying the killer's moniker.

One who the killer knew never would.

What circumstances would it take for Letty to choose swinging for a death she had not caused? What sort of person would she choose to do it for rather than reveal their name?

In some of the areas back in Boston that he'd trod in search of answers for clients, he'd met men and women willing to sacrifice themselves for family members. For lovers. Or because they lacked the courage to face the future.

All of Letty's immediate family was gone. Her extended clan had ostracized Kit and herself, scandalized over their father's bankruptcy.

No, if anyone in Boston learned of her predicament in Idaho Territory, they would conveniently forget she had ever been part of their world.

A lover then? She'd been Silas Rosser's property. Any fellow wishing to take her away from him would have found a quick grave. Upon learning of a beloved's death, would Letty have chosen to die herself?

His own history with her argued that she wouldn't.

Unless she'd lied about loving him two years ago. Only minutes ago.

If she'd simply been a woman in need of a lawyer and not the woman he still loved, would he be looking at this differently, Tal wondered.

Sadly, the answer was yes.

And yet, she said she loved him. If that was true, could his own reappearance in her life make her reconsider the logic of keeping the killer's identity to herself in the end?

Letty's lips had thinned, as though she needed to press them tightly together to keep the name from slipping free when he'd asked her once more to identify the culprit. She might be weakening, but he couldn't count on hearing that name drop free. He needed other and more likely suspects to muddy the courtroom waters. Better yet, he needed the true culprit to step forward and shoulder the blame.

Perhaps Letty wasn't supplying the name exactly for the reason she'd told him yesterday. No one would believe the word of a whore. It was what she'd become; whether it had been out of necessity mattered little. She'd allowed her body to be sold for a man's pleasuring.

Didn't that indicate she hadn't given up on life after Kit's death? That she had wanted to live, no matter what doing so entailed?

What had changed that she was giving up now?

More importantly, would she tell him when he asked that question?

Tal was footsore by the time he ran Linus Strand down along the creek where the claims were. The sound of water rushing down the mountain, the rustling of newly leafed bushes stirred by a light breeze, of pine branches swaying to the same tune, filled the air. The call of birds mixed with the voices of men hard at work with pans, sluices, and rockers. The air was fresh, both with the scent of tumbling water and forest, the combination of dust and mud in the camp proper finding no harbor in the woods, though new rills tumbled toward the creek, courtesy of the storm the evening before. With the clouds dispersed and the sun throwing dappled shadows on the ground, there was a chill in the air that made Tal glad he had abandoned just his coat to Letty's care, not his jacket.

Although he had not done so largely because of the spare pistol buried deep in the pocket. Simply by representing Letty's interest, he'd made a few yet unmet enemies. It behooved a man to stay alert and ready should trouble find him.

He'd learned to be that man back in Boston while visiting the most disreputable areas of the city, the places where his *pro bono* clients lived. The ability had been honed even further the past two years of drifting. His level of awareness of danger was well ingrained now.

The sheriff was in discussion with a couple of men

with shaggy winter growths of beard, straggling unwashed and uncombed hair that hung to their shoulders, worn cotton shirts, and trousers of every make and pattern a tailor fancied featuring in his shop. Hats ranged from bowlers to top hats to newsboy caps. He and Strand were nearly standouts with their wide-brimmed felt slouch hats. Tall, time-scarred riding boots with trouser legs rammed into the shank were the norm. In most cases, both boots and trouser legs were damp from men wading into the shallows to hunker in place with a gold pan, swirling water over the trace of creek bottom scooped up, waiting for particles of gold to separate from the grit.

When Strand spotted him trudging along the water's edge, he waved the men he'd been speaking with back to their work, scowled, and let his hand rest on the butt of his Remington six-shot. "You go and find someone else who's committed or is the victim of some crime I overlooked in addition to the ones you already mentioned?" he demanded.

"*Pax*!" Tal shouted. "Just came to let you know I'm going to scour Rosser's place again in search of those markers that haven't shown up. That or a ledger. One or the other has got to be somewhere on the property. Knowing who was in debt to the man should supply a few more people to interview."

Strand's brows were practically meeting above his nose now. "You interview or me interview?" he demanded.

Tal grinned at him. "If you don't mind, I'll go first. My client's clock is ticking. You can lay into them after I've long since left the vicinity, if you wish. Now, do you mind if I do a search or not? The mayor, in the event you hadn't heard, is ready to measure for curtains to claim the building as the new city hall. You got an *old* city hall?"

"Not so much as far as the camp is concerned. Ebner's got a large tent he built around his buckboard. Calls it city hall, home, and accommodation for his horse," Strand said. "Hell, I don't care if you turn Si's building on its tail end. For all we know, he kept all the information in his head, and you won't find a scrap of paper anywhere. Search all you want, just don't dig any bodies up from under the floor."

"It's a dirt floor," Tal reminded him. "I doubt a grave would have gone unnoticed."

"By you, but by most of the camp? Doubtful," Strand declared. "We're not talking Harvard men, here, you know."

"Making any progress in your current investigation?"

Strand adjusted the set of his hat so that it tilted forward over his eyes, sheltering them from a ray of sunlight pushing through a gap in the pines around them. "Remains to be seen. Suppose there might be some grains among the grit. Shifting it free will be the trick."

Recognizing it for the gold he sought when it did tumble free would be the true feat. "Justice can be a cruel bitch," Tal agreed. "But she's got loving arms."

"You know a hell of a different goddess than I do," Strand grumbled. "Not that I don't agree with you in part. Go on. In pursuit of evidence, I give you leave to do everything but burn Rosser's building down. Mind the roof doesn't fall on you when you pull the rafters free."

"I'll keep that in mind," Tal said, grinning. "You be back in camp about the time Mrs. Foley is ready to serve up her latest concoction?"

"Why?" The sheriff looked and sounded suspicious.

"Thought you might like to join me for vittles."

"So you can pump me for what I learned today?"

"For convivial company and conversation," Tal insisted. "I do, however, have a request for you to ponder before then."

Strand's eyes remained narrowed in distrust.

Which he had a right to be, Tal admitted to himself, considering what the request entailed.

"How much am I going to dislike this request?" the sheriff growled.

"Probably a lot," Tal said. "I'd like to take Miss Kittridge with us to the Gilded Moon so she can eat at a proper table, not off a plate balanced on her knees. I'm sure Foley can give us a table back in a corner. You can wedge her into the seat farthest from the door and you and I will sit on either side of her. I'll even let you shoot me if she makes a bolt for it."

"Best offer I've had all day in regard to you, Cain," Strand drawled. "I'll think on the rest."

"It's all I ask," Tal assured him and headed back to camp.

****

Even with the sun beginning to take an interest in what might be inside Rosser's open front door, it was still damn dark in the saloon's interior. There was just the lone lantern to use, though hooks in the rafters indicated there had once been more. Probably scavenged after Rosser's demise, either by Gately or some of the other fine residents of the camp, Tal mused. He considered trailing to the opposite side of the road to get a few more from the Bergens, then decided to make do. Hell, even if he did buy the damn things, when he wasn't on the premises they'd be stolen anyway. Considering the moment Letty's trial was over he would do his horse the unkindness of driving his spurs into its sides to leave the camp at a full-out gallop, he had better things to do with his money.

Right now, what he needed was a plan. He needed to think like the bastard Rosser had been, a combination of animal cunning and distrust of his fellow man—no doubt based on his own sadly lacking code of morals.

When he and the sheriff had scoured the building in search of Rosser's money belt and poke of gold, they'd searched every inch of visible space and hadn't found anything. Short of bearding Mos Gately about whether he'd helped himself to a ledger or a handful of promissory notes, it meant looking for a cache hidden where no one suspected it to be as well as within easy access should some fool walk in the door with the gold or greenbacks to redeem his markers. Easy access yet out of sight.

Tal lit the lantern and hung it from the centermost hook in the rafters. Went back and opened the door to the bedroom, then unbarred the shutters to supply a secondary spill of light.

Rosser wouldn't have wanted anyone to see him open the as yet mythical cache, Tal decided, perching on the top of the table that had served as his desk just hours ago, his feet on one of the stumps that made a pretense of being seats. That meant Rosser wouldn't use the saloon proper. But if he was renting out Letty's body to men, it also meant the back room wouldn't always be available. Which left him with the outhouse, and Tal could not see Rosser excusing himself from a man with money in his hand on the excuse that Mother Nature needed to have her way with him.

Of course, Rosser could retrieve markers prior to an evening's entertainment and keep them handy in his trouser pocket.

Doubtful that would happen. Wherever he hailed from, be it rural or urban, sometime in his youth Silas Rosser had no doubt begun his career of nefarious transactions. If he hadn't been slick-fingered enough to do the pulls himself, he would have known countless lifters who could empty a gent's pockets with him none the wiser. No, Rosser wouldn't have kept precious markers in his trouser pockets. He wouldn't have trusted anyone in camp enough to relax his vigil.

Was Strand right? Would Rosser have kept the knowledge of who owed him and how much they owed him locked in his mind? If so, the man had had one hell of a memory.

There was no way around it, he decided. He needed to ask Letty more questions about the dead man.

****

The mayor had his feet on Strand's table and the lone chair tipped back against the wall. When Tal strolled through the door, he shifted his feet back to the floor, let the chair thump back on all four legs, closed the book he'd been reading, and set it aside on the table. June Gilchrist had been right. He was reading Walter Scott's *Ivanhoe*.

"Well, you weren't gone long," Ebner said. "Come to relieve me of my duties?"

“Strand wouldn’t trust me to stand guard,” Tal reminded him. “Conflict of interest. And much easier to get my client off by simply swinging her up behind me on my horse and hightailing it out of camp.”

“A sight more dramatic, too,” Melton added.

“You read too many novels, Mr. Mayor,” Tal said. “I won’t be long. Just need to ask Miss Kittridge about Rosser’s habits.”

“Like did he pick his teeth, hit the cuspidor when he spat tobacco juice toward it?”

With the memory of Sheriff Strand’s evil eye on him earlier when he’d walked into Letty’s cell wearing iron, Tal unsnapped the holster cover at his belt and removed his Colt, placing it and his knife next to Melton’s book on the table. Since the day before he hadn’t let on that the Colt wasn’t his only handgun. The Smith and Wesson stayed hidden. “In what corner of the world would Silas Rosser own a cuspidor?” he demanded.

The mayor chuckled. “Not a one,” he agreed and tilted his head toward Letty’s cell door. “She was trying to catch a nap, but I’ll bet she heard your voice and will be up. Door’s open, so go on in.”

Tal knocked respectfully and waited for her to invite his intrusion rather than barge in. When she gave it, he pulled the door open, catching her in the act of folding his greatcoat and placing it neatly at the foot of the bunk.

“I’m sorry to disturb you,” Tal said. “Melton said you were trying to rest.”

“Trying,” she agreed, arranging her skirt and taking the straight-backed pose that spoke of her upbringing in a far different world. “Succeeding? I’m afraid

Morpheus has abandoned me. How can I help you, Mr. Cain?"

Tal scooped up the long coat he'd lent her and moved it back against the wall so he could sit next to her rather than on the floor as he had the day before. Then, he hadn't been sure of how she felt about him, had wanted to give the illusion of distance rather than make her feel overshadowed. Today was different. There had been a moment earlier when they had once again been the star-crossed lovers from Boston. He wanted them to be that couple again, though this time with the future before them and no complications to keep them apart.

He'd left the cell door open, ensuring that no one could accuse him of passing her a weapon or hiding either the questions he needed to ask or the answers she would give. In the outer room, the mayor picked up his book again, making himself at home in Strand's office. Considering he already knew Ebner Melton kept a close ear on everything that happened in the camp, the pose was a blind. Tal knew the mayor would absorb every word they said.

But with the man's back to the cell door, it gave Tal the opportunity to take Letty's hand in his. To stroke his rough, calloused, dirt-stained fingers over her long, soft ones before entwining them with his.

"Tell me what Rosser's day was like. What he did from the time he got up until he shut the saloon up and called it a night," he requested.

She frowned at him. "I don't understand."

"I'm looking for a pattern. I need to find the markers he kept."

"Not markers," she said. "He kept a ledger."

"You've seen it?"

She shook her head. "If you mean, have I seen the entries, no. He was very secretive about it. But I did see him making notes in it once or twice. I never saw where he kept it. He'd make notes in it every night. It was never in sight when Gately was there, so I doubt he knew it existed."

"Which brings us back to my original question," Tal pointed out. "Did Rosser have certain things he did every day, particularly when only you were around?"

"I can't help you find the ledger, Mr. Cain. I've no idea…"

Tal lifted their joined hands to his lips, placed a gentle kiss along the back of hers. "Think, darlin'," he urged.

She closed her eyes. Took a shallow breath and let it out slowly, forcing herself back into the time when she'd been Rosser's property. He hated asking her to do it, but he needed answers only she could supply.

When her head tilted slightly and her lashes fluttered, he knew she'd found a clue for him in those memories.

"I'm not sure this will be helpful," Letty warned. "It's more an oddity. When Gately came in, he always checked the contents of the barrels with taps, but never the upright one. Silas always said it was still aging to…well, gut-eating consistency, if you'll excuse such common language."

Tal held back the chuckle of amusement that threatened to escape at the resurgence of her proper upbringing.

"But I caught Silas shifting it more than once, always after the last customer and Gately had gone."

Once again Tal envisioned the saloon proper. There were indeed large barrels behind the makeshift bar, currently four of them. Three were mounted on cross bars, much like the sawhorses in his father's barn. He'd noticed one had developed a slow leak, bad whiskey dripping to a growing muddy spot on the dirt floor, continually freshening the scent of alcohol in the air. But the fourth barrel—it sat upright, untapped and waiting, a few tin cups resting on the round, securely nailed-in-place top.

"That can't be where he kept the ledger," Letty said. "I know it was possible to hear liquid swishing inside it. Gately tried to shift it aside once to retrieve a coin that had bounced behind the barrel. Silas thundered at him about disturbing the contents before they were ripe."

"It's worth checking," Tal said. He dropped another kiss on her hand before disengaging his fingers from hers. "I'll report on my findings over dinner."

She didn't move when he got to his feet, merely looked up at him. "More mystery meat in a thick gravy with a lone piece of potato or turnip?"

Tal grinned. "Welcome to the frontier version of Young's Hotel, Miss Kittridge."

She returned his smile. How few times he'd seen it since walking back into her life the day before. It was still the most beautiful sight he'd ever seen. "Young's chef would be appalled," she said.

"But if he was hungry enough, he'd ask for second helpings," Tal said and left her to her solitary thoughts once more.

Chapter Thirteen

Back in that other time, back when she and Tal had briefly believed they'd be able to spend their lives together, he'd frequently said that planting a seed of doubt in the jury's mind was nearly all he could do for his *pro bono* clients. The police tended to believe that if a person seemed to look guilty, they were guilty.

Considering she had been covered in Silas Rosser's blood only the day before, she looked extremely guilty. No matter how many paths Tal followed in his search for those seeds of doubt in her case, Letty could not see them providing sufficient fruit to convince any man on the jury of her innocence. They would simply convict her.

Praying would not save her. The Almighty knew she was blameless in the matter of Silas's murder, but surviving in the months since Kit's death had tarnished her, qualified her for exemplary citizenship in Hell. Her choice had been to sin or to starve to death. Sin had been preferable.

"Mr. Melton?" she called to the man reading in the outer room. "Do you think Mr. Short will return with the judge yet today?"

She heard the legs of his chair thump down on the wooden planked floor. Rather than get to his feet, the mayor leaned forward, peering at her through the door Tal had left open. "Wouldn't count on it, Miss

Kittridge. 'Diah might be in a hurry to return to the fold, but Brevard'll drag his feet and be more willing to take his time."

"Tomorrow then?" she asked.

Melton sighed deeply. "That, my dear, I'm sorry to say is quite likely, but we can hope the judge is on one of his drinking bouts and isn't up to the journey quite yet."

Perhaps she should pray for that. A reprieve, if but a brief one. The only thing to live for now was time spent with Talmadge Hammond.

Or she could give him the name he sought and damn another soul to Hell in her place.

It was something she simply couldn't do to the person who had inadvertently pulled the trigger during a struggle with Silas Rosser. The true killer was suffering enough, though doing it silently. Their desire to live was much stronger than hers was.

Even with Tal back in her life.

"Will Mr. Brevard be content with lodging in one of the dormitories?" Letty inquired. Anything to keep her thoughts from spiraling toward despair. She had made her choice. Her courage needed to be focused entirely on keeping to it. That didn't mean she had to contemplate it, though.

Melton chuckled. "That he will not be, Miss Kittridge. If we had a hotel, he'd expect to be granted free use of the best room. In fact, he's likely to complain that we are a backward community because we lack such a fine facility."

"Then where will he stay?"

"Given his rathers, it would be up at June Gilchrist's, but considering his wife made the trip to gold country with him, Brevard must forego his rathers in the matter. He'll get a tent, a cot, and a bottle of Foley's finest to keep him warm."

"Is the tent where the trial will be held as well?"

"No, ma'am. We'll be using the Gilded Moon. It has the largest square footage for a single room in camp. Fintan plans to stack the tables outside and has sweet-talked the other saloon owners into lending him chairs. You'll have to forgive me for mentioning this, but your trial is likely to draw men from every camp within easy tramping distance," Melton said.

"Perhaps in addition to a hotel, a theatre should be built then, sir. That way crimes would not need to be committed to supply the community with entertainment," Letty suggested dryly.

The mayor nodded. "Point well taken, my dear. I do miss the theater. Saw Edwin Booth in *Hamlet* before I heard the siren call of the goddess Aureus."

"Aureus? I don't believe I've ever heard of an ancient goddess of that name," Letty said.

"There isn't one," Melton admitted, "but there should be. I've merely requisitioned the Latin word for gold."

"An excellent usage of the language then, sir," she murmured. "Would you mind terribly telling me a tale of this newly born goddess?"

In answer, Melton got to his feet and shifted the chair so that he faced her directly. "Be delighted to, my dear. I picture her as—"

He halted when Letty raised her hand, indicating he should pause. "What is that?" she asked.

The mayor twisted in his chair, turning to look back at the closed street door. He got to his feet, crossed the small front room, opened the door. Took two steps outside, looked toward the south. She saw his shoulders slump, then he returned inside and quietly closed the door behind him.

"I'm sorry, my dear. That is the sound of silence. They've finished building the hangman's scaffold."

****

Tal had visited Burl Bergen and his wife often enough to feel they were old friends. Ones with whom he didn't care to socialize, but familiar as all hell anymore.

"I need a hammer or a small crowbar," he announced when Bergen looked up from rearranging a selection of buckets and panning equipment. "You got such a thing?"

"'Course we got such things. This camp's got buildin's goin' up faster'n ya can spit."

"I can spit pretty fast," Tal said. "Think I've got 'em beat on time, hands down."

"Whatcha want them things fer?"

How nice it would be to tell the man to mind his own business, but considering the size of the camp, and the fact that Rosser's building was across from the mercantile, there was no sense in playing his cards close to his chest on this hand. The gossips would invent their own truths.

"I'm checking Rosser's liquor supply to see if my client can make a profit selling any of it to one of the other saloons," Tal said. It was a partial truth. Personally, he doubted the Gilded Moon or the Friendly Gal would be interested in Rosser's brand of poison. The Spent Bullet might, though. Of course, he was basing that supposition purely on the quality of men he'd seen entering the Bullet's premises.

"Greedy bastard, ain't ya?" Bergen observed, but he did maneuver through the seemingly illogical arrangement of goods, returning a moment later with both a clawfoot hammer and a crowbar barely fifteen inches long.

Unsure about which would best do the job he needed, Tal said he'd take both without asking the price. Bergen would gouge him either way.

"Anythin' else ya need, Cain?" the shopkeeper asked as he scooped up the currency Tal dropped on the counter.

Tal glanced at the stock visible on both shelves and counter. "Looks like you have a nice selection of shirts."

"Need one?" Bergen growled. "Take yer pick. The wife makes 'em up."

"Nice sideline," Tal observed.

"Ya want a shirt er not?"

He did, Tal decided, but not for himself. "Yes, I do, and a pair of trousers with braces, if you have any." Letty would need traveling clothes when they left camp. If the Fates were against him and she took the long last walk, he'd give the items to 'Diah Short. The lad was in desperate need of duds that fit better than his current kit, which was both battered and short at ankle and wrist.

This time when he tossed the required monetary exchange on the counter, Bergen picked up one of the bills and stared hard at it. "Hell, another o' these things? Probably ain't worth the pulp it's printed on."

Tal glanced at the bit of paper currency holding Bergen's attention. The front pictured Lincoln on the left, a woman he took for Lady Liberty on the right, and an eagle with its wings extended at top center. "It's one of the greenbacks Congress put into circulation," he said. "Worth the same as any other ten-dollar bill, thanks to the Legal Tender Act of 1862."

"Trust a lawyer ta know somethin' like that. I seen 'em afore. There's a few floatin' around camp. Don't mean I have ta like gettin' 'em," the shopkeeper grumbled, but he shoved it into his pocket, not bothering to give Tal change on the transaction. "Don't go lookin' at me, Cain. If'n ya want any coin back, take it up with them fellas in yer precious Congress who didn't see fit ta press somethin' that jingles in yer pocket."

"You had coin enough to toss on the table last night while playing cards," Tal said.

"And if'n ya'll recall, I warn't the one walkin' home with 'em after that, neither," Bergen snarled.

Which was true, Tal admitted. There also hadn't been many of the recently issued greenbacks tossed into the pots, either. In fact, those that had made it in had been the lower denomination ones he'd brought with him from Virginia City.

Hefting his purchases, he nodded at the man. "'Preciate your help, Bergen. By the way, have you seen Gately lurking around Rosser's today?"

"Ain't had a reason ta keep an eye out fer him. Why?"

"Just wondering if he'd been by to do some thieving across the way," Tal said.

"Hell, if he did, wouldn't bother me none," Bergen admitted. "If'n ya find Si's liquor supply worth puttin' up fer sale, I'd be glad ta act as yer agent fer the transaction, Cain," the shopkeeper called after him as Tal headed through the open door.

"I'll think on it, Bergen," Tal said, then added under his breath, "for about two seconds." He'd already been gouged enough that day. There was no reason to promise himself a further gouging in the future.

****

He needn't have purchased tools, Tal found after wrestling the barrel in question away from the wall and prying the lid up. The contents were ripe enough to make a man pass out from just breathing the fumes, but the level of liquor in the barrel was gallons shy of full. Which made it easy to shift. Rosser's modest-sized ledger was tucked into a niche scraped into the ground beneath it.

The ledger and a well-packed leather wallet.

Tal was glad he'd closed the front door and wedged it shut before beginning his search. It wouldn't do for a passerby, or Bergen across the way, to learn Rosser had a cache of crisp, uncirculated, government-issue currency. Fifty greenbacks in all, each of the same denomination, the lone spread-winged eagle on the left-hand side identifying them as something few citizens ever saw—the newly issued 1862 hundred-dollar bill.

What the hell was Silas Rosser doing with five thousand dollars, and where in this godforsaken camp had he come upon it?

Unless he'd come to camp with it.

Just what he needed. A further mystery to sort out.

Hoping there might be the hint of an answer in the ledger, Tal stuffed the money back into the wallet and set it aside. At the rate he was uncovering the dead man's hidden funds, Letty was growing wealthier by the moment. If, that is, the current addition wasn't the proceeds of an armed robbery somewhere far from Idaho Territory. He needed to add a new feature to the questions he asked about Silas Rosser, such as did anyone know where his journey to the gold camp had begun?

Rosser's simple accounting system in the ledger made for interesting reading. Or would have if he'd known who the men mentioned were. The tally of names was a hell of a lot more than he'd ever need to shift suspicion from Letty when the court convened.

Unless some of those same men were among the twelve chosen for the jury. He'd have to see how Strand felt about having the names of jurors bandied as possible substitute culprits in the matter of Silas Rosser's death.

One of the most interesting entries in the book was the one carrying Kit Kittridge's name. Rosser's hand was as unformed as a schoolboy's but easy to read. On the twenty-first of January that year, Kit had handed Rosser fifty-two dollars and seventy-five cents, thus paying off his debt in full to the man.

The following morning, Kit had been found dead.

Frozen and with a scarf he hadn't worn earlier in the evening nevertheless twisted about his throat.

All of which meant he needed to formulate further questions, Tal decided. How much had Kit won that fateful night? How many men had he owed money to, and how much had each tally been?

How much of his winnings would have still been in his pocket when he'd, quite possibly, been accosted, rendered unconscious or murdered by strangling with the mysterious scarf, and then had his pockets emptied?

And exactly how much had Silas Rosser made by Letty debasing herself, considering her brother hadn't left any debts for her to cover?

Tal got out his notebook once more and began scratching down names and amounts. The larger the amount owed, the more reason a man might have to get in an argument with Rosser, one in which a gun came into play. He'd have to turn the ledger over to Strand rather than hold on to it, so he pulled the lantern closer and worked quickly. In the end, he narrowed the possible suspects down to three. Each had run up debts well over a hundred dollars, one coming in at over five hundred. Now there was a man with whom Lady Luck held no traffic, yet he borrowed against his claim's possible worth recklessly, apparently believing she'd come around.

If the man was actor enough to sell a pathos-loaded lie, Tal could see Letty thinking she was doing him a favor by going to the rope in his stead. Perhaps he'd spun a melodramatic tale about a wife and children back East, then sworn to never place another bet. A vow no doubt broken within hours. To men with that sort of debt, gambling was as sweetly tempting as an opium pipe, and just as addicting.

Pathetic as such a story might be, Tal couldn't see Letty sacrificing herself for a chance-met stranger. No, whatever her reasoning was for refusing to name Rosser's killer, it was for a reason that he couldn't yet fathom. But he would, Tal decided. If nothing else, he had the carrot of a shared future to keep dangling before her. He thought her gumption was springing leaks. Hopefully it would crumble by the time the judge reached camp, and she'd supply the necessary name.

The only traps to avoid then would be the true culprit's disappearance or the judge's refusal to accept the word of the accused.

At least he had more ammunition to fire in her defense with the information in the ledger pointing fingers at men who owed Rosser outstanding debts. There was a further suspicious notation next to the final name on his own list that Tal was sure Sheriff Strand would find tantalizing.

He was just about to close the ledger when he noticed Rosser had tucked a ragged edged bit of folded newspaper between the blank pages at the back. He wouldn't have found it at all if it hadn't shifted position and come out of hiding.

Curious over why the late saloon owner had saved an article, Tal unfolded the piece and found he was looking at the front page of the St. Louis *Packet Messenger* of June 11, 1862.

DARING ROBBERY! Two Men in Custody! a double headline blared in large letters.

Three employees of the Mississippi Merchants Bank made off with $100,000 prior to the opening hours early today. Thaddeus Colehardt and Morton Ordown were apprehended, but Ambrose Speke is still at large. A substantial reward has been offered for his capture and the return of the stolen currency.

The currency ranged from lower denominations to the highest. According to Mr. Sylvester Pomfrey, bank president, the money stolen was largely in government-issued greenbacks.

Mr. Pomfrey says the bank usually does not keep amounts this large in the office. An exception was made at the request of General Halleck to enable the Union quartermaster funds to replenish troop supplies.

Few of the bank's employees were even aware of the treasury shipment.

More details will be available in today's late edition.

Odd how Bergen had just been disparaging the paper currency that Washington had begun issuing last spring. Since Virginia City did business with San Francisco, the new bills were quite familiar in his adopted town. Tal hadn't thought anything about seeing them mixed with the older paper money issued by various banks that was still in circulation in the territories. Yet Silas Rosser had seen fit to save this bit of newssheet.

And had a wallet hosting crisp new hundred-dollar bills.

The story wasn't the only thing featured on the page. He had barely glanced at the roughly sketched portrait of the man who had gotten away with the money nearly a year ago. Too used to heading straight to printed details, Tal decided. The curse of his profession. Now he looked closer at the fellow pictured. A man identified as Ambrose Speke.

A gent who hadn't been using that name when he arrived in this godforsaken camp shortly after gold had been found the previous August.

Tal refolded the page of newsprint, but rather than replace it in the ledger, he tucked it into the inner pocket of his vest. He'd present it to Sheriff Strand as a parting gift before he rode out of camp. He wasn't sure Strand would be pleased to receive it. But for Tal, another mystery was now laid to rest. He knew from where and from what source Silas Rosser squirreled away funds to finance a life elsewhere with Letty in tow.

He'd been blackmailing the mayor.

****

This time when he stopped by the sheriff's office, Ebner Melton was gone and Linus Strand was in possession of the premises.

"Success," Tal announced, dropping the narrow ledger he'd concealed under his jacket on the man's desk. "And a bonus."

Strand turned from the stove where he'd been pouring himself a fresh cup of coffee. "A what?"

"Something I wasn't expecting, much less looking for," Tal said. "More money."

"And I didn't even see a rainbow for you to trail to that pot of gold," the sheriff drawled. "How and where in tarnation did you find the ledger?"

"Just asked the right questions of my client. She'd never seen Rosser unearth the thing or tuck it away, but she had seen him tallying entries in it. After that, she made a damn astute guess."

"You'll excuse me if I find that in itself suspicious," Strand growled. "You mentioned more riches as well?"

Tal extracted the leather wallet from his inner pocket and tossed it on top of the ledger. "I'll wager that the contents are stolen and stolen from someplace far from here."

When Strand opened the wallet, and glanced inside, he whistled. "The hell you say. You count it?"

"Yup," Tal said. "Five thousand. You got someplace really safe to tuck it?"

"No, and the sooner someone in camp decides to

purchase a safe, or we get ourselves a proper bank, the easier my mind will be," the sheriff muttered.

"Miss Kittridge awake?"

"Was when I relieved Ebner," Strand said. "Knock on her door and find out."

She was seated, her stance the one he associated with the woman she'd been in Boston: back ramrod straight, shoulders back, chin high, feet together, her hands at rest in her lap. She was also curious. "You found money as well as the ledger?" she asked, getting to her feet quickly.

"You heard what I told Strand?" Tal asked, stepping just inside the cell.

"It's a very small building, Mr. Cain," Letty said. "I thought I knew Silas. He was cruel, arrogant, and brutal, but suspect him of being deviously clever? No, I wouldn't have thought it of him."

Rosser was surprising them all, Tal thought and decided "deviously clever" was a tepid description of the dead man. "Cunningly vicious" was what suited Silas Rosser best.

Of course, whoever had killed the saloon owner was manipulative as well as vengeful. They had preyed upon Noletta Kittridge's sympathies prior to the shooting.

The camp was crammed with people deserving far from admirable adjectives.

Other than Letty, he absolved only Ebner Melton for the murder. Mostly because, while the mayor had a very good reason for wishing Rosser dead, Tal couldn't see Letty going to the rope in Melton's place. Besides, anyone standing near Rosser when he was shot couldn't have avoided the man's blood. Melton had been the first person he talked to upon arrival, and while a bit the worse for wear, the mayor's clothing had not sported anything more than mud and spilled whiskey.

Whomever Letty was protecting, Tal was sure her reasoning was grounded in emotion. Perhaps it hadn't been an accident as she said but a cleverly played-out part that would place her in the position of taking the rope in the true culprit's place.

"You recall any miner in particular applying to Rosser for credit?" Tal asked her. "I've got three possible names, but none of them mean a thing to me."

Letty sank back onto the cot, taking a seat at the end nearest the cell door. "I'm afraid I knew very few of the men's names," she admitted.

"But I know every damn soul in camp," Strand said. "Who are you looking for?"

Tal fished out his list. "H. Yager, R. Krauss, and F. Cusack."

The sheriff propped a shoulder against the wall. "Hiram Yager contracted the ague over the winter and died around Christmas," he said. "Rig Krauss has a claim he's working upcreek a ways, but either he hasn't got the knack for panning or he's staked out a lousy spot. Either way, he's not taking much out of it. Drinks away what he does find at the Spent Bullet most nights."

"None of the names mean anything to me," Letty confessed.

Mentally, Tal made a note to visit the Spent Bullet that night to ply Krauss with a shot of bad whiskey and a few questions. "And Cusack?" he asked.

Strand shrugged. "Never heard of him."

"Perhaps Silas wrote the wrong name," Letty

suggested. "The few times I saw him entering things in his ledger he appeared to be doing so from memory. All that name says to me otherwise is medicinal care."

"Medicinal care? As in a patent medicine?"

She nodded. "I believe there was a bottle in the backroom. Cusack's Miracle Tonic. Silas dosed himself with it for stomach problems."

"I'll look for it, though how it relates to our mysterious debtor will be difficult to sort out. I'm more inclined to believe our F. Cusack was known to Rosser previously and is using a different name in camp," Tal said.

Strand snorted. "You are the most distrustful cuss I ever did meet," he snarled. "For what purpose would a man set on panning for gold decide to not use his own name?"

"Possibly for the same reason that Rosser's ledger claims the man owes him five hundred dollars," Tal said. "He could be dodging debts elsewhere."

"You hoping to foist Rosser's death on this Cusack, then?"

"If he did it, the answer is yes," Tal allowed, "but I think it's much more likely he is responsible for a different man's death."

"Whose?" Strand demanded.

Tal glanced at Letty, at the way her face was turned up to his, her eyes curious. He wished there was a way to ease into the answer but couldn't find one. "Miss Kittridge's brother," he said quietly. "Per the notations in Rosser's ledger, Kit Kittridge paid off the debt he owed Rosser the night he was killed. F. Cusack handed over nearly a hundred dollars on his account the next day. I suspect those proceeds originated in Kittridge's pocket."

"Hell," Strand snarled.

Chapter Fourteen

'Diah Short arrived back in town just before sundown that night, both tired and buoyed up with news regarding the arrival of Judge Brevard.

Strand had allowed the cell door to be left open after Tal departed once more, but Letty was careful not to move far from her bunk. There were limits to what a lawman would sanction even as he attempted what he perceived as the gentlemanly thing to do. How differently he treated her compared to when he'd roughly hauled her from Silas's saloon the previous day. The only things that had changed since then were that she was dressed decently and Strand had begun calling her Miss Kittridge once more.

Seeing her turn from where she sat at the end of the bunk, 'Diah whipped a battered hat off, leaving a spill of greasy black hair straggling nearly to his shoulders.

Letty doubted Mother Short would have approved of the sadly depreciated state of 'Diah's clothing and hygiene. She wondered briefly whether the Short siblings had headed west after the matriarch's death. Or whether she'd sent them off to make their own way in the world in a section of it she deemed less risky. To Letty's mind, hieing children west was certainly preferable to sending them east into the slaughter of a battlefield.

"Ma'am," 'Diah greeted with a courteous head

bob. "Know ya ain't gonna like ma news, but…"

"But Mr. Strand is in need of it," she finished for the young deputy.

"Stop with the jawing," the sheriff ordered. "When should we expect Brevard?"

'Diah's narrow shoulders straightened. "Promised he'd start out at dawn er shortly thereafter t'morry. Cain't say he was much pleased at the idea o' beddin' down in a tent but said long as we keep him in whiskey und supply decent meals, he kin give us two days, tops."

A reprieve of possibly another full day, Letty thought. Would the trial be held shortly after the judge's arrival or on the day after? Whichever, they would have her buried before he left camp.

Would Tal leave immediately or stay merely because he'd sought refuge in a bottle of bad whiskey? If it was the latter, she pictured him downing it while seated on the ground next to whatever marker they used for her grave. She should wring a promise from him not to grieve, not to stay, but to leave before she mounted the scaffold. As much as she wanted his face to be the last thing she saw, it was impossible to wish the situation upon him. She loved him too well.

"Lucky us," Strand said. "Brevard is the most pompous windbag I ever did meet. Hate to have to inflict the camp with him, much less force Miss Kittridge to bear with him."

At 'Diah's befuddled expression, the sheriff hitched his head in the direction of her cell. "Miz Pearl," he said. "That's what that damn lawyer of hers has got us calling her again."

"Agin?"

"Ah, that's right. You weren't here when the hullabaloo over her brother's death happened," Strand murmured. "Miss Noletta Kittridge, that's who she is."

"Not Pearl?" 'Diah seemed stunned to find she had another name.

Letty took pity on him. "Pearl is what Silas chose to call me," she explained.

"Well, dangnabit. If'n I knew, miss…"

"It is all right, Mr. Short."

"I jest thought…"

"That I'd always been a whore?" Letty asked. "No, Mr. Short. In order to survive, there are times when a woman alone must do whatever is required, no matter how distasteful."

'Diah's head bobbed. "Yes, ma'am. I knows that well. Ma told me somethin' like, once."

"She is no doubt a very wise woman," Letty said, then turned her eyes to the sheriff. "Perhaps Mr. Short should join us for dinner so he can deliver his report in Mr. Cain's presence as well?"

Strand snorted. "'Tween you and that lawyer, my longing for a good bottle of hooch just keeps growing and growing," he muttered. But as he pulled his pocket watch free and consulted it, Letty knew it wasn't whiskey he currently craved, but Moira Foley's cooking.

"You ever set a fork to a meal at the Gilded Moon?" the sheriff asked the deputy.

"No, sir. Cain't afford nothin' ah ain't catched und cooked maself," Short answered.

"Tonight will be an exception, then," Strand said. "You're back on prisoner watch duty. The counselor has talked me into strolling Miss Kittridge down to

Foley's place for a meal. But if she makes a bolt for it, you've got my permission to shoot her."

The deputy's eyes widened at the mere suggestion, then dropped to the floor. "Ah ain't never owned a pistol, Mr. Strand."

"Know how to shoot one?"

"Ma older brother let me try his a time er so," 'Diah admitted.

"Good enough for me," the sheriff declared, and moved out of Letty's sight. When he returned, it was with a weapon Letty recognized.

'Diah stared at it rather than take the gun from his mentor. "That there's Rosser's shooter," he said.

It was more than that, Letty knew. It had once belonged to her brother Kit. She'd watched him lovingly clean it, studiously practice with it for months the previous year. She knew the feel of it in her own hands as he'd attempted to teach her how to shoot. She'd been too leery of the weapon.

Rosser had requisitioned it as his own faster than he'd acquired her services in his bed.

It served him right that the weapon had taken his life.

'Diah stared at it, making no attempt to wrap a hand around the polished wood and metal grip the sheriff presented.

"Don't get superstitious over an iron, boy," Strand said, slapping it into 'Diah's palm. "It's a tool. The tool of a lawman. I cleaned it free of gore and replaced every bullet. It's in top shape. Carrying it makes you my authorized representative as much as a tin badge would, if we even had tin badges in this backwater camp. Just be careful where you point it, lad."

Gently, the sheriff pushed the muzzle to face the floor. "It ain't cocked, so you can just shove it in your belt 'til we get a holster for it. Apparently, Si didn't have one for it."

"He didn't," Letty answered. Kit had, though. She wondered whatever had become of it. Her brother had gone armed in the camp, only shedding the pistol and its protective holster in her presence, because the weapon had made her uneasy. Odd that the lone time Tal had come into her cell armed in a like manner she hadn't felt the same. It was sad that, despite everything she and Kit had endured together, she had always considered him careless. Had expected something ill to befall him because he did wear a gun.

Tal's pistol, by comparison, was a part of the man he had become. One far more competent in everything he did than even the man he'd been in Boston.

"Mayhap Bergen's got a holster that's not ta dear," 'Diah said and shoved the long muzzle of the revolver into the gap between waistband and belt.

Strand grunted an answer and checked his watch once more. "You ready, Miss Kittridge? It's about time we were meeting your counselor for some grub."

"Of course, Mr. Strand," she said, reaching for the paisley-figured shawl to drape around her shoulders. "I wouldn't want to keep Mr. Cain waiting."

"Personally," the sheriff confessed as he wrapped a hand around her upper arm, "it's Moira's cooking that I don't want to keep waiting. 'Diah, pull the door closed behind you, then take the prisoner's other arm, will you? Wouldn't want the camp to think we're letting law enforcement standards down just because her lawyer is bribing us with a meal."

"No, sir," Short said. A moment later, Letty was sandwiched between them.

****

Tal knew his guests were en route when men on the street beyond the Moon's front windows stopped what they were doing to stare back toward the jail. A few inside pushed back chairs and left their seats to peer closer out the window.

"Dang," one man exclaimed. "It's like a damn parade out there."

"Ain't that Rosser's gal, the one that kilt him just yesterday?" another demanded.

"Looks like they's a-promenadin' this way," a third fellow noted.

Tal got to his feet, pushing his own chair back as Letty and her escort moved past the front window. 'Diah Short was back in town and filling the duties of deputy once more, he noted. The mayor would be relieved that he'd be free to roam the town at will looking for a fool willing to stand him a drink rather than be sequestered in Strand's front office making a pretense of keeping their prisoner in place. Briefly, Tal wondered why a man who had made off with a fortune from a St. Louis bank tended to depend on the kindness of his camp constituents to cater to his thirst. Had there been other men Melton paid off to have made it this far from Missouri with his ill-gotten gain?

It was a question he'd already decided to never ask. The mayor had played no part in landing Letty in jail for Silas Rosser's death. Tal couldn't see any connection the former bank employee had to Kit Kittridge's death, either. Melton's—or was it Speke's?—crime would only come to light when he passed the sheriff the newspaper article before riding out of camp after the trial.

Unless Melton slunk out of the place before then. Considering he rather liked the rapscallion, perhaps a dropped hint of the coming disclosure would give Ebner an opportunity to move on if he wished to avoid taking Letty's place in the narrow cell.

"Stay where you are, boys," Strand said as he issued his current prisoner through the door, 'Diah dogging her footsteps. "We're just here for a meal. Then the lady is headed back to the jail."

All the same, he hustled her across the room to where Tal waited. "Move aside, Counselor. Now that 'Diah's back, we'll be the men boxing Miss Kittridge in. You can sit across from her."

"Fine with me," Tal said. "The view will be better."

"Yer back'll be ta the room, though, Mr. Cain, und not everyone likes what yer doin' fer Miz Pearl," 'Diah said.

"As I see you're armed now, lad, I'll trust you to gun down anyone who makes an attempt on my life." Tal grinned and moved his gaze to the sheriff's sternly set features. "I know for sure Strand doesn't care if someone takes a pot shot at me."

"In that you're wrong," the sheriff drawled as Letty took her place at the table. "I prefer to reserve that honor for myself if the need arises."

Tal pulled out the chair opposite Letty and sat down as Strand and 'Diah dropped into the seats on either side of her. "You won't have to put up with either Miss Kittridge or myself much longer. Since 'Diah's back, I take it the judge will be arriving shortly?"

"T'morry," the boy said.

"Which means that whatever questions I still require answers to will need to be sorted out in quick order," Tal said. "You ready to tell us who actually did pull the trigger on Rosser, Miss Kittridge?"

Rather than answer, she pressed her lips together so tightly they paled. Her gaze centered on the tabletop rather than him or either of the two men bracketing her.

Tal sighed. "Okay, then I move on to other options. 'Diah."

The youngster jumped in his seat in surprise. "Yes, sir?"

"I neglected to ask you what you saw when you arrived on the crime scene yesterday. Where was Miss Kittridge standing in the room and where was Rosser's body?"

'Diah looked at Letty, then at the sheriff before focusing on him, Tal noted. "I weren't one o' the men helpin' Mr. Strand that mornin'," he said. "Was out settin' traps. Only got back inta camp after Miz Pearl was already locked up."

Letty nodded in agreement. "Mr. Short arrived at the sheriff's office only moments before you did, Mr. Cain."

Tal scowled at Strand. "Then who the hell did you instantly deputize yesterday morning?"

Strand leaned back in his chair. "Didn't deputize anyone," he said. "Fact is, if I hadn't bolted from my office the moment I heard the shot, the fellas who'd burst through the door before me would have strung your client up on the spot."

"No, they wouldn't have," Letty insisted softly. "They would have used me first, then lynched me from the rafters."

Fortunately, Fintan Foley arrived with a couple plates of his wife's latest stew concoction, making further comment ill-advised. But, Tal mused, she was quite right about what could have occurred. He suspected once the men had begun, there would have been little Strand could have done to stop them, short of putting a bullet in each one. He doubted the sheriff would have exercised such forethought. He'd been totally convinced of her guilt the day before.

Perhaps he still was, Tal admitted to himself. He hadn't found any evidence to prove she hadn't pulled the trigger. It was beginning to look as though, unless Letty finally gave him the name he sought, he never would.

Before Foley left to bring the next plates out, he stopped the man. "You have any idea how much money Miss Kittridge's brother won the night he died?"

"That's a while back, Cain. Don't know. P'haps two hundred or just shy of it. Why?"

Rather than answer the question, Tal asked another of his own. "You ever meet a fella named Cusack?"

"Cusack? Hell, don't think so," Foley muttered and excused himself to return to the kitchen for the rest of their meal.

"Who's Cusack?" 'Diah asked.

"Someone who owed Silas Rosser quite a tidy sum of money," Tal said. "And someone only Rosser seems to have known. That makes this Cusack one suspicious fella, in my book. Particularly since he was in this camp the day after Miss Kittridge's brother met with an unfortunate accident."

Although Foley had honored her with the first

serving, the sheriff receiving the second, Letty hadn't touched the fork next to her plate. "You really think Kit was murdered, don't you?"

Tal nodded.

"There's no evidence..." the sheriff began, then stopped to savor a mouthful of stew.

"There's plenty of circumstantial evidence," Tal insisted. "Kittridge should have had money in his pockets even after paying off debts that evening. Miss Kittridge says he wasn't the sort of man to leave her destitute or leave himself without the wherewithal to place bets on the next card game he encountered. But both you and Bergen have told me his pockets were empty when he was found the next morning. Not a greenback nor a coin in any of his pockets. The only thing of value he had was his pistol, and that was probably because it was recognizable. What happened to it, by the way?"

Letty claimed her fork as Foley returned with plates for 'Diah and himself. "Mr. Short has it tucked in his belt presently," she said, listlessly stirring through the meager fare before her. "Before that it was discharged into Silas's chest."

In the act of sampling his own meal, Tal stopped. "He was killed with your brother's weapon?"

She frowned at him before stabbing the tines of her utensil into a lump of something unidentifiable on her plate. "Why do you think everyone believes I killed him, Mr. Cain? Silas confiscated it as the only item of value Kit possessed. The revolver was the only firearm in the room, I was supposedly familiar with handling it in the past, and I was covered in..." Her voice faded away. Letty released the fork, letting it rest where it was, impaling a piece of gristly meat. "I'm sorry. I'm afraid I am not hungry, gentlemen."

The saloon proper was quiet, every man in the room engaged in eavesdropping on her words. Foley disturbed it by placing a bottle of whiskey in the center of the table and a fine china cup and saucer before Letty. Apparently unaware she was the focus of every man's gaze in the room, Noletta Kittridge took a ladylike sip of whatever was in the delicate cup.

Tal leaned back in his chair. "The only *firearm* in the room, Miss Kittridge? What of Rosser's infamous Bowie knife? Where was it?"

Her eyes raised to meet his. "I suppose it was where he always left it. Close at hand, hanging in its sheath over the bedpost."

Tal turned his interrogative eye on the sheriff. "It wasn't at the scene when I visited, which was barely an hour after Rosser died. Did you take it from the scene as well as the murder weapon?"

"No reason to," Strand said, "though if I'd seen it, I doubt I'd have left it there."

"Then you didn't see it," Tal pressed.

"Guess not."

"Then where is it? Could Rosser have caught someone in the act of thieving and gotten shot for the effort?" Tal asked.

"Hell, it's possible," Strand conceded, "but who in their right mind would try to steal anything from Silas Rosser?"

"Someone who was new to camp. Someone who didn't know him," Tal suggested. "It occurs to me that I have never asked Miss Kittridge to describe the sequence of that morning, to tell how she came to be standing close enough to get bloodied yet not pull the trigger herself. Did you ask her, Sheriff?"

Strand's face was stormy as he reached for the whiskey bottle and poured a shot into one of the tumblers on the table. "No, I didn't," he admitted. "But it didn't seem to be a question that needed asking, considering how things looked."

"Does it now?" Tal demanded.

Strand tossed off the whiskey, then turned to Letty. "Miss Kittridge." His tone sounded resigned and rather peeved, Tal thought, but didn't blame him. Even in Boston he doubted the police would have conducted their investigation any differently than Strand had. If a person looked guilty, then they were guilty. Questions be damned!

Letty lifted her chin. Although she had reason to feel beaten, her Kittridge pride kept her backbone stiff, her resolve absolute. He was proud of her.

"Yes, Mr. Strand?"

The sheriff cleared his throat. "Did you pull the trigger on your brother's revolver and kill Silas Rosser?"

"No," she said firmly. "I did not."

Chapter Fifteen

"I have a new question," Tal announced once they returned to the miniscule building wherein her cell held sway.

"You haven't run out of wind yet, Counselor?" Strand grumbled.

Releasing the grip he'd kept on her arm, he allowed Letty to return to her cell of her own volition. Though where else had she to go? she wondered.

"Go on. Spill it, Cain."

She took what had become her regular seat at the foot of her bed, observing the men in the office proper through the open door.

Tal had parked his shoulder against the wall and folded his arms across his chest. The sheriff already had his chair tipped back to rest against the adjacent wall, a location that allowed him to keep an eye on the comings and goings of miners dipping their heads to enter the Friendly Gal across the way. 'Diah was on his knees, feeding wood into the potbellied stove, stoking it for the night. While the weapons resting in holsters on both Tal and Strand's belts looked like they belonged, the revolver shoved into the youngster's belt was alien. Not because of its placement—the few times Silas had added the firearm to the arsenal he carried, he'd thrust the gun into the waistband of his trousers. No, what bothered her was that 'Diah Short, the deputy Letty judged as still shy of twenty years old, was now the owner of her brother's pistol.

"I'm a trained lawyer," Tal told Strand. "Questions and answers are my stock in trade."

The sheriff sighed deeply. "Is it about Rosser's knife?"

"No," Tal said, "but perhaps it should be. Seems likely that whoever helped themselves to it—whether it was before Rosser died or shortly thereafter—knows something about what went on yesterday morning."

"I'll keep an eye out for it," Strand said. "'Diah here will as well, won't you, boy?"

The young deputy nodded vigorously. "Sure will."

"If you see a fella wearing it, don't ask him about it, just find me. I'll do the asking. Hopefully before Cain tackles 'im," the sheriff growled, then eyed Tal again. "If this latest burning question isn't about the knife, what is it about?"

"The scratch on Rosser's face," Tal said, then looked beyond the sheriff, his eyes moving to where she sat watching them. "Had you delivered it, Miss Kittridge?"

"Do you mean did I have a reason to attempt to fight him off, Mr. Cain? No. Silas never forced me to do anything I hadn't already agreed to. The idea of even trying to ward him off is rather ludicrous. He was tall, broad, strong, and vicious to cross. All of those things made him a dangerous man," she answered.

"Then if you didn't deliver the scratch, who did? It looked fresh when I looked him over."

"A scratch?" Strand pushed to his feet, grabbed up his hat and slammed it in place. "Hell, now I've got to go roust Bergen to pry the damn coffin open. We were all set to plant Si in the morning. 'Diah, you stay here with Miss Kittridge. Cain, you're coming with me."

Tal pushed away from the wall. Put two fingers to the brim of his hat in a slight salute. "Miss Kittridge, I'll wish you a good night and see you for breakfast in the morning."

Letty nodded. "Good evening then, Mr. Cain. Sleep well."

As the door closed behind them, 'Diah finished fiddling with the stove and closed the door. "Is there anythin' ya be needin', ma'am? A cuppa coffee, mayhap?"

"I'm fine, Mr. Short," she assured him.

But she wasn't.

With Judge Brevard expected to appear the following afternoon, she knew Tal still hoped her thus far stoic resistance to identify the person who had pulled the trigger would waver.

In that he was right, she admitted, but only to herself. Part of it was the very natural fear of dying, dying for something she had not actually done, though she condoned the act. That was her crime: to have wanted Silas Rosser dead.

The part of her that wanted to shout the name of Silas's true killer longed for the clock to spin backward. To land her back in Boston. She should never have simply given herself to Talmadge Hammond, desperate to have a memory so precious of their time together that it was burned into her soul. She should have handed him a portmanteau packed with her things, should have run away with him.

But she hadn't, and not having done so was as much a crime as wishing Silas Rosser dead.

Would they hang her at dawn the day following the trial?

Would they wait a day to ensure that the crowd was larger, consisting of men from other camps, men who hadn't known Silas Rosser yet thrilled at the prospect of her hanging? The judge had promised to give the camp two days of his time. Even with Tal presenting a host of other possible suspects, a second day wouldn't be needed. The culprit had had no reason to kill Silas.

Until the morning when they did kill him.

Which meant every question Tal asked, every trail he thought worth following, would not supply the name she harbored.

Would continue to harbor.

She'd given her word to do so, and even the sheriff thought that bond surety enough.

"I want your promise not to attempt to escape, Miss Kittridge," Strand had requested earlier that day before leaving Ebner Melton as her guard. The position was now held by the newly armed 'Diah Short. Considering she had nowhere to go, stationing anyone in the outer office was for appearance's sake and nothing more. If the cell had held a man, neither the mayor nor the young deputy could have kept him in place with simply a promise. A man would never be given the courtesy of an unlocked door.

"Was your journey to secure the judge a pleasant one, Mr. Short?" Letty asked, simply to have another voice break the silence.

"'Twas rough country, miss, but the path was clear 'nuff. Since Mr. Strand sent me off later in the day, had ta bivouac last night after the light failed," 'Diah said.

"Weren't far ta go this mornin', which is why I made it back fer the sun set. Be nice ta sleep in my own bed agin. Guess I'm not a body what takes to campin' lessin' I gots ta."

"Yes," Letty agreed. "Although I slept on the ground once my brother and I were part of an immigrant train into the territories, I confess I always feared there would be wildlife crawling beneath the blankets with me."

"Me, too," 'Diah declared, delivering the flash of a smile. "Snakes in particular's my fear. It's why I shell out fer one o' the beds in the bunkhouses 'stead o' pitchin' a tent."

"Is it difficult to get by without your brothers at hand?" Letty asked.

"Some," the deputy admitted, "but in other ways it's better. They didn't much cotton ta havin' me trail along with 'em, miss. Ma, she insisted, though."

"I can understand her reasoning if she was attempting to keep her older sons from joining the forces in the east," Letty said, "but to send her youngest away as well?"

'Diah's gaze dropped to the dusty floor, to the few clumps of mud that had journeyed in from the path outside the door. As if mindful of domestic chores, the youngster took up the dilapidated broom in the corner and began sweeping. "Ma had her reasons, ma'am."

"She sent her children away and remained behind alone," Letty mused. "Was there other family to help her on the farm, then?"

Head bent to the self-appointed chore, 'Diah's answer was so quiet Letty nearly missed it. "She was dyin' und didn't want us witnessin' it, miss. We was sharecroppers, didn't own the land nor the house nor nothin' else. Truth tell, none o' us was very good at farmin' neither. With the boys und me gone, Ma said the fella what owned the place couldn't demand what we couldn't pay him. Said the preacher'd see ta her buryin' when the time came. 'Spect she's been gone a piece now."

"I'm sure she was at peace, Mr. Short. She wanted a better life for her children," Letty said.

"Yeah, she did that, ma'am. Ain't one of us found one, though."

Letty was certain that statement was true in relation to 'Diah Short. Whether it was to the older Short brothers she could not guess, nor did she care. In casting the youngest of the brood off to fend alone, the elder siblings had definitely cast 'Diah into a life that would not only be no better than that of a sharecropper's child but one that would undoubtedly be far worse.

She got to her feet. "Thank you for sharing that with me, Mr. Short. If you don't mind, I believe I will retire for the night. Perhaps it would be best to close and secure the cell door. I'm sure Mr. Strand would prefer those conditions."

'Diah put the broom aside. "If'n that's what ya want, miss. Jest leave the observin' hatch open fer light und air?"

Letty nodded slightly.

As the deputy closed the door, she slipped beneath the bulk of Tal's greatcoat, her head cushioned by one of the blankets he had provided. Sleep would not welcome her that night. For all she knew, morning might well signal her final hours.

In the outer room, the main door slammed back against the wall. The sound of men's boots as they pushed inside broke the silence.

"What ya think yer doin'?" she heard 'Diah demand, followed by the sound of a blow and a body falling to the floor.

"Come ta enjoy Si's gal 'fer we hang her," the gruff voice of Mos Gately announced, followed by rough chuckles from other men.

"Yer cain't—" 'Diah snarled, then was cut short as something thudded against the cell door.

Letty quickly slipped from the bunk and swept up the bucket used for her ablutions. When the board was tossed free of the brackets on the outside of the cell and the door was pulled open, she dashed the remaining water in the face of the first man through the portal.

****

Tal held the lantern, ensuring the light fell on the dead man's face. Both he and Strand had neckerchiefs up, covering both nose and mouth, yet the scent of the body in the simple coffin still wrapped around them. Bergen was the smart one, Tal decided. He'd stayed outside the shed with the second lantern and a pipe of foul-smelling tobacco providing a smoke screen to cloak the smell.

The sheriff had griped and sworn during their short journey to Bergen's place, but he hadn't balked at prying the lid from Rosser's coffin. He had knelt next to the box to give the wound on the corpse's cheek serious consideration. Now he exhibited all the signs of a man considerably irritated that he hadn't noticed the mark earlier.

"Hell," Strand snarled. "Doesn't look like a knife

did this. Not uniform or as deep as I'd expect of a carving. A splinter of wood? I can see her grabbing up something to swing at him. Something still raw and ragged."

"*She*?" Tal echoed. "I believe Miss Kittridge said she did not attack Rosser. In any case, it doesn't look like the sort of mark made by wood. There are three distinct gouges, all parallel to each other."

Strand tilted his head, eyeing Tal. "You got something else in mind, Counselor? If so, spit it out."

Tal stared at the nearly hidden marks along the dead man's jaw. "I've seen scrapes like this before," he said. "Back East I had several clients with claw marks."

"Doesn't look like an animal—" the sheriff began.

"Human," Tal corrected. "These particular clients were men and women engaged in domestic battles. Wives and husbands, men and their sweethearts, occasionally two women fighting over a man."

Strand turned back to study the wound. "You implying there was another woman present?"

"I simply told you why and in what circumstances I am familiar with similar wounds," Tal said.

"Sure you did," Strand grumbled as he pushed back to his feet. He dropped the coffin lid back in place and turned to Bergen. "You can nail it up again, Burl."

"Like hell," the shopkeeper spat. "Ya opened 'im, ya kin seal 'im up agin."

The sheriff snarled but caught the hammer Bergen tossed and pounded the nails back in place. "You know how few women we've got in this camp, Cain?"

"Damn few?" Tal offered.

"Damn few," Strand admitted. "I can't see any of them but Miss Kittridge having a bone to pick with

Rosser."

"Coulda scratched hisself," Bergen offered.

"Could," the sheriff agreed. "Somehow I doubt it."

"Miss Kittridge has already said that she did not inflict such a wound," Tal reiterated. "And that she did not put a bullet in his chest."

"She was covered in his blood," Strand insisted.

"Merely evidence that she was standing near him when the shot was fired. As I understand it, you were among the troops in the late war with Mexico. Was every man covered in the blood of a man he killed on those battlefields?" Tal demanded.

The sheriff stomped out of the shed, thrust the hammer back into Bergen's hand. "Only the unlucky ones," he admitted. "All right, I'll concede that your client *might* have merely been a witness, but if she didn't do it, why isn't she telling us who did kill the bastard?"

"I can think of only one reason," Tal said. "She's protecting someone. And if it is indeed another woman, that makes far more sense than if it was a man."

"But which woman, if indeed it is a woman? Pearl was the only female working at Rosser's. No gal in her right mind would leave the comforts of June's parlor house to work for Si, and why would any of the few good women in camp have any traffic with him?"

Tal trailed the sheriff from the mortuary shed, handed Bergen the borrowed lantern, and turned back to secure the door. "For the same reason many of the men who owed Rosser money did. They'd gone to him for a loan."

"You saying the scenario is a gal in need of cash didn't like taking no for an answer?"

"Would a man?" Tal countered.

"A man wouldn't kill him for refusing a loan," Strand said.

"One desperate enough might." Tal turned to Bergen. "Winter put a kibosh on panning, didn't it? I'll bet several folks ran up a tab at the mercantile during that time. Any of them men with wives hauled along for the venture?"

The shopkeeper shrugged. "A few, but now that the pans are workin' agin, debts are bein' chipped away."

"All of them?" Tal asked.

"The wife handles that," Bergen said. "But don't go thinkin' she'd be inclined ta cross ta Rosser's side o' the street ta deal with 'im. She ain't that sorta gal."

Once upon a time, Noletta Kittridge hadn't been that type of woman either, Tal knew. Circumstances pushed many people to do the unthinkable.

As Bergen stomped his way back inside the residential part of his building, Strand brushed dirt from his trouser knees. "You have the idea that another woman was involved all along, Cain?"

"Wish I had. It would have saved considerable time," Tal said. "But no. I noticed the scratch on Rosser's face, but my focus has been on finding someone more likely to plug him than Miss Kittridge. A man would tend to use his fists. Women claw their victims. At least they did in the cases I knew in the past."

"For what it's worth, I agree with you," Strand admitted. "Despite everything you've brought up, none of it means Pearl didn't pull the trigger, though. She's still got the best reason to shoot him. He could have gotten clawed in a separate incident."

Which was equally as likely, Tal mused silently, but it didn't seem to fit the timetable. That scratch had looked fresh the day before. Delivered shortly before the pistol was fired, by his estimation. Letty claimed Rosser's death had been an accident. The clawing could have occurred at the start of a struggle that ended in a grab for the revolver that had then gone off when Rosser attempted to disarm his assailant.

It also made far more sense to him that Letty would assume the blame to protect another woman. A woman she judged as having far more to live for than she did.

With the judge due to arrive the next day, he had bare hours to convince her to identify the real killer. There was always the chance that the jury would take the circumstances leading to Rosser's death into consideration and not demand hanging as the punishment for the true offender. He doubted the same consideration would be given to Letty herself, though. The camp had condemned her within minutes of Rosser's demise.

"I still think the answer is within the ledg—" he began.

That's when the first shot was fired, followed closely by a second.

****

"Get the damn gun away from that kid," Gately shouted to his companions.

"I'm a-tryin'!" another of the intruders yelled back, then yelped as 'Diah pulled the trigger on Kit's revolver once more.

For her part in the battle, Letty swung the now-empty bucket, connecting nicely with her assailant's jaw, then threw it at Gately's head. He fended it off with an arm, but she'd already taken in hand the privacy screen Kit had built for her, swinging it to keep the men out of grappling distance. Once they closed on her, she knew all would be lost. She'd be overpowered, probably struck down by fists, rendered insensible if not unconscious.

The gunshots were sure to bring Tal and the sheriff back to the jail, but would they be able to overpower the men accompanying Gately?

Would they be in time to save her from whatever he had planned? She remembered all too well the combination of hatred and lust he had leveled her way since Silas had brought her back to his saloon in January. True to his word, Silas had stood between her and those he deemed unworthy of the pleasure of her company. Her protector had barred Mos Gately from being among those chosen few.

Letty swung the folded screen at the first man through the cell door. It splintered against the intruder's shoulder, leaving her with ragged pieces of wood trailing bits of cloth like pennants, ones that appeared to denote surrender since the petticoat used in the construction had once been white.

When Gately pushed his confederate to the floor, stepping over him to come at her, she stabbed the rough pronged stick in her hand at his face. The former bartender feinted back and swept it aside. She let the makeshift weapon follow through on the arc and brought it back up into his groin.

Which is when 'Diah pulled the trigger once more and Gately pitched forward, knocking her to the floor. Pinned beneath the large man, Letty tried to squirm free, but he was a dead weight pinning her in place.

The loss of their leader gave the rest of the men pause, which worked in Sheriff Strand's favor. He stepped through the open door, his pistol in hand, Tal at his back in a similar stance.

"Stand down!" Strand thundered. "Don't, and either Cain or I will take great pleasure in putting you down. Him in particular."

Through the open door of her cell, Letty saw Tal, his Colt steady in his hand, a grim expression on his face. His lips lifted at one corner in a grin she identified as one of pleasure over the idea of putting a bullet in one of the men who had come to accost her.

"Now," the sheriff ordered. "I want every gun, every knife on any of you dropped in a pile in the middle of the floor. Do it slowly, boys. Cain and I both have rather itchy trigger fingers, and you're all within dandy distance for us to do serious damage."

'Diah lay against the wall where someone had tossed him a moment before, but he scrambled hastily to his feet.

"You okay, boy?" Strand asked without taking his eyes from the men who had accompanied Gately.

"Yes, sir," 'Diah avowed. "Tried ta stop 'em."

"You did good," the sheriff said. "Put your weapon on the table and help Miss Kittridge get out from under Gate before she suffocates."

The deputy looked none too steady as the revolver was placed on the sheriff's desk and he maneuvered around the men who had considered him no threat.

"Y'all right, miss?" 'Diah asked, falling to his knees next to Letty and Mos Gately's still form.

"Yes, Mr. Short. Thank you for what you did," she said.

’Diah shoved at Gately’s shoulder as Letty attempted to both push the man’s weight off her and squirm from beneath him.

“Oh, Gawd!” ’Diah gasped. “I plugged ’im in the back.”

The shot had done more than that, Letty knew. She’d had time to ascertain her attacker’s condition. “He’s dead, ’Diah,” she said softly.

As Gately’s body rolled to the side, the young deputy began shaking in earnest. “Gawd, no!”

Letty scooted back against the cell wall and wrapped her arms around the deputy as he began to sob. Helpless to do anything else, she simply held him until Strand entered the room.

The sheriff hunkered down next to the body but didn’t roll it back on its face. Instead he issued another order. “’Preciate it if you’d take the boy into the office, Miss Kittridge. I’m going to need your cell for a piece, to keep Gate’s troops corralled. Force a swallow or two of the whiskey in my saddlebag down ’Diah’s throat, will you?”

“Of course, Mr. Strand,” she said and scrambled to her feet. She had to help ’Diah up, as the youngster was still shaking badly in reaction.

In the office proper, Tal had the other three men under the watchful eye of his leveled Colt. He stood resolute, on alert rather than relaxed back against the wall as he had been earlier.

“Bartender dead?” he asked without looking away from the prisoners.

“Yes,” Letty answered. She had to put Strand’s lone chair back on its feet before forcing ’Diah into it. The sheriff’s saddlebags hung on a hook nearby. She found the bottle of whiskey but had to nearly force it down the deputy's throat. 'Diah gasped and sputtered but swallowed it. Proof, she felt, that while he'd haunted the saloons since arriving in town, beer rather than hard liquor had been the drink of choice.

'Diah looked up at her with still damp eyes. "I didn't mean ta kill 'im," he said.

Letty busied herself by resealing Strand's bottle of whiskey. "I know," she murmured, then stood back against the wall, away from all the men in the room.

****

Strand had the same problem he'd had the day before. With an alleged murderess secured in his lone cell, he had no place to jail others who broke the law. He did the only thing that came to mind. He fined the hell out of their gold pouches and then let the men disperse. But not until they'd carted Mos Gately's body to Bergen's mortuary shack.

Tal hadn't formed a part of the parade delivering the latest dead man. He stayed behind at the jail, 'Diah once more manning the front office while he sat with Letty on her bunk. She'd picked up a smear of Mos Gately's blood on her dress, he noticed. Nothing like the splatter from Rosser, but it wouldn't look well to come bloodstained to the trial. It was good to know she would not have to, now there was a gown waiting for her at June Gilchrist's place.

Using the recent contretemps as his excuse to comfort her, he gathered Letty close in his arms, holding her a complacent captive against his chest.

"From Strand's interrogation of Gately's associates, it sounds like you held your own for a bit there," he murmured into her hair.

"Considering I've had more than enough time to contemplate what I could do should the occasion arrive, I was prepared," she admitted. "Actually, Silas insisted I be able to defend myself, even if it was for only moments. While he trusted to his reputation to protect me, there were times when he wasn't at the saloon and I could be considered easy prey. Gately wasn't the only man to whom he refused access to me."

"Apparently, both 'Diah and you surprised the hell out of the batch of them."

She shook her head, rubbing her cheek against the nubby fabric of his weskit. "Not Gately. He knew Silas had given me a few suggestions. What he didn't expect was to find Mr. Short armed with a pistol and the courage to fire on them."

"The kid did some damage, though. The close quarters probably helped, but one man's got a bullet in his calf and another had his ribs grazed."

"And Gately is dead," she murmured.

"'Diah's shook up about that," Tal said by way of agreement.

"He'll recover," Letty said.

He thought she sounded detached, almost cold the way she pronounced it. Like a fact. Living in the wilderness had certainly changed the way she viewed violence. Was it a result of her time as Rosser's property, or had she learned how to distance herself from emotion in certain circumstances, thanks to events on the trail west itself?

Or had it been Kit's death that had closed her heart to sympathy?

She repeatedly told him she was no longer the Noletta Kittridge he'd known in Boston. Tal was ready to accept that now. She was still the only woman he would ever love, though.

"I think you should leave the camp," she said. "Leave before the judge arrives. I don't want you to watch what happens to me. Remember me as I was in Boston, not as I am here."

"I'm not leaving, Lett. I've got new leads to follow and—"

She tilted her head back and pressed a soft, brief kiss against his mouth to halt the words. "They won't lead you to the person who caused Silas Rosser's death," she murmured.

"But could prove Kit was—"

"The sheriff has already promised to follow through on that investigation," she reminded. "If it is possible to identify whoever waylaid and robbed Kit that night, leaving him for dead, Mr. Strand will find them."

"It could all be tied together," Tal said.

"It isn't."

"Lett. You can't—"

She pressed a finger to his lips this time. "I want you to take the money requisitioned from Silas's estate."

He nearly laughed to hear anything termed an *estate* in connection with Rosser.

"No."

"And the ring you gave me," she continued, ignoring his refusal. "I don't want scavengers appropriating it after my death."

"I'm not leaving," he said. "Both the mayor and Strand accepted my offer to act as your representative for the trial."

"A trial that would never have been held but for your insistence," she reminded him. "If you hadn't arrived yesterday, I would already have been hanged and buried."

He snorted. "It took them a full day to fell trees, prepare the timber and build the scaffold."

"Without Mr. Strand's interference, the rafters at Silas's would have sufficed."

"But Strand did stop them."

"Temporarily. Please, Tal. Leave. Take what funds I have. Take the ring. Forget you ever saw me. Remember only our last day together in Boston."

"Remember the day you sent me away?" he demanded. "No, Miss Kittridge. That I do not choose to do. Fate, the gods, luck, call it what you will, gave us another chance. *This* chance to have a life together. You can either trust me to find the answers on my own or make it easy on me and tell me who the hell shot Rosser."

Although he couldn't see her face, pressed as it was against his lapel again, he knew her lips were thinned, that she was probably biting the bottommost to keep from speaking the name he needed.

"A woman killed him, didn't she, Lett?" he said softly against her hair.

When she didn't answer, he knew he was right.

Chapter Sixteen

Sheriff Strand looked weary when he returned to his office after turning the latest body over to the mercantile owner's tender mercies. The only thing Burl Bergen would like about the arrangement was the fee he would be paid to build another coffin and dig another grave in the small cemetery west of the camp. Letty wasn't surprised when Strand shooed both Tal and 'Diah off to their own beds. The deputy looked ready to drop from exhaustion, but Tal, she knew, planned to work his way through the three saloons in town hoping to find someone who remembered a miner named Cusack.

Even if he located such a man, Silas's most mysterious debtor knew nothing about the murder she was accused of committing.

But Tal's question—or was it merely a guess?—regarding the gender of the person who had pulled the trigger worried her. If enough time remained, the hunter she'd always known lay beneath Mr. Hammond's professional exterior would sniff out the culprit. He had the scent, though fortunately there were other trails that appeared more likely avenues for him to pursue at present. Would he even tell her which ones he had eliminated? Somehow, she doubted it. Tal would want to startle her into giving the secret away while they were before the judge.

A man due to arrive the next day. Would Mr. Brevard arrive when the sun was high or as it was setting? If the latter, she had a longer reprieve. If the former, dawn would likely be the last one she saw.

Except, confined in the windowless room, only the gleaming that reached the open hatch in her secured door must suffice.

No longer would she enjoy the brush of a forest-scented breeze caressing her cheek, tugging locks of modestly bound hair loose to dance to its secret tune.

No longer the long-missed feel of Talmadge Hammond crushing her to his chest, or covering her mouth with his, teasing the fire within her alive.

That fire flickered already, accepting that it would soon be extinguished. But not until she lured him once more into making love to her. If she was in truth the temptress some now thought her, considering what she'd become under Silas Rosser's patronage, she would know how to entice Tal. Unfortunately, she was no Lorelei. They had shared the ultimate intimacy only once, yet she remembered every caress, every brush of his lips, his hands. Would he have accepted the offer of herself that day in Boston if it hadn't been what they'd thought was their final parting?

He had refused the offer of her body as payment for legal services. She must make him reconsider. He'd brushed away the idea of accepting the funds he'd laid claim to for her from Silas's cache. She must pass it into his keeping secretly, slip it in the pockets of the coat he'd lent her, that kept her warm with more than merely its weight. The only thing she knew he was likely to leave the area with was her ring. Unless he slid it back in place on her hand when she lay in the coffin.

He wanted nothing from her but the name of the person who had shot and killed the man who had owned her.

It hovered so near to escaping that she felt choked holding it captive. Yet every hour that passed, the reasons she had given herself to hold the secret seemed less viable. She could escape the noose, leave this Godforsaken wilderness behind, and finally have the life she had once craved. One shared with Talmadge Hammond.

She could condemn another to that final fate on the gallows.

Someone who still dreamed of a better future. Who had not lost hope. Who still wanted to live.

With the cell door once more secured and the only sounds those of the sheriff settling in for the night, Letty pulled Tal's greatcoat around her. Savored the scent of him that lingered in the fabric. Let brief memories flit through her mind.

Tal in formal clothes, backlit against the glitter of a ballroom full of mirrors, flowers, and the fluttering flames of candles, his gloved hand reaching for hers, requesting her as his partner in the figures of a dance.

Tal smiling lazily as they strolled across the Common, her hand tucked in the crook of his arm, his hand covering it possessively. Of his laugh, deep, amused, and so warm and natural she'd fallen in love with that alone at first.

Tal grim-lipped, his stance still and stiff in response to her parents' refusal to allow him to call.

Tal supporting himself on muscled arms as he introduced her to the ways of love. His patience, his tenderness, his passion.

Tal walking away from her that day in Boston, the

scent of their lovemaking on her skin urging her to call him back. To tell him there was only one way she could countenance his leaving, and it was to take her with him.

She had bitten back the words rather than call after him.

What a fool she had been. A fool several times over. She had blindly followed Kit west. Had agreed to Silas Rosser's terms.

She had stopped living a long time ago. Had lost hope. Doubted that a better future awaited her.

Even one with Tal Hammond once more at her side.

The name fluttered in her chest like a captive bird seeking to escape, except it fluttered in fear that she would release it.

Because it did, she would not.

****

He started at the Spent Bullet, the only saloon in camp he'd never visited. The clientele reminded him strongly of the boyos in the Boston stews. He'd observed the Bullet's custom coming and going since first arriving in the camp and had chosen to keep his distance. They wouldn't like having him among them. He didn't care to rub shoulders with them. Yet here he was, mounting the boardwalk that ran the width of the building, his attitude alone daring the men around him to take exception to his presence.

The noxious smell of the place swept out the open door, trying to get him in its clutches. Spilt bad whiskey, sour beer, strong smoke puffed into creation by packed pipes, cheap seegars, hand-rolled cigarettes, and ill-spat tobacco juice took him back to the Black

Sea area in Boston, where brothels, gambling, and alcohol were the rule. All that was missing from the miasma of the Spent Bullet was the smell of dead fish, the shrill notes of a fiddle, and a mix of newly arrived immigrant accents clashing with those of New England. The fetidity of hygiene-deficient men was most definitely in place.

He'd been in worse places, Tal decided, and stepped through the portal.

"Know a fella name of Cusack?" he asked the bartender once a shot of spuriously murky whiskey had been poured.

"What ya want with him?" the man snarled.

"So you know Cusack?" Tal persisted.

"Never said I did. Asked what ya want with him, mister."

"Found his name among Si Rosser's list of men who owed him. Just wanted to assure him that the debt is forgiven. Miss Kittridge has no intention of pursuing the matter," Tal said.

"Kittridge? Who the—"

"Pearl," Tal clarified.

"The gal we're fixin' ta hang," the bartender said. "What the hell's she got ta say over a debt owed ta Rosser?"

"Do you know Cusack or don't you?" Tal countered.

"Don't," the man said. "Ya drinkin' that er jest keepin' the glass out o' circulation?"

Tal forced the poison down and allowed what pocket change he still retained to drop in number by slapping payment for a refill on the bar top.

It was a nicer bar top than that at the Friendly Gal

but several grades below the one Fintan Foley polished at the Gilded Moon. Otherwise, Tal figured the aesthetics of the Spent Bullet were on a par with what Rosser's had been, except the long bar was better and flooring had been laid in.

With drink in hand, he wove a way through the closely packed tables, observing the various games in play. He found Ebner Melton's map of the area nailed to the rough wall toward the back of the place. It took purchasing a below-grade seegar to have reason to strike one of his few matches, though rather than light the smoke, he let it burn down nearly to his fingertips while scanning the names of men who had staked claims along the nearby creek. Cusack was not among them.

That didn't mean the man didn't exist, merely that he hadn't filed a claim under that name.

Tal watched a group of men play checkers, then casually asked, "Any of you seen Cusack around lately?"

"Can't have seen a man who don't exist," one of them told him. "Sure ya got the name right?"

The fellows engaged in a game of cribbage basically told him the same thing, as did the poker players. Leaving both the unsmoked seegar and the untouched second dollop of whiskey as payment for the only man to offer him a lead, Tal headed for the Friendly Gal to follow up on it.

Half an hour later, he felt he'd have gotten further along on the investigation by shooting himself in the foot.

The mayor sympathized with him but, after ensuring that Tal would supply a bottle rather than a lone glass of tarantula juice, confessed that considering he'd been one of the first men to arrive at the site after the discovery of the creek's hoard of gold and he'd never met a fellow answering to the name, looking for someone named Cusack was a waste of time. Despite dropping queries after the seemingly nonexistent debtor at tables around the room, Tal agreed with him.

The night was winding down when he pushed through the Gilded Moon's door. While Foley corralled spent bottles and empty glasses from around the room, Tal leaned back against the curved and lacquered edge of the upscale bar, his left boot heel hooked on the freshly installed brass foot rail. He figured Moira's hand was behind the numerous upgrades, and that having them increased the custom at the Gilded Moon. A man could make do with a place like the Spent Bullet, but he wouldn't feel civilized until he entered a place like the Moon. "I know you told me this once, but tell me again. Ever heard of anyone named Cusack?"

Foley swiped a cloth over one of the tabletops. "Did some thinkin' on that, and never heard of one in this camp," he said. "Did know a Cusack back East somewhere."

"Where somewhere?"

"Now that's the trick of it," Foley admitted. "Was a while back. Hadn't married Moira yet. Drifted a lot. Laid some track, tried my hand at ballyhooing patent tonics, tended bar. Did some bare-knuckle boxing. Been thinking on where I might have met this Cusack but haven't pinned him down. Doubt it would be much help even if I did recall the where, Cain. He ain't in these parts."

"But someone named Cusack was in these parts,"

Tal insisted. "Otherwise Rosser wouldn't have his name in his book of debtors."

"He had a *book* of names?"

"Yeah, a ledger. Found it earlier. This F. Cusack owed Rosser quite a chunk of cash, and he likely wintered here since he put a hundred bucks in Si's hand back in January and some more on account in a much smaller amount since then," Tal said, then straightened. "It's enough to give a man a pain in his nether regions. Mind if I pour myself a fresh drink? I'm in desperate need of washing the taint of everyone else's liquor off my tongue."

Foley went back to cleaning tables. "Go on ahead," he urged. "Nice to know my alcohol is better'n everyone else's."

"Food's better here, too," Tal said, rounding the counter. He swept up a bottle from beneath the bar and a fresh tumbler. "That cobbler your missus whipped up nearly took me back to my mother's table."

"Nearly?"

"Well, it's damn near impossible to top a man's mother's cooking." Tal poured a modest finger's width of whiskey into what he considered a fairly clean glass. It would not have passed his mother's quality control when it came to washing up, either. "While I'm pouring, can I get you a dose, Foley?"

The Gilded Moon's owner swung a chair off its feet, upending it so the seat rested on a tabletop and the legs reached for the ceiling. "Not often someone else is pouring for me. Appreciate it, Cain. If you can't find this Cusack, what's your next move? We could be having yer gal's trial tomorrow if the judge rolls into camp by midday."

Tal pushed a second tumbler across the bar in Foley's direction. "Sleeping on that," he admitted. "Hoping the judge lingers over the breakfast his wife whips up for him."

"Will if it's anything like my Moira's cookin'," the bar owner said.

"I'll drink to that," Tal seconded. "Fact is, even your whiskey leaves a better tang on a fellow's tongue. Probably doesn't eat my gut away as quickly as what I suffered through at your local competitors' establishments this evening."

Fintan chuckled. "Moira's secret family recipe. The fact that her father brewed up a mean poteen made her a lass well worth courtin'."

"Same mix, is it?" Tal mused. "Hell, considering I found a couple bottles with the Gilded Moon label slapped on them at Rosser's, he preferred your poison over what he foisted on his customers, too."

"Si had bottles of our whiskey?"

"Yeah. Does that tone of voice indicate he was more likely to have nicked them than paid for them?"

Foley shrugged. "Could have taken them off men who came in the door with one in hand. No barkeep wants a customer bringin' his own mash in the door."

"Since I didn't sample it, be damned if I'd have known it was from your barrel but for the label," Tal said. "Don't often see labels on the house's own product. Not even back East."

Foley chuckled. "Moira's idea. Advertising, she calls it. If a fella walks away with one of our bottles, shares it with his mates and they all want more, the label tells them where it's sold. At least in this camp. By the time we grow inta a city, Gilded Moon will be the drinkin' man's choice fer fine whiskey. Think she got the idea off a patent medicine bottle. They've got labels with the flogger's name for the liniment or tonic in big letters and the host of ailments cured or relieved in smaller print. 'Course there's usually a hell of a lot of sicknesses tallied up."

Tal savored a final sip from his glass. "During your spell as a medicine man, what were you pushing? Pills, drops, liniment, tonics?"

"Bit of it all," Foley said with a grin. "'Course when I got run out of town er had a passel of pitchfork-carryin' farmers on ma tail, I changed the product."

"Wise man," Tal agreed, and bid his host a pleasant good night. If indeed Judge Brevard rolled into camp sooner than he'd like, he had one hell of a day ahead of him saving Letty from the rope. Whether he'd manage to get any rest with that anticipation hovering over him was any man's guess.

****

The skies had been clear throughout daylight hours, but clouds covered any glimmer a distant star cared to make now that night had fallen. Tal was just shy of his temporary quarters at Rosser's former saloon when a light rain began falling. Rather than risk twisting an ankle in one of the permanent ruts in the street, Tal tilted his hat forward over his eyes and turned the collar up on his jacket for the short distance he'd yet to travel.

Across the way all was dark at the Bergens' facilities, both mercantile and funereal. As he glanced back down the length of the camp, what few lamps still burned were being extinguished one by one. Doors were secured, beds were sought.

Life went on as usual, if usual meant increasing the tally of bodies in need of burying could be considered *usual.* Letty was now the only former resident or employee of Silas Rosser's saloon still drawing breath. And if he didn't come up with some dazzling misdirection to tilt the opinion of the soon-to-be-chosen members of the jury away from convicting her, she'd join Rosser and Gately in the camp's scratched-out boot hill.

When he lit the lone lantern, he found scavengers had been to visit again. Fortunately, they hadn't appropriated his saddlebags or bedroll, nor found his rifle in the rafters. They had made off with the barrels of bad whiskey, the potbellied stove, the pipe that vented smoke beyond the roofline, the pile of split wood ready for use, and the tools he'd purchased earlier from Bergen. If the rain kept up, the saloon proper would soon be damp as well as dank. It would also be a night where what warmth remained inside would soon take itself outside through the previously filled hole in the roof. There would be no shedding of jacket or shirt or boots that night. The blankets of his bedroll had an uphill battle to fight in keeping him cozy. He almost wished he hadn't given Letty his greatcoat.

Wished he could be sharing its warmth with it sheltering the two of them.

Soon, he promised himself. All that was needed was to dazzle the jury of men who'd already made up their minds about her guilt, and plant suspicion on the fellows they called friends.

Hopefully, Brevard wouldn't be as much of an ass as the judges before whose gavels he'd argued in Boston. From what he had heard of the man thus far, the frontier judge would be obnoxiously high and proud of his authority despite the fact that his knowledge of the law equated to not much more than a glancing blow.

Oh, yeah. He needed to be in top form to confuse the issue sufficiently to win Letty free. Lacking a name, he'd have to fall back on overloading these simpletons' minds with possibilities, make them doubt their previously held belief enough to absolve her of guilt and simply kick them both out of the camp.

For that, he needed a clear head. Rest. A hell of a lot less whiskey.

And Letty's sweet whisper dropping that cursed name in his ear. The name that would put the guilty person in her place on the scaffold.

Considering there had been uninvited guests at Rosser's in his absence, Tal decided to see if anything other than the whiskey, stove, and wood was missing. Since the front door had been as he left it earlier, a wedge of wood tapped beneath the bottom to hold it closed, the thieves had likely used the rear door. Hidden from view, a wagon could easily have been maneuvered into place for the weighty stove's extraction, for the barrels to be carted out. Sure enough, when he brought the lantern closer, the back entrance swung loose on its leather hinges, the securing wedge on the inside kicked to the side. That meant they'd entered through the window in the back room, knocking the shutters free, and only left by the door. The mayor had probably been by, stepping off the measurements prior to claiming the place, and forgotten to drop the board in the brackets to keep the shutters in place. With the street door facing the hive of activity Bergen's mercantile tended to be, he figured anyone entering from the front would have gone unremarked, including himself.

As though in answer to his suspicion, there was a creak, a bang, and a thump in quick succession in Letty's former room.

It was damn spooky when he pushed the inner door open and lifted the lantern high. The mattress still lay half on and half off the makeshift bed, the ruined bedding still spilling toward the packed earth floor. Rosser's discarded clothes were where the dead man had dropped them days ago. As he'd guessed, the board across the shutters rested against the wall. One shutter swung open as he stood in the doorway, banging back against the wall, rain seeking entry on a breeze. If there had been curtains hung, they would have appeared to be reaching ghostly, billowing arms toward him.

Damn but he was tired. Living at the scene of a man's death was making him fanciful. At this rate, he'd soon expect either Rosser or Gately's reanimated corpse to step free of the shadows like Mary Shelley's literary monster.

Tal put the lantern on the floor and hefted the broad piece of wood. Taming the swinging shutters with an elbow, he dropped the plank into the waiting brackets, securing the building against both weather and further intruders.

Sleep, he needed sleep, Tal decided, rubbing a hand along the tight muscles in the back of his neck. What little rest he'd caught the night before barely counted as repose. His mind had been too full of newly gathered information. There was nothing like the need to save the woman he loved to put a man on edge. Since he and Letty were attempting to appear to be strangers, there were very few minutes in his day where he ceased to play a part. Although he needed to be alert and line perfect before a judge and jury very soon, there was every reason to believe sleep would play the avoidance game again that night.

His hand rested on the curve of the lantern's handle when there was a thud on the main door. Tal glanced toward it, wondering who in the hell wanted him at this hour.

He'd taken a step forward when the door to the back room smashed into his shoulder, knocking him off his feet, and into the saloon proper. The lantern landed next to him, on its side, the glass shattering, spilling flame-licked oil across the dirt floor. Hastily rolling away from the fire, Tal knew he'd chosen the wrong direction when something solid smashed into his temple. A shadow hovered over him, its arm raised for another strike. Hell, Tal thought blearily. Silas Rosser's ghost *had* put in an appearance and was damn irritated with him now.

But it was a very solid man of flesh and blood who leaned toward him. A man in common dark clothing and a neckerchief pulled up to hide his lower face.

"Cusack sends regards," a man said as the next blow descended.

Then pain and the void claimed Tal.

****

As much as she wished to welcome sleep, it avoided Letty's efforts to claim it. She was having difficulty remembering when last she'd drifted into a peaceful slumber or dallied in sweet dreams. Had the nightmares come with Kit's death? With the loss of wealth and status in the aftermath of their parents' demise? Or did they date further back, to Tal's leaving, to her parents' refusal to give him her hand? It was difficult to remember the last time she had lacked contretemps in her life.

The sheriff's snores in the outer room were a minor deterrent to sleep. Silas's had been much worse. With the observation hatch open in the cell's door, they drowned out any hint of nature's murmur. She could hear no early courting song of newly awakened insects, no hoots of owls or cries of their prey. No lonely howl of a wolf.

Letty sighed deeply, drawing the always-fresh scent of pine-drenched air into her lungs.

The expected fragrance was mixed with something familiar yet unwelcome. There was more than merely the forest represented. There was a hint, one that grew as she gasped in recognition, sending fear rushing through her veins.

Tossing Tal's long coat aside, Letty scrambled from the bunk to the door. "Mr. Strand," she called, urgency in her voice. "Mr. Strand!"

She heard him stir but couldn't be sure he had wakened, though his snores stopped with a snort. "Linus!"

The volume of her voice roused him this time. "What?" he snarled.

"Do you smell smoke?" Letty demanded.

She heard him inhale, then scramble free of the blankets on his cot. He yanked the office door open, stepping out into the street. In quick succession, farther up the camp shots were fired into the night, followed by shouts of "Fire!"

The sheriff dashed back inside, tossed the securing board across her cell door aside and pulled it open. He pulled his boots on as he spat instructions. "Go no farther than the front office, but get to where you can keep watch in the event the fire spreads. I won't have prisoners being roasted on my watch, so if necessary, retreat north toward the Gilded Moon and bring the weapons and ammunition with you."

"I will, but only if the fire threatens," she promised.

Strand dashed south moments later.

Letty hastened to the window. It was impossible to see what building was burning, but the reflected glow of the flames lit the business across from it—Bergen's Mercantile.

Silas's saloon was on fire.

"Oh, God, no!" she gasped. *Tal!*

****

The Devil was dancing a real foot stomper in his skull, Tal decided as he drifted back to consciousness. It had to be Old Scratch, for it felt like he was in Hell. Even behind closed lids he could sense the flames licking about him, hear the demon cackle of their glee.

He rolled to his side, pain stabbing like pitchforks in his brain, and opened his eyes. In the room behind him, the sad excuse for a mattress and blood-caked bedding dissolved like tinder to the hungry flame. It was already chewing on the bed, licking at the walls. Next to him the shards of glass from the broken lantern reflected dancing red-gold light, though they no longer lay within flame themselves. There hadn't been enough fuel left to sustain or cause the inferno that raged around him, yet the scent of coal oil was strong. Whoever had hidden in the saloon waiting for his return had fed the flames, making sure the saloon would writhe in its death throes.

As he would in his own if he didn't escape the building.

Tal flinched away from the heat. His equilibrium swam as he pushed to his feet and stumbled toward the rear door, the nearest possible escape route. No flames licked at it yet, but when he fell against it, hoping it would swing open, it resisted. Of course it did, he snarled at himself. He'd kicked the wedge into place only minutes before. But when he dropped to his knees, his scrambling hands found no wedge. Back on his feet, Tal wasted time ramming his shoulder into the door, again with no result.

Whoever had attacked him and set the fire had ensured that there be no exit from the rear of the building, but had they done the same at the front?

The rear door swung outward, but the street-facing one opened inward. Hopefully, he could pull it free of any wedge tapped in place from the outside.

He stumbled while crossing the saloon proper, now hemmed in by flames licking up the walls, and he coughed in rapid succession on the gathering smoke inadvertently inhaled too deeply when pain racked his brain at the near fall.

The fire hadn't reached the front of the building yet. His murderer had concentrated on igniting the rear and side walls. Once the flames reached the roof, they would begin eating their way forward. If he didn't make it to the street soon, he'd be fodder for the inferno.

And Letty would go to the rope with no one to defend her.

Tal tugged his own neckerchief up, a meager and less than efficient barricade to the rising smoke, and forced himself forward. Reached for the latch. It gave, but the door refused to swing open on its leather hinges. Tal tugged on it. Put a foot against the wall and pulled back once more.

Hope died in his heart when it remained solidly in place. He sank to his knees; rolled his back to the wall beside the door. The only way out was via death. It hovered on dark wings in the dancing flames. He could almost see it grinning at him. Or perhaps it was the ghosts he would soon join, those of Silas Rosser and Mos Gately. Of Kit Kittridge.

Tal was barely aware when gunshots were fired in the street outside and voices he recognized shouted the one word that struck fear in the hearts of any community that consisted of closely built wooden buildings. *Fire!*

He heard the thud of a body hit the door. Felt the wall flinch with the impact. Then the door swung open and men were dragging him free, into the street and the sweet chill of the gentle rain. They dropped him nearly in the same place he'd stood that first morning when Letty had been thrust from the saloon beneath the eyes of a hungry crowd.

People in nightwear, in their drawers, in trousers but shirtless, tumbled from buildings. Men from the dormitory-like lodging just feet from the saloon scrambled out, carrying their possessions rather than chance losing them should the flames grow ravenous for another structure. A ragtag assembly line of buckets passed from horse troughs hand-to-hand to those stationed nearest the fire. Tal recognized Strand in the forefront, backed by the mayor and Bergen.

And by the light of the conflagration he saw what

had caused the thud that had distracted him before he'd been attacked.

Driven into the center of the main door was a Bowie knife, the scabbard dangling from where it was impaled.

Rosser's lost property had been returned.

Considering few knew he'd asked about it, Silas Rosser's killer had just made a mistake.

Chapter Seventeen

The rain didn't turn into a deluge until after the roof of Rosser's saloon fell in. By then everyone who lived in the camp proper was in the street and had taken a hand in either the bucket brigade, at the well pump, or in tossing water on the flames. Fortunately, while the bunk house next to Rosser's sported singed marks, it hadn't caught fire. The real luck, everyone agreed, was that rogues had acquired the liquor barrels earlier in the day. If they'd been in place, an explosion could easily have spread the fire to the rest of the camp.

The storm was short in duration, but it squelched the last of the flames. Tired and drenched, the camp's residents trooped back to their disturbed rest, leaving Tal to follow Strand back to the sheriff's office. His head was throbbing, but his determination to bring the elusive Cusack to justice burned as brightly as Silas Rosser's building had, shortly before.

The glow of lamplight in the jail's street-facing windows was a welcoming sight. It promised warmth, shelter, and the possibility of a scalding cup of coffee, all things that took second place to seeing Letty's face again.

He was surprised to find her hovering in Strand's sanctum rather than in her cell. He was even more pleased when she threw herself into his arms, and further when she shared the desperation all too present in his kiss.

Strand slipped through the door behind him and silently closed it, ignoring the intimacy between client and counselor in a gentlemanly fashion.

When Letty came to her senses and stepped out of his arms, he saw her eyes flicker to the wound on his temple, to the minor burns on his hands, the singed spots on his now-drenched clothing.

Unable to help himself, Tal let his knuckles stroke soothingly over her soft cheek. “I’m fine,” he said.

“You’re damn lucky Ebner and ’Diah were out answering nature’s call and roused everyone. That boy’s new pistol is getting a workout since I handed it to him,” Strand said, then glanced at the items resting near the door. “Good girl,” he told Letty and dropped an approving pat on her shoulder.

Tal surveyed the pile. Prominent among the items was Letty’s worn carpetbag, though it no longer cradled her own meager possessions. It bristled with items that had no business being in her care, things that made it impossible to close securely at present. Boxes of ammunition, Strand’s revolver and holster, Rosser’s ledger, and items of clothing Strand hadn’t donned when he hastened into the night crowded each other in the valise. The sheriff’s saddlebag, rifle, and the bedding from both his and her bunks were piled near the door for quick extraction should the fire have spread. Only now did he notice she was wearing his greatcoat. He hoped she’d filled the pockets with Rosser’s cash and gold stash. As much as he hated to do so, he’d probably need to borrow some of it to replace everything he’d lost in the fire.

His Sharp’s rifle in particular. At least he hadn’t

divested himself of the Colt or his hunting knife prior to the attack. The weight of the Smith and Wesson .22 in his jacket pocket was equally assuring.

Strand pressed him down into the lone chair. Letty turned her attention to stirring the coals in the stove and restocking it with wood. Tal closed his eyes and let the pain have its way with him.

"Care to tell me what happened?" the sheriff said.

Tal touched the spot on his temple that demanded attention. His fingertips came away painted with blood, though he had felt the beginnings of a scab already forming. "Cusack's friends came calling. At least the fellow who bashed my head in said Cusack sent his compliments."

"The Cusack everyone claims never to have heard of much less know," Strand noted.

"Yup. Apparently it wasn't enough to scatter assurances everywhere that the debts owed to Rosser were forgiven."

Letty reached for Strand's coffeepot and peered inside. "I don't believe Cusack is a person, actually," she said. "Or at least not one in camp, outside of the product carrying the name."

Tal sat forward in the chair. The sudden movement set new lightning strikes of pain ricocheting in his head but, other than flinch, he pushed the discomfort aside. "The product?"

"Hmm. I mentioned Silas had a couple bottles of tonic he used for stomach pains and any other illness that threatened. The label called it Cusack's Tincture," she said, then turned to the sheriff. "I'm afraid there are only dregs of coffee left, Mr. Strand. Would you possibly have tea? I can competently heat water, but brewing coffee is not one of my talents."

In answer, Strand flipped the flap open on his saddlebag and removed a bottle of Gilded Moon whiskey. Pulling the cork free, he offered Tal first pull on the restorative. Conscious of the chill eating its way from his damp clothing into his bones, Tal accepted with alacrity.

"If you don't mind removing to your cell and closing the door, Miss Kittridge, Cain and I can shed our wet duds and scramble into some dryer things. Fortunately for you, Counselor, we're of similar build and height and I've got sufficient kits to lend you a change."

"Appreciate it, Sheriff," Tal murmured.

"Do you also have something to bind Mr. Cain's wound, Mr. Strand?" Letty asked. "If not, I'll destroy my petticoat to create one."

"No need, ma'am. I've had reason enough to need a supply of bandages more than once in the past."

She nodded acceptance. "Once you gentlemen have changed, I'll see to the damage then, Mr. Cain. Please call out when you are ready."

Tal watched as she drew the cell door closed behind herself, though he noticed the hatch in it stayed open. She didn't want to miss what they might say in her absence.

Strand pulled off his boots, then unbuttoned the fastenings down the front of his clinging damp longjohns. "Think she knows anything about dealing with wounds?" he asked.

"I think whether she does or she doesn't isn't going to stop her from wrapping my head up," Tal said as he set his Colt aside on the table and attempted to ease out of his jacket without setting off the fireworks in his head.

"Considering the welcome you got, I'm inclined to agree with you," Strand murmured. "You think this Cusack is someone in the camp?"

"I think it's worth checking to see if Bergen carries a patent tonic with that name on the bottle and, if he does, where he gets it from," Tal cautioned. "Could simply be the attacker muddying the trail."

"Could be," Strand admitted, "but considering he had you sealed in that inferno nice and tight, why even mention this Cusack? You weren't supposed to live through that little campfire he set."

"Damn," Tal growled. "I hate when you're right."

Strand was buttoning a pair of dry trousers in place, but Tal had only managed to remove his jacket. He turned his fingers to the task of releasing the buttons on his weskit and found his hands shaking.

"I hate it, too," Strand said. "Means someone I have a nodding acquaintance with just tried to kill you and didn't care whether the camp was destroyed in the process."

"Damned inconsiderate of them," Tal agreed. "Damned telling, too. If all that was at stake was an unpaid debt, why try to kill the man spreading the word that it was forgiven?"

"Unless they heard you were trying to tie Cusack to Miss Kittridge's brother's death and didn't mind nursing a guilty conscience over the matter."

Tal finished dealing with his vest but winced again as he removed it. "Right now, I'm nursing quite a hankering for a chunk of ice wrapped in flannel to ease the drum tattoo in my head. You think among the delicacies at the Gilded Moon, Foley's stocked up on any over the winter to cool his wife's larder?"

Strand shoved his freshly buttoned shirt tails into his trousers and hoisted the braces back in place. "I can find out," he said, reaching for his jacket and his hat. From habit, the sheriff ran his fingers over the brim rather fondly before tilting it over his eyes.

Tal sighed. He'd been wrong about missing his rifle the most. He was going to miss his hat more. His head had been training it for over two years now. Funny that a single item like that could take on new meaning to a man on the frontier. Back in Boston he'd owned several hats and had never gotten melancholy over a one that he'd left behind.

"Neither Fin nor Moira should have drifted back to sleep yet. Dealing with our recent excitement will keep a good many folks restless for a while. I'll be back in a bit," Strand promised, and slipped out into what was once more a gentle rain.

He'd barely left when Letty peered around the cell door. "Could you use some help?"

Resisting the natural inclination to nod, Tal grunted. "I'd probably pass out making an attempt on my boots," he confessed.

She had removed his greatcoat, he noticed when she left the cell. Her gray calico skirt swirled around her as she knelt at his feet. "You'll be glad to know that while I'm hopeless with coffee, between dealing with Kit and Silas, I do have some experience in removing a gentleman's footwear," she said.

"Rosser was no gentleman," Tal said.

"Silas was inebriated enough to have a nodding acquaintance with many of Father's friends, and Kit's as well, back in Boston."

"But you weren't called upon to remove their boots," Tal murmured.

"Of course not. They had valets or butlers or footmen to deal with such things," she responded. "Now which would you prefer I deal with first? Left or right?"

He let her choose and simply clenched his teeth against the protest his abused brain made.

"What's this?" she asked, shaking separately bound piles of greenbacks from his boots.

The size of each had dwindled greatly, but as it had been to loosen tongues in the saloons or to supply her with minimal comforts, the money had been well spent.

"The remains of my travel fund," he said. "Not everything I've accumulated. The bulk is waiting for Adam Cain in a Virginia City bank vault."

"Then you returned to your trade?" she asked.

"Found I had a knack with a deck of cards," he corrected. "Other than yours, I haven't taken on a case since I left Boston. Avoided the temptation to do so."

"Because you felt you'd lost—what did they call it? Hammond's Magic?"

He chuckled, then immediately flinched, put a hand to his battered head. "Ooh, bad idea, that. Only the kind ones called my glib tongue that. Hammond's Balderdash was probably the most repeatable of the more common wits' opinions."

"Is that what you'll use in my defense, Tal? Balderdash?"

"I've few facts, a landslide of suppositions, and, yes, a hell of a supply of balderdash for the performance, Lett. If you'd just—"

"Give you the name," she finished. Carefully, she set his boots aside beneath Strand's makeshift desk.

Tal sighed. "Can you at least tell me if I'm right about it being a woman?" When she didn't respond, but plucked instead at the buttons of his shirt, he lost his patience and gripped her wrists, preventing her from helping further with his damp clothing. "Is it, Miss Kittridge? I know you. Not just the Noletta Kittridge of Brahmin Boston but the woman she was forced by circumstances to become. That woman might buy a man's excuses if a family's safety was involved, but Rosser never let you get close to anyone in this camp once he dragged you beneath his roof, and from what I can learn of your life in camp before that, you kept to yourself, to your cabin. The only true congress you had with residents here were those with the few wives who made the trip to the territory. So, which of the *good* women are you protecting, Lett? Moira Foley? Bergen's missus? One of the miner's wives? Who among them killed Silas Rosser that morning?"

She stared into his eyes unflinchingly. He realized the grip he'd taken on her wrists would leave them bruised and released her. When she didn't turn away from him but rose gracefully back to her feet, he was surprised.

"None of them," she whispered, then cleared her throat. When she continued, her voice held the pitch of a woman making polite conversation. "Can you deal with the rest of your things without aid, Mr. Cain? If so, I'll remake Mr. Strand's bed. Do you wish a pallet made up out here for yourself, or will you share my blankets with me?"

When he didn't answer, she gently touched his

face. “I would prefer the latter,” she said. “There is every chance that I will hang before nightfall tomorrow. I can think of no better way to spend my last night than with you.”

As much as he wanted to shout down her calm acceptance, at heart he knew she was right. The men of the jury, the residents of the camp and of those nearby, and probably the judge once he heard about it, had decided her fate nearly two days ago when she’d stumbled in the street before Rosser’s place, covered in his blood. He faced an impossible battle in the makeshift court. If he lost…

“I’ll share with you,” Tal said softly.

****

Strand was not surprised at the agreed-upon sleeping arrangements when he returned with a chunk of ice about the size of a billiard ball though it was far from round in shape. Once it melted, the bar cloth Foley had wrapped it in would be decorated with forest detritus, judging by the bits of leaf and twig visible beneath the frozen surface. It was a welcome comfort to his pounding head, Tal claimed. Unfamiliar with the treatment of head wounds, Letty decided she would take him at his word. She’d already cleaned the spot on his temple, applying a salve the sheriff swore was a miracle cure, and bound Tal’s head with one of Strand’s proffered bandages. Fintan Foley’s donation would soon leave the bandage soaked, but the sigh of relief Tal had made when the chill of the ice pressed against his temple soothed her fear for him. With a hand to his head to hold the compress in place, he accepted her help when she slipped beneath his opposite arm, escorting him to her cell.

"I'm afraid there aren't sufficient blankets to make up both the cot and a pallet on the floor, Mr. Cain," she told him, though it was for the sheriff's benefit, not Tal's. "The flooring is hard, but I've spread one blanket to block any drafts that might creep between the boards and folded another for use as a pillow. I didn't think it wise for you to do without such comfort, considering your wound."

"Very thoughtful of you, Miss Kittridge," Tal murmured.

"There is still one blanket to use as a cover, but considering the chill you took tonight in the rain, I suggest it be augmented by the greatcoat you lent me."

"Beautiful and wise," he said. "I bow to your will. Figuratively, of course. I'm afraid at this point doing so literally would pitch me headfirst at your feet."

"Something to be avoided, then," she agreed. "Do you need assistance getting to the floor in a less dramatic way?"

"I'll make it," he assured her, but he sat on the denuded bunk first, then eased his way down to the meager bed she had created.

Letty lifted the glowing lantern and turned back to where the sheriff was already slipping beneath his own blankets in the dark outer room. "I'm going to close the hatch in the door, Mr. Strand," she said. "I doubt Mr. Cain will appreciate the morning light, even if it is dulled by clouds."

"As you wish, ma'am," he mumbled, and turned his back to her.

"Mr. Strand?"

He sighed deeply but didn't move. "Yes, Miss Kittridge?"

"Thank you for trusting me earlier."

"It was that or let you roast. Besides, I did notice you were saving my things, not your own, so you have my gratitude on that."

"All the same…"

"All the same," he echoed.

Letty blew out the light, set the extinguished lantern on the floor next to her cell, and quietly closed the door.

Her days in residence made her very familiar with moving about the small room in the dark. Although she had not disrobed to sleep in days, Letty removed her dress and boots before slipping in next to Tal, wearing just her chemise and petticoat. As though it knew the way, her head found his shoulder and nestled against it, her arm resting on his chest.

"I love you," she whispered.

She felt him move, felt the blanket and the weight of his greatcoat shift as he drew them up over her bare shoulders. "But not enough to have a future with me," he murmured.

"Yes, I do," she said. "If circumstances were different—"

His lips cut her words off.

They were gentle at first, simply tasting her mouth. Was he imprinting the feel of her to fuel his memories? She had done so that afternoon in Boston long ago. She had thought then that it was the last time they would be together. Now it would be one in truth.

Must they always have *last* times?

When his tongue glided over her bottom lip, moved to trace the contours of the upper, Letty welcomed him, her mouth eager for his. It was the dance she had shared only with Tal. Other men had used her body, but kissing she had never allowed. Not even with Silas, who had held her in thrall, who could have simply taken that intimacy as he did the other. Yet had not. Had been content to concentrate his attentions below her chin.

But not Tal, never Tal. She savored the memory of every kiss they had shared. From the first, audaciously stolen, to the passionate, soul-claiming farewell.

The farewell that had become an until-we-meet-again. This night—or would it be in the early morning?—they would share the true farewell kiss.

Holding back the desperation that filled her, Letty's tongue met his, entangled with it. Each breath she breathed, he swallowed like a man fearful of drowning. What remained of her life, she gave to him. To sustain him in the coming battle; to harbor against the loss she saw as inevitable.

She had promised to love him until an unspecified future. The *until* that was arriving on far too fleet a foot.

Tal groaned softly, allowing her to absorb the sound, to keep it from escaping into the night. His arm drew her closer, near enough to sense the quick tempo of his heart, feel the rapid rise and fall of his chest as he tore free of her mouth and, rolling to his side, buried his face against her throat. She arched it, allowing his lips to range at will. For her own part, she took advantage of their new position to pull the tail of his borrowed shirt from his trousers. Her fingers took full advantage, reacquainted themselves with the feel of hard muscle across his shoulders, the contour of his back from nape to lean waist, of flesh both warm and slightly foreign to her touch.

"Let me undress you," she whispered into his hair.

"No," Tal murmured.

In the dark she found his bearded cheek, gently trailed her hand down it, her palm cupping his jaw, her fingertips caressing the planes of his face, the pad of her thumb tracing his lower lip. "I need more than memories tonight, Tal."

She felt his mouth tilt. He was smiling, though she couldn't see it, only sense it. "I'm a gentleman, Lett. And a gent allows a lady to go first."

Wounded as he was, Tal Hammond was teasing her. Was not letting their night together assume the nature of a shroud. Only she saw it as a requiem, one sung for their love, for her life. It should be a joy, a rejoicing that they did love, that brief though their time together was, it was a celebration of hope. Even if that hope was fleeting and misplaced.

"All right," she said. "I'll indulge you, but only because you're an injured man."

"More than merely injured, surely. Let's term it grievously wounded," he corrected. "But do feel free to indulge away. I'm only sorry I won't be able to view the process. Would you mind disrobing slowly?"

"You can't see me, Tal."

He ignored the reminder, ran his hand down her bare arm from shoulder to wrist. Moved to the curve of her hip, continued up over her chemise. "In my mind I can, battered as it is. I can feel that your dress is no longer a barrier. Just a single layer left." His hand glided from her arm to her hip, tracing a new path. "Petticoat and chemise?"

"Yes," she said, the answer more a sigh than a word.

"Pull the ribbon free first," Tal instructed. "What color is it?"

For answer, she slid her leg over his, nudged him to lie on his back, then sat up, straddling him. Pelvis to pelvis she was very aware that despite the ill-treatment it had received that evening, part of his body was quite alive, hard, and accessible to her needs. Tal's hands found her bent knees and glided upward over her petticoat-draped thighs.

"It's a blue ribbon," she told him. "A deep sapphire blue, like your eyes." In truth, the shade had long ago faded to a sickly pastel. He would only know that if, prior to placing her in a coffin, they divested her of the silk dress June Gilchrist's seamstresses had made. And only then if he stayed for her burial. Which he would even if she forced a promise from him to leave prior to it.

"The bow is slipping away, leaving the ends dangling free." She took his right hand in hers. Drew it to her breast. "Should I disentangle the tie or would you prefer to do so?"

His fingers found the spot where the disparate pieces entwined and drew them free at a maddeningly slow pace.

"Top button, please," Tal requested once the job was completed.

Letty complied, one hand holding the placket while the other pushed the fastening free.

As if he had seen the action, Tal murmured, "Next one."

Precious minutes were lost as each button in turn was dealt with to his specification. Though he couldn't see her, the slow measure of the exercise left her breathless, as though with each release Tal had been privy to more and more of her flesh. When the last was free, the backs of his fingers brushed between the valley of her breasts, then slid within the open garment to glide across one mound until he cupped it.

"Lean forward," he said.

She braced her weight on her arms, her hands resting on the blanket beneath him just above his shoulders. Tal brushed the cloaking fabric aside. The cool, damp air of the night leaching through miniscule gaps in the mud-caulked timber walls touched the exposed tip of her breast, drawing it to attention. His mouth covered it a breath later, suckling pleasure that tugged a fresh desire into being deep within her. His tongue laved, his teeth grazed over it lightly, teasing, tempting, arousing. Claiming.

In Boston, they had been rushed, all too conscious of minutes slipping by, their passing marked only too well by the mantelpiece clock's measured ticking. She had not known pleasure could be delayed, built upon. The men who had used her these past months had cared only that she was available; Rosser allotted little time for what they crudely termed *a poke*. Even Silas took his pleasure quickly.

But Tal…

Pleasure was a shared event that he had no intention of pushing to its close that night. When he switched his attention to her other breast, giving it equal attention, Letty arched, her head thrown back, her lips parted as a shuddering sigh escaped her throat.

As though in answer to an unspoken command he'd read in her muted voice, Tal's hand found its way beneath her petticoat. His fingers found the center of her longing and nearly wrung an audible cry from her.

Her breathing ragged, Letty swallowed. Ran her tongue over parched lips. Parched for water or for his kiss, she wondered, then decided the answer was both.

"I thought you wanted to go slowly," she whispered.

"This is slow," he said against her skin, though it felt nothing like that to her.

"You intend to kill me by degrees?" she asked.

"Something like that," he agreed. "Sit up. Let's rid you of all this confining cloth."

Rid implied a quick removal, but Tal had no intention of increasing the pace. He gathered a handful of cloth, but it was merely to tug the hem of the chemise from confinement beneath the petticoat. When it was free, his fingertips traveled gently from her waist to her ribs, brushed the lower curve of her breasts.

"Kiss me," he instructed.

"With pleasure," she murmured. In leaning forward, her hips lifted from his. Her hair spilled over her shoulder, a cascade that fell veil-like about them both. She teased his bottom lip lightly, taking it between her teeth to tug. His groan was part baritone chuckle, part passion. She brushed her mouth over his, retreated, brushed again. Their breaths mingled briefly before she claimed him with a punishing caress. It lacked gentleness, it demanded passion. Tal pulled the chemise so that it bunched around her shoulders, but he didn't remove it. Instead his hands sailed her rises and falls, settled on her hips, and guided her back into place. Through the rough texture of his borrowed trousers, the stiff pressure of his shaft argued for a quick release from confinement. Promised a joining that would be sweet, joyful, more branding than their first act of love.

And then he peeled the chemise over her head, tossing it aside in the dark.

She heard the hiss of hastily inhaled air. “Ooh, shouldn’t have done that,” he said. “Moving too fast for my sluggish brain.”

Letty found the tangle of his hair, traced the edge of the cloth she’d bound about his head. “You’re not well enough for this exercise,” she soothed. “We should stop. Let you rest.”

“No,” he whispered, sounding both angry and frustrated. “I’m afraid if I pass out, I won’t wake up. That I’ll miss the only chance to make love to you in this Godforsaken camp.”

She heard what he did not put voice to: that he would fail to do what he had promised, that he could not prove her innocent with the information he had.

He needed the information she kept from him.

To keep him from asking, or from vowing they would have a future together, she cupped his face between her hands and kissed him deeply. Tal’s arms encircled her, pulled her close with a desperation he’d held at bay thus far. When she released him, he buried his face between her naked breasts and inhaled the scent of her.

The cure, temporary as it would be, rested in her keeping. Letty reached for the cord that secured her petticoat, pulled it free. As though coached in a part, Tal pushed the fabric down over her hips, uncovering her navel, her stomach, the uppermost edge of the golden thatch that guarded her woman’s mound. With touch alone, he guided her up on her knees. The petticoat fell away from her hips, from her seat. But for the dark, she was on display, her legs spread wide as she knelt above him, her back straight, her breasts aroused.

When his palm cupped her intimately, Letty steeled herself to be still. She was his living statute, warm, willing, and waiting.

"You are so perfect," he breathed softly. "So lovely."

"So lacking in decorum when in your arms, Mr. Hammond," she said. "I am also unclothed, while you…" She plucked at his shirt.

Rather than make a move toward the shirt's fastenings, his fingers caressed her hidden folds. "You're wet," he said.

"Hardly surprising, considering…" she murmured.

"Considering," he agreed. He probed further. "Shall I stop?"

Now, it was an inconceivable idea. "No," she said, though the word was expelled as a sigh. "Perhaps I could…" She played with the topmost button he had fastened. It rested in the center of his chest.

"Could," he conceded, letting his other hand glide over her bare hip and around to her buttock. He was holding her in position, rocking her gently forward, backward, forward again.

She released the first of his buttons. "You're distracting me."

"Um-hmm."

"Maddening man. Isn't your head bothering you?"

"I'm distracting me, too," Tal said. "If this wasn't Strand's shirt, I'd say rip the damn thing."

"You wanted to go slow," she reminded.

“With you. Not with me.”

She leaned down to kiss him, her fingers moving more quickly down his shirt. He found further ways to make her forget what she was doing.

Rather than push his shirt aside once it was open, she moved to the buttons on his trousers. Tal made no effort to stop her.

He had borrowed outer clothes, not a set of longjohns or drawers, she realized when her fingers encountered warm flesh. “Oh, my,” she breathed in surprise. “Can you lift your hips so that I can remov—”

Tal’s hands grabbed her waist, lifted her, and impaled her swiftly. Shocked, she gasped, but he was already sliding back down her canal, guiding her into the rhythm that felt more like a dance than an invasion.

His breathing sounded like a rattling gasp, but hers was none too steady. “Lett,” he whispered.

She kissed him, their tongues mimicking the motion of their mating. She no longer needed guidance to give him pleasure, to share in his pleasure. She moved slowly, letting him slide nearly free before drawing him back within her body. In answer, Tal’s hands found their way into her hair to prolong their kiss, and then they were back on her hips, forcing an increase in the tempo.

Music swirled around her, created by their ragged breathing, by the rush of blood through her veins, through the motion of their bodies as each sought, retreated, claimed. She had been born to tread this dance of love with Tal Hammond. Now she gave it to him as a gift. The most precious thing she owned. Her love for him.

And then her body did something it had done only

once before, and only with him. It self-destructed, taking Tal with her into perdition.

In the aftermath, she lay across him, gasping for breath, her body only now noticing the chill in the room, that she was slick with sweat. His arms were around her, holding her close. Holding her as though he would die before releasing her.

She clutched him in return, pressed a gentle kiss to the center of his chest.

"I love you," he said quietly. "Don't let them take you from me."

Letty bit her bottom lip. Pretended she was already asleep. There was only one way to do as he asked.

It was to condemn another in her place.

Chapter Eighteen

The sound of Sheriff Strand moving about in the outer room woke Tal. Letty curled at his side. His arm was around her, the fingers of her hand entangled with his. Slowly he slid free of her grasp. She didn't stir, didn't wake.

Strand had opened the hatch in the door, possibly to check on them, possibly to see if she'd killed him in his sleep. While the sheriff was now convinced that someone, possibly the mysterious Cusack, had murdered Kit and had turned Rosser's saloon into a dandy pyre that Tal had been lucky to escape, he still wasn't convinced Letty was innocent when it came to Silas Rosser's death.

Having the hatch open allowed the scent of coffee to waft into the cell. It was luring him from his hard but warm and shared bed. Tal lifted a lock of Letty's tangled hair and placed a soft kiss on her bare shoulder. His head still ached, but not to the same extent it had the evening before. Apparently, a healthy dose of romantic exercise and a good night's sleep could cure what ailed him. Slipping from the combined comfort of blanket, greatcoat, and warm bedpartner, Tal got to his feet slowly. When the building didn't attempt to tilt sideways, he was relieved.

Doing up the front of his borrowed trousers and rebuttoning the shirt, Tal figured all he needed was to find his own clothing had dried before the heat of the stove overnight and that Moira Foley had mixed up a fresh batch of biscuits for breakfast. Having both of those wishes come true might allow him to be as close to a complete man as his battered head would allow.

There was a hell of an agenda to accomplish before the judge rode into town…if he rode in at all that day. A visit to Bergen's to replace the things he'd lost in the fire came in second to visiting the remains of Rosser's saloon. He hoped the gentle, though consistent, rain had cooled the scene enough for him to pick through it. Although the label wouldn't have survived the conflagration, he hoped to find the bottle that had held Cusack's tonic. If the patent medicine had a decent enough reputation, there was a chance the bottles were specially ordered and carried not only the manufacturer's name but the location that Cusack called home. If the bottles hadn't been specifically molded with those details, he had nothing to go on but his attacker's words and Letty's mention of the Cusack formula being Rosser's favorite remedy when he was feeling poorly. Otherwise, Cusack was just a name jotted in a journal by a man who might have been helped along the road to Hell by the fellow most in debt to him.

"Morning," Strand greeted when Tal slipped from the cell, closing the door softly behind himself. "Duds are dry. If you're lucky, that wool weskit didn't shrink none."

"If I'm lucky," Tal agreed, testing the rolled collar of his vest. It might be dry, but it still smelled of coal oil fumes and soot. "You mind if I keep this kit and buy you a new one?"

"Sentimental about it now, are you?"

"Sorta," Tal admitted.

"Fine with me," Strand said. "Want some coffee?"

"Thinking more along the lines of one of Moira Foley's specials."

"Don't blame you," the sheriff drawled, and handed him a cup of steaming liquid anyway. There was the faint aroma of chicory rather than ground beans rising from it, which made Tal wish there was a place to discreetly dump the brew rather than be forced for politeness's sake to drink it.

"You think Brevard has started on his way here yet?" he asked.

"Sure of it," Strand said. "He'll be looking for both a fee for wielding a gavel and time away from his missus. Bet he started at first light."

Tal glanced out the window at the sky. It was gray with clouds, but first light had shown up hours ago, if his farm senses were still in good stead.

Strand took a careful sip of his steaming mock coffee. "You got a plan?"

"I've got a jumble of puzzle pieces," Tal admitted. "Hopefully the plan will fall together before court's in session."

"You're going to need that breakfast at the Gilded Moon," the sheriff said. "How's the head?"

"Mending," Tal allowed. He was careful not to move too quickly when he reclaimed his boots from beneath Strand's table. "Considering the alternative, I'm dandy."

"You better be, after the tender care you got last night."

It was impossible to keep the smile from his face

after that, Tal decided, and stopped trying to keep it hidden. "Yeah," he agreed. "Say what you will about ointment, recovery's all in the nursing."

"Amen," Strand murmured, and lifted his cup in a silent toast.

****

Moira Foley fussed over him, offering to redress his head wound, an offer Tal politely turned down. He asked that breakfast be sent to the jail for both Miss Kittridge and the sheriff, and made short work of his own, anxious to accomplish what equated to herculean feats before Brevard selected his jury. Before he could be on his way, the mayor pulled out a chair and settled in for a bit of jawing.

"You're looking fairly alive for a man who got his edges seared last night," Melton said.

"Thanks to you and 'Diah," Tal countered. "'Preciate the rescue."

"Apparently, the frequent visits to the necessary required by my uncommon thirst are a blessing in disguise," Ebner allowed.

"All the same, I owe you a bottle of Foley's finest in thanks," Tal said.

"Won't turn it down, dear boy."

Tal thought the man would make an exit, but Melton stayed where he was.

"Brevard's expected not long after noon," he said. "You know what you're going to do yet?"

Tal leaned back in his chair. "I figure to get Miss Kittridge off scot-free, buy her a horse, and hightail it out of this hellhole."

"Not the most detailed of plans, then."

Tal sighed. "No, it isn't. I'm hoping my luck

wasn't totally used up by your timely call to nature last night."

"And if we hang her?"

"I'll ride out even faster."

The mayor nodded as though it was the most profound thing he'd ever heard. When he didn't make further comment, Tal wondered what was up. Ebner Melton, alias Ambrose Speke, usually was the most talkative man in the camp.

"Something on your mind?" Tal asked.

Melton cleared his throat. "You ever find those markers at Si's?"

"Why?"

"Did you find anything…let's say, out of the ordinary tucked out of sight?"

"Such as?" Tal drawled.

"A bit of newssheet."

"Like an article he might have saved?"

"Something like that," the mayor admitted.

"And if I did?" Tal said.

"If you did, I was wondering if you'd be interested in a bit of company when you leave town. A partnership, if you like," Melton offered.

Tal leaned forward, his forearms on either side of his empty plate. He dropped his voice to a conspirator's whisper. "If that's a bribe, it's very ill disguised, Mr. Mayor. But I like you. You've been kind, in your own way, to Miss Kittridge. Which is why I suggest you break camp and move on, *Ambrose*. I'm honor bound to pass Rosser's bit of blackmail along to Strand, but it doesn't mean the man whose visage is immortalized on it has to be present when I hand it over."

Melton inhaled deeply, then released it in a sigh.

One that sounded suspiciously like relief to Tal. The older man pushed back his chair, slowly rose to his feet. Offered his hand. “It’s been a pleasure to have known you, Mr. Cain.”

Tal pushed his own chair back. Shook the mayor’s hand.

“Now, if you’ll excuse me…” Melton said.

“You’ve got packing to do,” Tal finished for him.

But before Ebner scuttled away, he turned back. “I don’t believe she did it,” he said.

“She didn’t,” Tal agreed. “Now I just have to convince the rest of the camp that she’s innocent.”

And do so before they could hang her.

****

Letty was surprised to find Tal had vanished when she woke. Considering the condition of the blow he’d received, she thought he’d linger a while before returning to his quest for something to prove her innocent. If nothing else, he had to be dealing with a blinding headache.

The hatch in the cell door was closed as she had requested it be the evening before. Having no idea of how long she had slept, Letty half expected Strand to check on her soon. Considering the only thing between her skin and the cool temperature in the room was a lone blanket and the bulk of Tal’s greatcoat, finding the clothing she’d shed was of paramount importance.

As it was, she was still doing up the buttons down the front of her dress when the sound of new arrivals in the outer office penetrated the cell. A moment later, she recognized Maisie Flagler’s voice.

“Miss Kittridge?” the young dove called, knocking politely on the door. “May I come in?”

Sweeping up the makeshift bed on the floor didn't improve the cell's appearance but did provide her guest with room to move. "Please do, Miss Flagler," she answered, wondering why the seamstress had come to visit.

Then she remembered. The judge was expected sometime that day. Maisie had no doubt brought the silk gown for her to don.

But when the door opened, Maisie stood aside while two unknown men carried in a full-sized plunge bathtub. While not as luxurious as the delicately painted, boat-shaped one in her dressing room back in Boston, it was an unexpected extravagance in this wilderness outpost. The tub filled the cell, leaving very little room between it and the bunk attached to the wall.

To remove herself from the men's path, Letty sat down and swung her legs up onto the bunk.

"The boys will need to be in and out a bit with buckets of water," Maisie said from the open doorway. "I'm afraid the water will be rather cool since Mr. Strand's stove can't heat a sufficient supply, but I brought Madam's perfumed soap and our cotton towels along. I'll help you wash your hair and comb it out. If you'd like, I'll help you bathe, or give you privacy, miss."

Although there had been maids to attend both her mother and herself at the Kittridge home in Boston, she had performed the task herself for long enough now to feel uncomfortable being nude around strangers. She had never been entirely naked around Rosser or any of the men who paid to use her. Considering the night had concealed her the evening before, even Tal had only seen her unclothed once, and that had been on their stolen afternoon nearly two years ago.

"I don't deserve either your or Mrs. Gilchrist's consideration," Letty told her visitor, "but I would appreciate assistance with my hair. If, as you warn, the water is cool, bathing will be swift and more easily accomplished on my own. Thank you for the offer, Miss Flagler. This is indeed an unexpected treat."

"Madam June thought freshening up would help you remember you aren't Pearl any longer. We all know you didn't kill Si, and Mr. Cain is going to ram that down that jury's throat."

Letty wished she could believe it. However, although she would enjoy the feeling of being clean once more, it would be of short duration. They'd still hang her.

Best to keep that belief to herself and enjoy what she could of the rest of her life.

The men moved back and forth through the sheriff's front room, each carrying buckets in both hands. Were they emptying newly filled horse troughs? She'd never know. The men accomplished their job silently as well as swiftly. Their job temporarily completed, the men trooped out the door until needed to empty the tub and reload it on the wagon. Letty had no doubt of their destination. It would be the Friendly Gal Saloon, directly across the way.

"I didn't bring your dress with me, miss," Maisie said, bustling into the room, a basket of essentials over her arm. "This place offers too many chances for it to get snagged. I did bring a spare dressing gown for you to wear after the bath, so you won't have to put on what you're wearing."

"You are all too kind," Letty murmured.

"No, we ain't," Maisie insisted as she removed towels and soap from her basket, then turned with a dropper to add a subtle hint of perfume to the water. The thoughtfulness of the gestures extended to her by the women at the parlor house were enough to knot Letty's throat with emotion.

"We're just women, and women need to watch out for each other. Sure as hell no man's gonna do so," the dove declared, personal experience obviously fueling her words with a touch of vitriol.

But Letty knew one who would. One who would be close to destroyed when he failed to rescue her.

Talmadge Hammond.

****

Tal was surprised to find both Strand and 'Diah Short in the street before the jail rather than manning posts inside when he strolled up, en route to the remains of Rosser's saloon. The sheriff had his arms crossed over his chest as he leaned back against the hitching post. 'Diah had drawn himself up to sit on the long bar of it, shoulders hunched, hands resting on the wood while his dilapidated boots dangled a foot from the ground. Both had their hats tipped forward over their brows, though the sun was still at their backs.

No doubt 'Diah had done so simply to mirror Strand's stance but had given in to a boy's joy of climbing by perching himself on the tempting stretch of pine.

Strand read the question in his expression before Tal gave it voice. "We been evicted. Maisie sashayed in with two of June's regulars toting a tub. The cell has been turned into a lady's bathing closet, so we were ousted."

“Right prudy thing it is, too,” ’Diah contributed. “Gots vines and flowers painted along the sides.”

“A real step up from a dip in the creek,” Tal agreed. “That mean you’re free to journey down to the site of my near demise, Sheriff? ’Diah’s beginning to get a reputation for plugging fellas. Think he can handle a couple women?”

Strand unwove his arms, pushed away from the hitching post. “Yeah, long as he promises to keep his finger off that trigger. Threatening’s one thing, boy. Killing’s another. I’d rather keep the body count down, if you don’t mind.”

The young deputy dropped back to his feet. “Yes, sir, I kin do all that.”

The sheriff gave a quick nod of approval. “Be back shortly,” he said. “Not like it’s far to Rosser’s.”

Which it wasn’t. Two of the three long bunk houses and another shack sat between the sheriff’s office and the charred remains of Rosser’s place.

Strand fell into step with Tal. Tilted his chin toward the stripped tree branch in Tal’s hand. “Nice piece of lumber, counselor. Too spindly for a club. Besides, you’re still armed with that Colt on your hip.”

“Didn’t search it out as a weapon but as a probe,” Tal said. “Doubtful the rain cooled all the embers. This should flip anything but broad rafters aside.”

“You looking for something in particular?”

“Be nice to find some of my possessions survived, but I have my doubts on that,” Tal admitted. “No, what I’m hoping to find is the bottle of Cusack’s tonic that Rosser held so dear.”

The sheriff nodded. “You’re hoping the glass is imprinted with something that might point a finger in a particular direction."

"Yup," Tal agreed. "Think I'm pissing in the wind?"

"In regard to your client's trial? You bet," Strand said. "So why bother?"

"Because there might be a connection to Kit Kittridge's death. This Cusack owed Rosser a heck of a lot of money. The ledger that, fortunately, was in your hands, not mine, clearly shows that a hefty amount was returned to Si the day after Kittridge's death. From that I posit that means Cusack likely killed Kittridge, either on purpose or accidentally. Whether Cusack then killed Rosser in a struggle over possession of the gun Rosser acquired from Kittridge's estate—if we can call what little he left as an estate—is still conjecture. However, Miss Kittridge says that Si was killed accidentally, and no, she wasn't the one to accidentally kill him."

"You *posit* that I was going to say that?" Strand drawled, pulling up at the edge of the arson site. The mix of ash and rain made for a murky soup in depressions and within bowls of partially charred timbers. Neither of them would escape being marred by fresh charcoal.

"In regard to my client, I can *posit* what you're thinking and what you're planning to say," Tal said and edged along the partially blocked alleyway between what had been Rosser's and the bunk house next to it. "I think the mysterious Cusack is our best bet for solving two killings with one culprit, though."

"*If* what you're looking for turns up," the sheriff cautioned as he surveyed the damage but made no attempt to step into the burned area.

"Won't know until it's found. Your presence backs

me up, proves I did find something rather than expect anyone to believe I did so." Working his way back to where the rear room—the bedroom—had been, Tal poked through the remains.

"You've got some of the durndest ideas," Strand snarled. "Where the hell'd you get them?"

"From the police," Tal said, prodding a different spot. "New ways of investigating crimes are coming into existence, and they're proving to be damn effective at corralling the guilty parties."

"Where'd you learn about them?"

Tal took a chance. "Boston," he said.

Strand grunted. "Not surprised in the least. You knew both the Kittridges before."

It wasn't a question, but a statement. Tal answered it anyway, as honestly as he would if sworn in before the bench, his hand on a Bible. "Yes," he said quietly.

"Let's get to it, then. The sooner 'Diah doesn't have the weight of the world on his shoulders in connection with your client, the better," the sheriff declared and kicked at a bit of burned-through wood.

A bottle rolled over in the muck.

"Damn," Strand snarled.

Tal looked over his shoulder at his companion. "Find something?"

"Not a medicine bottle, but a bottle, all the same," the sheriff admitted. He untied his neckerchief and used it to protect his hand from picking up a coating of ash. "Surprising one, though. Didn't know Si had a stash of Gilded Moon whiskey."

"It's still got part of the label on it?" Tal asked in surprise.

"Naw, but it's got a distinctive shape. Nicely

curved like a pleasingly plump woman. Always figured Foley bought a couple cases of them because it reminded him of his wife," Strand said, retrieving it.

When he whistled in surprise, Tal was temporarily distracted as he poked around what he guessed had once been the bed. "Don't tell me there's still alcohol in it," he pleaded.

"Not a drop," Strand assured, "but it's got something you're going to like even better."

In the ashes of what had once been Letty's bedroom, Tal identified a curve that had nothing to do with the structure of the building. He hunkered down to push his rustic probe deeper, looking for the neck of what appeared to be a bottle. It was small. He doubted the mouth would be wide enough to allow his bitterroot branch entry to maneuver it free. How would the judge view an attorney with soot coating his hands? Not well, probably, but there was no other way to snag what he hoped—no, prayed!—would be evidence damning enough to turn eyes away from Letty.

Following the sheriff's example, Tal put his neckerchief to work when enough of the small medicine bottle was visible.

"What's impressing the hell out of you, Strand?" he called across the ruins.

"Just the imprint along the one side," Strand answered. "Will take a minor scrub down to be sure, but I believe it reads—"

"Cusack Tonics?" Tal asked, reading the raised though soot-coated lettering that ran along the back side of the four-inch-tall, clear glass bottle now resting in his hand.

"Nope." The sheriff drew the word out. "This one

says whiskey. *Cusack's* Finest Whiskey."

Tal closed his eyes. Let a heartfelt sigh of relief escape his lungs. At last, he had something to take into the courtroom.

****

The judge drove into camp in a weathered buckboard drawn by a single, weary-looking nag. 'Diah burst through the office door to supply the details of Wakefield Brevard's far from impressive arrival and deliver a message. Rather than visit the sheriff's office, Brevard preferred to issue a strong request for Strand's presence at his table in the Gilded Moon.

Although his own attendance hadn't been requested, Tal decided he'd tag along, if for no other reason than to find out when the judge intended to bring the court to order.

Brevard was a dustier version of magistrates he'd argued before in Boston. A less hygienically inclined one as well. If the judge intended to shave before court convened it would take heavenly intervention. Currently he was dedicating himself to emptying a bottle of Foley's finest.

Or rather, Cusack's finest, Tal thought. When Fintan approached the table with tumblers and a second bottle for Strand and him to share, it was a Seven-Day Wonder to watch the sheriff maintain his usual façade. Foley would be taken by surprise when evidence of his true identity was revealed during the trial.

"We need twelve honest men," Brevard intoned, telling them what they already knew.

"Soon as you let me return to my prisoner, I can send young 'Diah out to round up fellas along the creek," Strand said. "They'll be expecting the summons, since we guessed you'd be arriving about now. Only question is when you want the trial to commence."

Brevard tossed off a shot of whiskey and refilled his glass. "Soon as the jury's selected and I can tell them what I expect them to do."

"Which is listen to the facts, view the evidence, and make a decision based upon what is said in the makeshift court rather than what they might have decided around the campfire or over a hand of cards?" Tal asked.

"Naturally," the judge said, though Tal doubted any of it would have been in the man's script prior to that. "Who are you, precisely?"

"Adam Cain," Tal said, offering his hand. "I'm representing the accused."

"Know what you're doing?"

"Ensuring that the camp doesn't hang an innocent woman."

Brevard frowned. "I meant, you got any acquaintance with the law? On the *right side* of the law?"

So the judge thought he looked like a miscreant himself? Tal nearly laughed. The last time he'd looked like a gentleman had been the day he boarded the train out of Boston. Since then his wardrobe had consisted of rougher, sturdier items. No one would mistake him for the gambler he'd become, but no one would take him for a lawyer, either.

His head still sported the bandage and his hair smelled of soot, but his trousers, shirt, and vest were all fresh from Bergen's Mercantile. Only his boots were as mistreated as Brevard's appearance.

"I've argued many a case," he assured the judge.

"I'll vouch for Cain," Strand said. "He's sharp and he's honest."

Almost honest, Tal clarified silently. He was traveling under an alias, after all.

Brevard removed a pocket watch from his vest. "Then as soon as the jury's in place, we'll start this show," he decided. "Say four o'clock?"

Strand nodded. "Four o'clock it is. You hear that, Foley? Time to start rolling out the tables. You're going to be out of business the rest of the day."

And, Tal mused, if all went well, for a good bit longer than that.

****

Letty was surprised to find the saloon proper at the Gilded Moon nearly cleared of furnishings and already crowded with men when she arrived, sandwiched between Sheriff Strand and 'Diah Short. While Strand stepped through the door ahead of her, 'Diah hung back and helped her restrain the billowing skirt of the deep lavender silk gown, making sure it didn't catch on any previously unnoted splinters on the door's molding. Rather than keep the cloth from harm, Letty knew the deputy's real goal was to simply have a reason to touch the richly glowing fabric.

As promised, Maisie and her fellow dove, the seamstress Alice Purdue, had returned to the jail to work the required miracle while the jury was selected. *Pearl* ceased to exist as *Noletta* reappeared when they brushed her hair and captured it in a fashionable snood that brushed her nape. June Gilchrist had even lent her a pair of heeled shoes, far more appropriate than her scarred boots for a silk gown. They had also supplied a pair of kid gloves, but she forewent using them. Maisie had buffed and shaped her nails earlier, returning her hands to near ladylike status. Her only ornament was the ring of pearl and emeralds Tal had given her as a token of their love.

Love she read in his eyes when they met hers from across the room at the Gilded Moon. He didn't approach her; didn't speak. He didn't have to.

"This the accused?" a grizzled man seated at the lone table growled.

"It is," Strand said.

"Stand her over there," the unknown man ordered, pointing to the same corner she'd eaten in the day before.

The sheriff complied, gripping her arm, though he did so lightly and, she surmised, for the sake of appearances.

The man she supposed was the judge picked up a clawfoot hammer rather than a proper wooden gavel and brought it down with a thunderous bang on the tabletop. "Court's in session," he announced. "Since we're lacking the usual judicial circus staff, I'm just going to tell you what we're about today. I'm Brevard, acting judge for the Territory of Idaho since there's nobody else at hand to do this. We're here today to decide if the accused murdered a man. That's her in the corner over there." He pointed the hammer at Letty.

Letty found eyes turned her way, some angry, some fearful, some merely curious.

Brevard redirected the hammer toward Tal. "And that's Cain, her lawyer," he said by way of introduction.

She had seen plays in the theatres in Boston where a narrator introduced the parts the actors would play.

The idea that any Kittridge, much less herself, could be on trial for murder was so foreign, this had to be a play as well.

But it wasn't.

The judge resumed his monologue, making short shrift of what was to come when the curtain went up on the first act. "I questioned and chose the jury earlier, and that's them lined up along the bar," he informed the audience. "Sheriff Strand will swear in those that haven't put their hand on the Bible yet but need to should the occasion arise. Any questions? If not, keep your trap shut and just listen to proceedings. Speak up and I'll toss your ass out of here. Got it?"

Although she'd never been in a proper courtroom, Letty doubted the men behind the bench in Boston's courts ever delivered speeches such as Brevard's.

"Strand. You made the arrest, so tell us about it," the judge ordered.

Linus Strand was as brief and to the point as Brevard had been. He explained that he and others had heard a shot fired at Rosser's place at a time of day when they all knew Si was likely still abed. Strand himself had been in his office at the time, which meant men stopping at Bergen's mercantile and some from the Friendly Gal arrived on the scene before he had. Brevard asked him to halt and dragged each of the men who had burst into the scene of the shooting to their feet to tell him what they'd found. There was a slight delay as each was sworn in, but Brevard kept the ceremony well clipped.

"Swear to tell the truth?" he asked each in turn, then accepted two one-word replies and a nodded head for the third.

"Found Pearl standing over Si. Hadn't even bothered ta move after shootin' him," the first man said.

Tal immediately took a step forward. "Objection. There is no evidence to show that my client was the shooter."

Brevard sighed deeply, then admonished the witness not to make damn-fool judgments on his own.

The second man kept that in mind but painted what he'd seen upon entering the room in gory detail. "Und the pistol was lyin' in the blood poolin' at her feet. Recognized it as Si's own gun."

Brevard turned stern eyes on Sheriff Strand. "We got the weapon in question?"

"As we're short on arms, Deputy Short has been issued it for use in performing his duties," Strand answered.

"You identified it as the property of Silas Rosser and as the murder weapon as well?"

"Mr. Rosser had been in possession of it for several months. Whether it was the murder weapon or not, I can't swear. It was at the scene and the barrel was still warm to the touch as though recently fired. It was also shy one bullet in the cylinder," the sheriff said.

"Sounds like we can consider it the weapon used," Brevard said, then turned back to the man currently sworn in. "Anything else to add?"

"Just that it weren't always Si's gun. He took it over after her brother died," the man explained, indicating Letty with the jutting tip of his unshaven jaw.

Brevard frowned. "Are you indicating that the accused was familiar with the weapon?"

"I'm sayin' she knew the damn thing," the witness insisted. "Probably knew how ta use it, too."

The men crowded into the saloon to watch the show murmured loudly among themselves, which earned them a thunderous bang of Brevard's makeshift gavel and a shouted demand for silence.

In the ensuing quiet, Letty heard Tal clear his throat. "Objection," he said. "Simply because the weapon was once the property of Miss Kittridge's brother does not necessarily mean that she was familiar with handling the revolver."

"Didn't have ta be ta shoot Si in the chest," the witness growled.

"Objection. It has not been determined that my client was the person who shot Silas Rosser," Tal contended.

They were just words, though, Letty thought. There were only three people in the room who considered her innocent: Tal, the sheriff—who had only absolved her a few hours ago—and the person who, in fact, *had* pulled the trigger.

Brevard shooed the witness back to his seat and turned his attention to the third man, who simply grunted affirmatively regarding what the two before him had said. As the man lumbered back into the crowd, the judge turned his eye on Tal.

"You got more to say on this, Counselor?" he demanded.

Letty wasn't surprised when Tal smiled. "I do indeed, Judge. I'd like to call Burl Bergen to the stand."

The crowd rumbled in low tones as the shopkeeper pushed to his feet and placed his hand on the Bible the sheriff offered. "Swear ta tell the truth as I knows it," Bergen said.

"Good enough for me," Brevard announced. "Mr.

Cain?"

Although Tal didn't move from where he stood, Bergen eyed him as he would a wild animal, cautious and very aware that an attack might be imminent.

"Mr. Bergen," Tal said. "You not only run the local mercantile but serve as the undertaker in the camp. Is that right?"

"Yeah," Bergen answered shortly.

"Did you examine Silas Rosser's body after his death?"

The shopkeeper scowled. "Did after ya und the sheriff kept draggin' him out ta gape at."

"Can you describe his injuries?"

Bergen sighed this time. "Hole in his chest."

"Anything else?"

Bergen's expression turned to a glare. "Scratches down the side o' his face."

"Scratches," Tal repeated. "Did they appear to be something he had acquired a few days earlier?"

Bergen glanced at Strand. "No. Was fresh. Sheriff thinks so, too."

The judge's eyes darted to Strand. "I do," the sheriff agreed. "Also determined it was delivered by a close-in attack, not the result of a run-in with an animal or an ill-planed door."

"Cain thinks a woman gave it ta him," Bergen offered.

"The accused?" Brevard demanded.

Tal took another step forward at the question. "If the court will be patient, the answer will become apparent shortly," he promised.

"Any more questions for this fella?" the judge asked. "If not, the witness is excused unless we need him to clarify anything further."

Bergen stomped back to his seat.

"I call Miss Noletta Kittridge to the stand," Tal announced.

Letty was unsure whether she was expected to leave the corner in which they'd placed her or step up next to the judge's table as the others had done. The sheriff took the option out of her hands by taking her arm and escorting her forward. Her hand on the worn cover of the Bible Brevard had supposedly brought with him, she swore to tell the truth.

"Miss Kittridge. Did you kill Silas Rosser?" Tal queried.

"No, I did not," she said.

"Do you know who did?"

She should have expected him to ask, but it still rattled her that he did. "Yes," she whispered.

The crowd moved beyond murmurs and whispers to a calliope of voices. Brevard's hammer brought them back in line, though slowly.

Once silence had been achieved, Tal asked his next question. "Was the person a man?"

How she hated to answer, but she had sworn to do so honestly. "No," Letty said.

Brevard pushed to his feet as his hammer fell, demanding silence when the crowd erupted this time.

"Silas Rosser was killed by a woman?" Tal persisted.

Knowing her response would sound breathless because the word caught in her throat, Letty responded. "Yes."

"Was it a woman living beneath the roof at Madam June Gilchrist's parlor house?"

Although she whispered the word, it seemed more like a shout in the absolute silence that reigned in the room now. “No.”

“Was it the wife of a man mining a claim along the creek?” Tal asked.

She couldn’t remember ever having met any of the miners’ wives, although she knew only a few had made the trip, dragged along by a man with a dream as she had been in Kit’s tailwind. “No.”

“Was it Mrs. Irene Bergen?”

The mere idea startled her so much, Letty snapped the answer, knowing she relayed a sense that the concept of Mrs. Bergen killing anyone was impossible. “No, absolutely not.”

“Was it Mrs. Moira…” Tal paused a moment before completing the question. “…Cusack?”

“N—who?” Letty stared at him in surprise.

There was a sudden scuffle near the doorway that led to the Gilded Moon’s kitchen area before two men, who had obviously been stationed there by Sheriff Strand to prevent the Foleys from escaping, dragged them back into the room.

It took repeated falls of the hammer on the abused tabletop before order was restored this time.

Tal appeared to be the only one not disturbed by the contretemps. When the hullabaloo receded, he repeated the question. “Did Mrs. Moira Cusack, also known as Moira Foley, kill Silas Rosser?”

“No,” Letty said firmly.

Tal looked thoughtful as he faced the jury. “If a woman killed Mr. Rosser but it wasn’t you, one of the doves, or any of the wives in the camp proper or along the creek, who was it?” he asked.

Letty bit her bottom lip.

"You are under oath to answer, Miss Kittridge," Tal reminded.

When she didn't speak, Letty realized he had stumbled on the secret.

"Is the woman who shot Silas Rosser in this room?" he asked.

Over the heads of the seated crowd, Letty's eyes briefly met those of the woman she'd attempted to protect, and once again she relived that terrible morning just days past.

****

Three Days Earlier at Rosser's Saloon

A clever sunbeam found its way through a gap in the wooden shutters, piercing the gloom of the room and finding Letty's closed eyes. She held a hand up to block it as she sat up in bed. For the light to have crept in meant it was midmorning. The density of the largely coniferous forest surrounding the camp kept light at bay for much of the day at the saloon. Considering that the man who owned her kept late hours, and expected her to, nothing beyond stray rodents and insects were abroad any earlier in the building.

Letty slipped from the bed, hoping to steal a few moments of her own before Silas roused. If she managed to be fully dressed prior to his waking, there was a chance he wouldn't decide to sample her for his breakfast. The sunbeam had other ideas.

"What the—" he growled, following the words with a string of vulgarity Letty had learned to block out.

Taking the opportunity to torture Rosser a bit further, she threw the shutters wide. Behind her, he snarled and threw an arm over his eyes to block the light, but she inhaled deeply, enjoying the cool, fresh scent of pine, fir, and spruce that wafted through the opening.

Since she'd slept in her drawers and chemise, Letty quickly slipped into her Balmorals. She'd finish lacing the sturdy high-topped boots once she was out of the room and don her corset out of his sight as well. After nearly three months as his possession, she knew quite well what would rouse Silas to an amorous mood and avoided doing certain things while under his eye, as much as possible.

She grabbed the blanket that had served as her only bedding while on the trail west, using it now in place of the silk dressing gown that had been sacrificed to a used clothing shop in Chicago when she and Kit had been short of funds. "I have to…" she told Rosser. She never finished the sentence. Ladies, her mother had taught her, didn't mention privies.

"Take the piss pot with ya," he snarled. "Smells like a damn latrine in here."

Even with the bucket emptied it wouldn't smell any better, she thought.

"Ya need ta clean the place up, Pearl," Rosser said.

She was already at the door, but Letty paused long enough to look back at him. "Cleaning is not the labor for which you acquired me. Perhaps 'Diah Short would be interested in the work."

Mr. Short made up for her shortcomings. Her talents lay toward things not worth a twig this far from civilization.

Rosser grinned widely at her, both his teeth and the beard nearest the corners of his mouth stained with tobacco juice. "Not a bad idea, honey."

"You disgust me," Letty said, hastily leaving the room.

It took very few steps to reach the rear door of the saloon. The path away from it was packed dirt like the floor within the building. It led to a narrow shack of an outhouse at the edge of the woods. Because it was used by the patrons as well as the staff at Rosser's, it smelled even worse than the small room that served as her working and living quarters.

As loath as she was to return to the saloon, it didn't do for a woman to stand around in her undergarments where any man could see her and decide to take advantage of what he viewed as an opportunity. Still, it took several minutes to fasten her corset, lace her boots, and deal with the disgusting bucket. She was still a distance from the saloon when she heard the voices.

Rosser was snarling at someone. The other person's voice was pitched at a quieter level, but it sounded like they were pleading.

Letty put the bucket down outside the building and slipped inside quietly.

"Get away from me, ya freak," Rosser snapped.

"But I love ya," the other person cried. "Look, ain't I female 'nuff fer ya, Si?"

Letty crept closer to the open door and was surprised to find 'Diah Short standing before Rosser, both calico shirt and longjohns open to display small but fully formed breasts.

Rosser shoved 'Diah hard enough for the disguised woman to crash back against the wall. "Don't worry, freak," he snarled as 'Diah slid to the floor. "Once I tell the rest o' the camp yer little secret, ya'll have more 'n 'nuff custom. When it comes ta enjoyin' a poke, most men out here don't care if a gal's got a face like a jackass and nary a soft curve ta squeeze."

'Diah scrambled to her feet and lunged at him, raking her nails down his cheek. Silas laughed as he tossed her aside once more. This time the young woman merely stumbled, but as she did, she grabbed up the revolver Rosser had set aside on the rough stool next to the bed. With a scream of rage, she swung the barrel toward him.

Freedom danced before Letty's eyes briefly before reason reasserted itself. Without Rosser to protect her, provide for her, what would become of her? Would the events that had led to her becoming a drab at his saloon play out once more?

Rosser grabbed 'Diah's hand, intent on disarming her quickly.

But passing herself off as a man had led 'Diah Short to doing jobs that gave her strength beyond that of an average female. Silas managed to edge the muzzle away from himself, but not to twist it from the furious woman's hand.

Letty dropped the blanket from around her shoulders and rushed forward, pushing between the two. "Cease this," she cried. "It's foolish..."

"Shut up," Rosser snarled, backhanding her.

The blow was quick and would have knocked her to the floor if she hadn't been pressed between Rosser and 'Diah. It took Rosser's attention away from the struggle for possession of the gun long enough for 'Diah to pull the trigger.

Fired close to Letty's ear, the explosion was deafening. She looked on in stunned shock as Rosser stared uncomprehendingly at her, then fell back across the rumpled bed, the shirt he'd half buttoned now matted with a spreading stain of blood.

Though still reeling from the sound of the shot, Letty heard 'Diah moan as she dropped the weapon to the dirt floor and leaned back against the open shutter in shock.

"I didn't mean ta…" the woman gasped, staring at the dead man on the bed, then at Letty. "Oh, Miz Pearl! Yer…"

Letty glanced down at her blood-soaked garments. They had only moments before someone in the camp burst through the door.

"I come ta see if'n there was any jobs that needed doin', but when I seen Si on his lonesome…"

Letty straightened her back. Squared her shoulders. "You were never here, Mr. Short. Kindly exit through the open window. No one from camp will see you from the road. Go into the forest. Check your clothing for blood splashes, and if you find any, disguise them by draping one of the animals you trap over it. Or destroy the garment. You can take your emotions in hand as you run into hiding. There must be no hint of your involvement."

"I never…" the woman mumbled.

"'Diah! Leave before the chance is gone," Letty snapped. She didn't dare go near the other woman. There was so much blood on her own clothing she couldn't be sure some of it wouldn't transfer to 'Diah. Glancing back over her shoulder at her protector's lifeless form, she thought the young woman hesitated, grabbing something from the head of the bed, and then she was in action, following Letty's instructions.

"Thank ya, Miz Pearl," 'Diah said as she swung

one leg over the windowsill. "I did love him."

"Love is an insanity," Letty counselled. She watched until the other woman melted into the forest. 'Diah had taken Silas's Bowie knife with her, she saw. Damning evidence that she'd been in the room. Letty took a deep breath. If need be, she'd lie about the blade, and she would keep 'Diah's secret. Considering blood coated her clothing, there would be only one outcome. She'd welcome it.

What option was there for a tarnished woman in this wilderness?

Letty stared down at Silas Rosser's still body again. "You damn fool. I hope you're happy you've managed to kill me," she snarled, though he was long past hearing the hatred in her voice.

A moment later, a handful of the camp's residents stormed through the street-facing door.

****

The Trial at the Gilded Moon

Tal moved to within a yard of her before making the inquiry that would force Letty down the path she had resisted for days now. "Did Silas Rosser force a situation that resulted in the shot being fired, Miss Kittridge?"

She still looked torn over the answer. Would she hate him for maneuvering her into swearing to tell the truth?

Her Kittridge backbone held her upright, had her unconsciously straightening her shoulders, lifting her chin. She looked straight at him, ignoring the judge, the jury, the spectators.

"Yes," she whispered.

It wasn't enough. He needed to push her further.

"Were you involved in this situation?"

Letty nodded.

"A verbal answer, please, Miss Kittridge," Judge Brevard ordered.

"Yes. I tried to stop it."

"Is that how you came to be covered in Silas Rosser's blood?" Tal demanded.

"Yes. I was standing between…them," she said, still not identifying the third person in the room that fateful morning. He had to push her, though she'd hate him for doing so.

"Was the person who pulled the trigger on the gun Miss Dinah Short?" he asked loud enough to be heard over the rising murmurs of the crowd.

"Who?" Brevard snapped, then hastily tumbled out of his chair, scrambling for safety.

From where she stood at the back of the crowd, 'Diah Short had pulled the revolver from where it was shoved into the waistband of her trousers. "I didn't mean ta kill 'im!" she shouted, aiming the weapon toward where Tal stood near Letty.

'Diah's hand was shaking badly. Tal expected the pistol would bark death whether the girl intended it to or not.

"'Diah! No!" Letty cried as those nearest 'Diah scrambled toward the sides of the room.

"Ya promised, Miz Pearl," 'Diah cried. "Promised not ta tell!"

Letty stepped boldly forward. "And I haven't, 'Diah. I've kept your secret. What happened to Silas was an accident. Don't make this worse by shooting someone else."

"Someone like *him*," the girl said, swinging the

barrel to point directly at Tal.

Chances were Dinah Short's shot would miss, but in missing him, it could strike Letty.

The woman he loved appeared fearless. Calmly she stepped between him and the weapon in the deputy's hand. From the corner of his eye, Tal saw Sheriff Strand ease a step nearer the men along the wall.

"Did you start the fire that nearly killed Mr. Cain?" Letty asked.

"Why would I do that?" 'Diah demanded, emotion sending her voice into a higher, more feminine register.

"That wasn't 'Diah," Tal said, hoping he could keep the young woman's attention away from Strand as he smoothly stole another step. "It was Foley. It's also likely that he killed your brother."

Distracted by the information, Letty broke eye contact with the young woman she'd attempted to protect. Over her shoulder, Tal read a decision in 'Diah Short's homely face as she turned the weapon toward herself, preparing to make a court decision on her fate unnecessary.

Linus Strand lurched forward, grabbing the revolver away, ensuring that the hungry muzzle pointed toward the ceiling rather than endangering anyone in the room.

Letty wilted in obvious relief while chaos reigned in the rest of the room. Wrapping his arms around her tightly, Tal let it all wash over them unnoticed.

****

Linus Strand had no trouble controlling the now sobbing Dinah Short. The young woman had been disarmed and her hands secured behind her back. The sheriff's hand rested on the handle of the revolver at his belt, daring any of those in the makeshift courtroom to make a move toward his latest prisoner.

The judge banged the clawfoot hammer against the tabletop in rapid succession to get order, making the tumbler and bottle he had near at hand jump at each thud. “Quiet!” he thundered. The crowd ignored him.

Strand drew his Remington revolver and plowed a bullet into the ceiling. “Shut the hell up!” he yelled. Only then was the noise reined in as men regained their seats.

When only a murmur of sound remained, Brevard pinned his gaze on Tal.

“Do you wish to continue, Mr. Cain?” he demanded.

“Yes, your honor, I would,” Tal said and turned back to where Letty stood alone, her shoulders squared, her chin raised, looking quite glorious in the deep lavender gown and very much the woman he’d fallen in love with in Boston over two years ago.

“Miss Kittridge. Did Dinah Short murder Silas Rosser in cold blood?”

Letty clenched her hands together, but she didn’t flinch. “It was an accident,” she said again.

“But Miss Short’s finger was on the trigger?”

He knew she hated to admit it, but she nodded. “It was.”

“What makes you believe it was an accident?”

“She didn’t mean to fire. She was upset. He had just rejected her, insulted her. Ridiculed her.” She turned toward the judge. “He was a murderer, a thief, and a liar. Silas Rosser deserved to die. Dinah Short does not.”

Brevard peered at her closely. “That’s for the jury

to decide," he said. "They sure as hell were ready to string you up, missy. Yet you kept quiet about what she did. Why?"

Tal wasn't surprised to watch her chin lift higher. "Because she had a reason to live," Letty said. "At the time, I did not."

"Now you do?" Brevard demanded.

Tal's heart swelled when her gaze moved to him. "I do," she said softly.

Brevard grunted, then cleared his throat. "The case against Noletta Kittridge for the murder of Silas Rosser is not worth spit. Any of you gents in the jury disagree with me on that call?"

The men in the chairs lined along the bar grumbled a bit, but their elected representative followed procedure and got to his feet. "No, sir. We're in agreement with ya on that."

"Good," the judge said and smacked the substitute gavel solidly against the now thoroughly marred tabletop. "Case dismissed. Let's say we move on to Dinah Short's crimes. It'll save me a trip back. Any one of you care to speak up for her?"

The room filled with the murmur of male voices and the shifting of both feet and chairs, but it was Letty who answered.

"Mr. Cain will," she said.

Tal smiled at her, not in the least surprised that she'd offered him up. "I would be honored to represent Miss Short's interests, Judge. If you could avail me of a few minutes to speak with my new client?"

"Done," Brevard announced and pulled his pocket watch out. "You got thirty minutes, Counselor. Then court will resume to deal with the gal first and then the murdering arsonists. We're adjourned, gents. Clear out, but don't go far." Then the judge exited, headed for the Gilded Moon's kitchen to forage for the meal Moira Cusack would not be serving.

****

The last rays of sunlight were disappearing behind the western set of mountains, though Tal doubted Letty was aware that night was about to engulf them. She stood silently at her brother's gravesite, a stranger in men's clothing.

June Gilchrist had offered her parlor house as a temporary refuge. Letty had accepted the offer but hadn't lingered. Freshly changed into a pair of men's trousers and a shirt and with her hair braided in a long tail that hung over her shoulder, Letty had stepped out onto the porch where he waited after barely thirty minutes. He wasn't surprised at the swiftness of her transformation from the resigned woman he'd defended in the make-do courtroom at the Gilded Moon to the bright-eyed woman who looked forward to her newly gained future.

A future with him, he hoped.

Besides the duds he'd purchased for her at the mercantile, she now had a wide-brimmed felt hat and a boxy jacket, though her feet were still shod in the only pair of lady's boots to survive the reduction in her wardrobe the year before. She was now the owner of a gentle roan mare, a mule, a small tent, and blankets. He'd made the Bergens very happy with the spending spree to replace what they had each lost, all purchases made courtesy of the late Silas Rosser's cash hoard. The only item he planned to replace the moment they arrived in Virginia City was the rifle. He really missed that Sharp's 1853 lost when Fintan Cusack had attempted to roast him.

East of the burying ground, lamps and lanterns were being lit, the small camp ceasing to resemble a collection of cut timber in favor of a fairy glade. The shadows would remain around the charred timbers of Rosser's saloon; all would be dark at the Gilded Moon. Business would be lively at both the Friendly Gal and the Spent Bullet, now the only spots for men to bend an elbow and gossip about events of the day.

Would it be one that went down in the annals of history? The day a man who had lacked purpose had won the life of the woman he could not forget; the day a forgotten girl had lost her life.

At least Dinah Short was content now. Despite his efforts, the camp hanged her swiftly. Silas Rosser had too many friends in the place to surrender their need for an Old Testament type of justice. Neither he nor Letty were in attendance. The young woman had barely been cut down when they'd strung Fintan Cusack up for the murder of Kit Kittridge and the attempted murder of himself. After Moira babbled incoherently that she and her husband had changed their surname due to a death back in Kansas, for the camp's safety, Strand incarcerated his favorite cook in Letty's abandoned cell.

It was only after the excitement had died down that anyone realized the mayor had departed sometime during the trial. Strand scowled over the belated delivery of the still slightly soggy news clipping regarding a robbery back East but said not a word in rebuke.

Letty made one request before she let Tal escort her out to the parlor house—that the young woman they'd known as Obadiah Short be buried next to Silas Rosser, the man with whom the girl fancied herself in love. Tal wondered whether she'd done it to please 'Diah's spirit or to irritate Rosser's. He fancied the latter himself.

Leaving the horses and the mule to graze on the first sprouts of spring, Tal moved to stand beside Letty. Kit Kittridge's grave was still mounded rather than flat, a result of his burial being delayed until the ground softened after the winter freeze. The simple wooden cross was a far cry from the memorial he'd have been given in Boston. Bergen had chiseled *Kittridge* and nothing more on it. If he hadn't walked into the camp three days ago, another marker would have been pounded in place next to it, one that said *Pearl* rather than give her real name. Tal glanced at the dimming sky and offered a heartfelt thank you to whatever providence had led his feet in this direction to save the woman he loved.

Although she kept her eyes on her brother's grave, Letty's voice curled around him as it had done over two long years ago back in Boston, caressing his name. "Tal, how did you know it was 'Diah?" she asked. "I was careful never to give her away, treating her as a young man, always calling her *Mr.* Short."

He nudged his hat back an inch. "I know you, Lett. The more I considered things, the more I realized that it would never be a man you were protecting. It would be a woman, and since Rosser didn't visit June Gilchrist's girls and none of the good women in town had anything to do with him, it had to be a woman who had disguised herself as a man for safety's sake. 'Diah was the only one capable of a successful masquerade because of her upbringing. Whether her brothers divorced themselves from her or she chose to go her own way, it seemed doubtful that she'd ever been treated as anything other than a boy."

Letty looked up at him. Tears glinted in her eyes, catching a ray from the setting sun. "But if she hadn't given herself away at the trial…"

Tal sighed. "They would have hung you because you would have refused to supply her name."

Her gaze dropped back to the grave at her feet. "Yes," she agreed softly, her voice quavering over the single word.

"Light's nearly gone," he reminded. "We'd best be on our way, though the distance traveled won't be far in the dark. We will be away from this hateful place."

She nodded. "There is one more thing I'd like to do before leaving Kit here."

"And it is?"

"Marry you," she said.

"We've no preacher, and I doubt Brevard—"

"All I need is family, and Kit's the best I can do. What could an official do other than have us repeat his words?" She reached for his hand, intertwined her fingers with his. "We already have the ring."

"True," he admitted. "The question is who do you want to marry? The fellow who stupidly left you behind or that Cain fellow who made one hell of a bunch of enemies by attempting to deprive them of a hanging?"

The first stars of the evening seemed to be reflected in her eyes when she stared up at him. He realized they were unshed tears. It was hard for her to leave her brother behind.

"I'd like to marry them both," Letty said. "But as I

fancied being Mrs. Talmadge Hammond, I'd rather like to become *his* wife, if it's possible."

Tal pulled her close. "It's possible. I'll still have to be Cain for a bit. That's who my bank account says I am in Virginia City. Once we hit wherever we're headed after that, the disreputable Adam Cain can cease to exist."

"He wasn't so disreputable. He was quite clever and very determined."

He kissed her lightly over the compliment, then took both her hands in his. "How shall we do this, Miss Kittridge?"

"Simply say the words, Mr. Hammond. Do you take Noletta to be your wife?"

"I do," he vowed. "Do you take Talmadge?"

"Most certainly I do," she promised.

"Then before the spirit of the one person who knew us both best…"

"And approved of our match," she added.

"…we become husband and wife."

"Until death do us part?"

"No," Tal countered. "Forever. *Until* sounds too much like a legal loophole, Mrs. Hammond, and I've no intention of letting you slip free of me again."

A word about the author...

Beth Henderson fell in love with history decades ago. Her first completed manuscript was a historical romance, although it went through many revisions before publication. She likes adventure mixed with mystery and her first loves are nineteenth-century men with guns on their hips. Having snagged a BA in American History, she has difficulty prying herself away from research. In a career that is 30+ years long now, romance is only one of the genres she writes in under two other pen names.

Visit her at:

http://www.4TaleTellers.com

~*~

Other Books by this Author

LUCKY
AT TWILIGHT
PARAMOUR
WICKED
RECKLESS

Thank you for purchasing
this publication of The Wild Rose Press, Inc.

For questions or more information
contact us at
info@thewildrosepress.com.

The Wild Rose Press, Inc.
www.thewildrosepress.com

www.ingramcontent.com/pod-product-compliance
Lightning Source LLC
La Vergne TN
LVHW020532100826
845148LV00010B/1427

* 9 7 8 1 5 0 9 2 3 5 5 4 4 *